HOUSE OF BREAD

Amanda Nicol

a®

Published in 2016 by Agent Press

A catalogue record for this book is available from the British Library

ISBN 978-0-9571449-1-0

Also by Amanda Nicol

Badric's Island
Dead Pets Society

www.amandanicol.co.uk

For my family, with special thanks to Bruce Nicol,
Hannah Walker and Steve Ashmore

'The madness of some of them has such a humorous air, and displayed itself in so many whimsical freaks, that it was impossible not to be entertained at the same time as I was angry with myself for being so.'

WILLIAM COWPER, on visiting Bedlam

'...And all tendernesses of the soul cast forth as filth & mire, Among the winding places of deep contemplation intricate, To where the Tower of London frown'd dreadful over Jerusalem, A building of Luvah, builded in Jerusalem's eastern gate to be His secluded court. Thence to Bethlehem, where was builded Dens of despair in the house of bread; enquiring in vain Of stones and rocks he took his way, for human form was none...'

WILLIAM BLAKE, from Jerusalem, Plate 31.

The Hebrew word Bethlehem translates as House of Bread. The priory of St Mary of Bethlehem was founded in 1247 in Bishopsgate and by the 14th century became a mental hospital eventually to be known as Bedlam.

1

Three full days

Dan opened his eyes. A face was looming over his, framed by a blinding yellow light. It was beautiful – smooth, brown, rounded and as shiny as a freshly split conker.

'Cigarette?' said the apparition, black eyes twinkling, a fluorescent anorak materialising from the golden glow.

'Oh, yeah ... cheers.' He took one and pulled himself upright, his head reeling. Patting an unfamiliar pocket, he pulled out an orange lid from a packet of Smarties. He focused on it. Strange, the letter was D...

'Is this what you're after mate?'

An old bloke appeared out of nowhere wearing a stiff brown suit circa 1950, the contours of his skull clearly visible beneath his wrinkled, greenish-white skin, some remaining hair in jagged white peaks. He struck a match and held a trembling flame to the tip of the cigarette.

'Just what the Doctor ordered, eh?' he said, leering at him, nodding and grinning.

'Yeah ... thanks.'

He slipped the lid back into his pocket, smoked the rest of the cigarette and stubbed it out in a twinkling green tin ashtray. An elfin-faced girl in a huge purple dress approached and held out another, already lit.

'We're not allowed to let the flame go out,' she said, gravely.

'Right,' he nodded, happy to chain-smoke. The dress billowed about her as she walked away.

'Can anyone tell me where I am?' he asked, but the question floated away like a bubble. He rubbed his eyes and ordered his head to explain itself, but his workhorse memory had just discovered open country. It was prancing about, pausing for just long enough for him to almost catch hold, when, with a snort and a buck, it was off again, galloping into the distance in a cloud of dust.

'Dan, could you come into the office with me, love?'

Focusing on a shorthaired woman in jeans and sweatshirt, he got unsteadily to his feet and followed her. She beckoned for him to sit down at a desk.

'How are you feeling?'

He tried to reply. Fuck! Now his tongue had turned into a trapped eel. Slamming his hand over his mouth, he stared up at her. Christ! He was dribbling! She went to a cabinet, took out a bottle, tipped a small white tablet into a tiny beaker and handed it to him.

'This'll help. It's just a little side effect,' she said, coolly. She gave him some water and watched as he took the pill. Wiping his mouth with the back of his hand, he managed to ask where he was.

'You're in hospital, love.'

Hospital! Hospitals were places with rows of beds, people in pyjamas and nice nurses in uniform. Obviously not that sort of hospital. That only left one other sort that he could think of... The woman held up a leaflet in the weary way of an air hostess re-enacting the safety drill and began,

'You are being held under Section 4 of the Mental Health Act...'

Sectioned? No way! He snatched the leaflet from her and started to read.

The small print swam before his eyes.

'Could I make a phone call please?' It seemed like the right thing to say. The woman offered him the use of the office phone. Who the hell was he going to call? His solicitor? He grabbed the receiver, then put it back, defeated. Without meeting his eye, the woman handed him a container and asked for a urine sample.

He stumbled out of the office, trying to focus on the document. He knew that it was important to know the score in this sort of situation, but he just couldn't get past the first few lines. He read them over and over again. Three full days, three full days... Three full days, three bags full, three blind mice, three ships sailing in... Three, three, why three? The more he thought about it the weirder the word became. Was three more significant than any other number? Why not four days? Why not two blind mice? He could get to the bottom of it, he was sure, if only he wasn't so wasted. He found the loo, grappled with the plastic container, took it back to the woman, then made his way to the TV room. He could feel his walk becoming robotic, alien. He slumped down onto the sweaty plastic couch.

He was woken by the sound of shouting. Hauling himself up, he saw the old, grey guy pacing up and down, jerking like a man-sized wind-up doll.

'...AND THE BLEEDIN' PLANES DON'T HELP! Are they just stupid or what? All day and half the flamin' night! Carving up the sky...' He stopped to look round at his audience. Following his gaze round the room Dan saw a collection of semi-comatose folk draped about the place, taking no notice of him whatsoever. Apart from the guy in the anorak, who was rocking from side to side like a sick animal in a zoo. Dan watched him. About twenty five, twenty six he reckoned, hair about two inches long all over – a cropped afro, an aristocratic face, like a prince from a small African country, the sort of black guy you got at Weybridge College, not the South London street look at all. How could he wear that jacket in this heat? Not to mention the v-neck Christmas present jumper under-neath. His shoes were like the ones his dad wore to work, grey slip-ons with buckles at the side. He looked down at his own feet which seemed to come to life as his gaze fell upon them, roasting in someone else's old tartan slippers. He kicked them off, repulsed.

You're a fake, baby,' Alec crooned, pointing at the old guy, who strode towards him, fists clenched. A rosy-cheeked woman curled up on a foam chair put down her book, saying, 'Now, now, boys, none of your nonsense. It'll be hot chocolate soon.'

The man sat down. His eyes were filling with tears.

'Now then Jack,' she got up and crossed the room, 'What's all this about, the planes and everything?'

'No one cares... No one gives a toss,' he said, miserably.

'About you love?'

'About the sky! HAS ANYONE BEEN LISTENING TO A WORD I'VE BEEN SAYING?' he roared, on his feet again.

'Was I the only person bothering to watch that effing programme?'

Bodies stirred and heavy eyelids opened, like dozing toads who'd just heard a splash somewhere in their pond.

'You just don't get it do you? ...It's solid... At least it was, protecting us from the invisible things. It was solid and now we've shredded it! I can see it... I wouldn't expect you to be able to...' he sighed.

'It was something about the ozone layer wasn't it?' she said.

'It's the planes, nurse, the bleedin' planes! Don't you see?'

From across the room the anorak piped up cheerily, *AIRPORT! Ooh-ooh-ee-ooh-ee-ooh AIRPORT! Ooh-ooh-ee-ooh-ee-ooh...'*

'Shush Alec!' she snapped. Jack and Alec, Alec and Jack. Dan forced the two names into his head.

Clinking and jangling, a trolley arrived. Diverted, Jack grabbed his hot chocolate and drank it in one draught, smacked his lips, slammed the cup down and brought one over to Dan.

'Hot drink for you, mate?'

'Thanks.' He felt it seep through him like an oil change. Water, sugar, nicotine. All a man needed to survive. After all, that's what he'd been living on for God knows how long and it hadn't done him any harm. In fact, sectioning apart, he'd never felt better in his life, more or less, he thought, adjusting his weight onto the buttock that wasn't aching.

The nurse came over holding out a little beaker of orange liquid. Thick, syrupy, with more than a hint of narcotic on the nose.

'Do I have to take it?'

'Yes love,' she said, 'it'll help you sleep.'

He shut his eyes and swallowed.

'I'll take you to your room now,' she said, leading him

towards the staircase.

He collapsed onto the bed. Now that he was a certified lunatic undressing would not be necessary.

2

Twenty eight days

'Dan dear, you've got a visitor.'

The words seemed to come from a long way off.

'Dan love, there's someone here to see you.'

He unstuck his eyelids to see Mat, his next door neighbour, looking really upset. Since he had no idea of the whereabouts of this hospital and Mat obviously did, Dan decided that he was in on it with the rest of them.

'Fucking Judas,' he hissed, the taste of his nasty breakfast still in his mouth. Mat sat down next to him.

'Christ, what have they done to you?' he said, picking up one of Dan's bruised wrists. 'I'm really sorry about all this man. It's all my fault. I should never have let you get into this state.'

Dan looked at him. God, the coolest dude was actually shedding a tear.

'Hey, don't get upset. I'm OK, honest. I've only got to stay here for three full days, apparently. I'll be back home, tomorrow maybe, I've sort of lost track of time. They've given me something so that I can have a bit of a rest, that's all. It's a seriously heavy buzz. You'd like it...'

Mat sniffed. 'Listen man, I'm supposed to be comforting you here! Me brought ya some stuff an' ting,' he said in his mum's best Jamaican, handing Dan a plastic bag containing forty fags and three of his finest homespun tapes.

'Thanks Mat... Do you think you could check the flat for me? Just make sure all the papers are in one place...' Anxiety clouded his face at the thought of his parents rifling through everything.

'I'll sort it. Relax man, that's what you're here to do... Hey – dig your groovy clothes.'

Alec came over and joined them.

'How'ya doing Dan, and who might this be?' he said, opening hostilities.

'I'm Dan's neighbour, and you are?'

'I'm Dan's friend.'

'Guys, c'mon,' said Dan, 'Alec this is Mat. Mat this is Alec.'

Mat put his hand out to Alec, who ignored it, his eyes boring into the visitor. Happy to be able to return some hospitality at last, Dan handed round cigarettes as if he had two hundred duty free. Some people asked if they could take one for later, how could he refuse?

'Steady on mate, I bought those for you!' said Mat.

Before long, he stood up and said he had to be going. Dan waited while he went into the office to get someone to let him out. He could hear Mat asking why he was looking so rough and saying something about him not being a bloody criminal, but he couldn't hear the reply.

On the way out Mat said, 'Listen man, you mind that Alec geezer, he's dodgy, believe me... And check out babe left. Take it easy mate. Laters.'

Dan looked to his left, seeing the elfin-faced girl applying a lot of make-up to what he suddenly noticed was her beautiful face. This compensated him for the loss of Mat and the irritation he was feeling at not remembering all the things he'd wanted to ask him, all the friends he wanted him to get in touch with. He approached her.

'I owe you a cigarette,' he said, holding out his pack.

'You don't owe me anything. Do you think I gave you

one so that I could get one back? That's what's the matter with people, everything has to be a deal. Why couldn't you just offer me one because you wanted to?' she said, crossly.

He couldn't handle this sort of mind game shit, especially with someone he didn't know. He withdrew the packet, said nothing and walked unsteadily back towards the television room. If she was that clever, then she'd have known that it was a ruse to get into conversation with her, and she would have taken it as a compliment. Why did women have to overcomplicate things all the time? He had to lie down. It was all too much.

He was woken by Jack.

'You'd better get your head together, Sherlock's here to see you.'

'What?'

'Doctor Holmes. This is your chance to get out of here so you'd better say the right thing. Just agree with whatever she says, even if it's not true.'

Suddenly the Elf girl was there, distracting him from Jack.

'Sorry about earlier,' she said.

'Forget it,' he said, smiling at her.

'You remind me of an elf.'

'What does an elf look like?' she smiled back at him.

'Like you.'

A team of important-looking people breezed into the room. Dan saw the guy that had taken such great care of his Walkman the other day. That had been one of the things nagging away at him. He went over to him and asked for it back.

'Not now, Dan, not to worry, it's safe in the office. The Doctor's here to see you. She's a very busy woman, so we'd better get on.'

'Look, if she's that busy, she doesn't have to bother with

me, I'm perfectly OK.' Looking back, he saw Jack shaking his head despairingly.

They led him into a small airless room. The doctor sat down at a table and indicated for him to sit opposite. She was filling in forms in a large, rounded, almost childlike hand. She looked at him and smiled briskly. He raised the corners of his mouth with difficulty. He was pretty sure she was the one with the giant hypodermic.

'Dan, do you know where you are?' she asked.

'...Yeah, sort of...' he replied cautiously.

'Do you know why you are here?' Difficult one.

'...Yes,' wondering whether this was the correct response.

'So you think that you are ill?' He could hear Jack telling him to agree with everything she said, but he just couldn't bring himself to say yes to this one.

'I'm a bit worn out, that's all. I've had a lot on my mind, you see I've got this project to organise... It's quite tiring really, I suppose I could do with a bit of a rest. I was ill, a few months back. I was desperate for help then and people kept telling me that I wasn't...'

'So you don't consider yourself to be in need of hospital treatment at the moment.'

'No I don't.'

He felt completely sure that she would realise that they would be wasting resources on him, and he would be free to leave. Then she asked, smiling in mid-sentence without reason, if he could take seven away from one hundred, backwards. He looked at her in astonishment. Was he ill if he could or ill if he couldn't? Was this the fail-safe and definitive test for insanity?

'I don't know... my head is fu... messed up with the medication...'

'Just try for me Dan, please.'

His heart started to thump. He wanted to get this right. Even if getting it right meant getting it wrong.

'One hundred, ninety-three ... em ... eighty-six ... seventy-nine,' He was breaking out in sweat, under the spotlight of a TV game show... 'Seventy-two ... sixty-five, fifty-nine, I mean eight, fifty-one ... forty ...er ... four ... thirty-seven, thirty, twenty-three ... sixteen, nine, two.' What a relief. Thank God she hadn't asked for the Fibonacci sequence.

The Doctor looked up and with another smile, she said he could go. Puzzled, he stood up and made to leave. His sweating hands slipped on the door handle. He wiped them on his non-absorbent trousers and tried again. After several attempts, the door opened. His tongue was misbehaving again and his eyeballs were trying to twist into the darkness of his head. Jack and Alec were waiting for him and saw him struggling.

'NURSE! QUICK! DAN NEEDS SOME KEMEDRIN, NOW!' bawled Jack.

Holding his hand over his mouth, eyes rolling, Dan slid down the wall and onto the floor.

A young bloke rushed over with a tiny plastic beaker containing a white pill, and a glass of water. Dan took the pill with Jack holding his hand. He was glad that the Elf wasn't around to see him in this unattractive state. His attack of the contra-indications began to subside.

'What did you say that pill was?'

'Kemedrin. It's the antidote to the other stuff you're on. In your case probably Largactil, maybe even Haloperidol. I think it's the Kemedrin that does for your short-term memory, but I can't remember! Ha, ha!'

'What's the other stuff?'

'The other stuff, my boy, is the big guns. Antipsychotic tranks, the gear they give to people in Broadmoor. You're lucky it didn't kill you mate. People have been known to drop down dead after a shot of that stuff. In the book it says 'EMERGENCY BEHAVIOUR CONTROL' at the top of the page... Easy to slip a bit into the water supply if necessary don't you think?'

Dan was freaked. To his relief he saw the Elf coming towards him, smiling.

'How did you get on with Sherlock?' she asked, sitting down next to him.

'I think it was OK, but I'm not sure.'

'As long as you said that you were definitely ill. That's your only chance of getting out,' said Jack, butting in.

'Hang on a minute, say that again. My only chance of getting out is by saying that I'm definitely ill? Surely if I say that I'm definitely ill then they'll definitely keep me here?'

'No, it doesn't work like that, you see, the thing about "mental illness",' said Jack, signalling inverted commas in the air with waggling fingers, 'is that if you've got it you don't think you 'ave. So if you say you 'aven't got it, then you 'ave got it. Get it? So you've gotta say that you've got it, for them to think that you 'aven't. Or at least think that you're getting,' more commas in the air, '"better".'

'But surely, if I said that I was ill, they wouldn't then say, OK, fine, off you go?'

'No, but they might not section you again.'

Right on cue, the nurse was coming back with a leaflet.

'Ahem, Dan mate, feeling a bit better now? Good.' He cleared his throat. 'We are holding you under Section 2 of the Mental Health Act... My name's Dave and if you've got any questions I'll be in the office.'

'28 days,' said Jack in his ear, as if to translate. 'Could be worse, could be worse...'

Into his other ear Alec warbled, *'Welcome to the Hotel California...'*

3

Summer breeze

He sat stunned, leaflet in hand, then stood up and pushed everyone away. Why wouldn't they all just leave him alone? He stormed into the office, banged on the desk and demanded his Walkman. Dave handed it to him and started to say something, but he wasn't interested, snatching it out of his hands. He stormed out in search of the bag that Mat had brought him. He was sure he'd had it before he'd seen the Doctor. He hunted around the foam chairs frantically, eyed by their zombified inhabitants.

'Has anyone seen a bag with some stuff in it?' he addressed the room. No one said anything. Then Alec appeared, holding it out to him.

'I was just keeping it safe for you while you were with Sherlock. Here you are.'

'Thanks,' said Dan looking inside. The batteries and two tapes were all that remained.

'Where's the rest of it?'

'What else was there?' Alec looked concerned.

'Another tape and some fags.'

He shrugged. 'Didn't see them. You've got to keep an eye on your things in here, you know.'

'Oh yeah, right. Thanks Alec.'

He guessed the fags would be long gone by now, but felt gutted at the loss of the tape. Maybe someone just borrowed it. He looked round to see who else was wearing a Walkman. An approximately seven-foot black guy with big headphones was ambling around. Every now and then would come the loud, discordant, *'BEEN AROUND THE WORLD AND I, I, I...'* Dan went over and tapped him on the arm. The giant looked down, surprised that someone had dared to disturb him.

'What's up stranger?' he boomed, freeing up one ear.

'Sorry, I don't even know your name, I was just wondering if you'd seen a tape... It was in a plastic bag...'

The bloke looked seriously displeased.

'You don't even know my name, but you're accusing me of teefing your tape, eh?'

'No, no, not tee ... stealing it, just seeing it somewhere. I'm really sorry. My name's Dan by the way,' he said, holding out his hand.

'Benny,' said the big guy, touching it with his fist. He took a radio out of his shell suit pocket.

'No tape in here,' he said, and turned away with another tuneless, *'BEEN AROUND THE WO-O-ORLD, LOOKIN' FOR MY BAY-AY-BEE...'*

Regretting his accusation, Dan sat down, closed his eyes and floated off again.

Another meal came and went. More medication was administered. Dan watched as Benny crashed onto a sofa, felled like a mighty oak. It was hard to keep track of Alec, Jack and the Elf, because they too were falling in and out of drug-induced sleep. It gave a strange sort of intimacy to the television room. It reminded him of an airport departure lounge, where a prolonged delay unites strangers, etiquette dissolving into grunts and bad-tempered attempts to get comfortable.

There was, in theory, the jolly diversion of ping-pong,

but the table was monopolised by the two ward champions. Jack introduced them as Krishna and Spiderman. The first on account of his baggy orange trousers and shaven head, the second his legendary ability to scale any wall.

'Is he really a Krishna?'

'Dunno. If it wasn't for the trousers I'd say more like National Front,' said Jack. He was right, they both looked pretty mean, but it could have just been concentration. Others would write their names hopefully on the list for their turn. When it came to it, more often than not the aspirant player would be in the TV room, snoring. Krish and Spide would look round, exchange grins, snigger, and begin a new epic tournament.

'Anyone for the garden?' Dave was opening a glass door onto the outside world. Dan leapt up, grabbed what was left of his things and was there in a flash.

'Why didn't you do this ages ago?'

'We do it every day at this time if the weather's good.' Dave was bending down to undo the final bolt.

'Not since I've been here you haven't.'

'Oh yes we have, you must have been out for the count... I mean asleep,' he said, blushing. The door swung open onto a high-walled patch of paradise.

Dan was enveloped in the warm, fragrant air of a summer's day. Somewhere nearby a lawn was being mowed, and the smell was an echo of a thousand summers, bouncing around his brain like tennis balls on a grass court. There had just been a tantalisingly brief shower. Just enough to remind the garden that it needed it, and make the leaves of a big horse chestnut twinkle. A million miniature rainbows decorated its branches. Never in his life had he been so happy to be outside. If he'd been a dog, he'd have rolled on the grass and kicked his legs in the air. The breeze washed away all the interference. He felt discharged, earthed. He went over to the farthest corner, which wasn't very far, lay down, put his hands behind his head and drifted away. He had the pleasant sensation of being on a lilo, gently bobbing on a lazy sea.

After a while he became conscious that he had company. It was Jack, deep in thought, chewing on a stalk of long grass. He sat up and looked around him. In the centre of the lawn, the Elf was sitting cross-legged, surrounded by a circle of large people, blinking in the sunlight like creatures fresh from hibernation. They were passing round a cigarette, taking one drag each, then lighting a fresh one with the end of the last.

'I'd like to know what she thinks would happen if she did let the flame go out,' said Jack. Dan watched, admiring her. They sat silently for a while, eyes shut, worshipping the sun like holidaymakers by the poolside.

'There's a lot of people on the big side in this place,' Dan commented.

'That's how we'll all end up, mate.'

'What do you mean?' He looked at Jack, holding his hand up to shield his eyes from the almost painful light.

'Well, what do think happens to a person whose system is pumped full of downers for years on end? It's all about blood sugar. You get your medicine, it wipes you out. You get the munchies – your body tries to sort it out with a sugar hit. Blood sugar soars, pancreas does its bit, blood sugar drops. That calls for another Mars Bar. In the meantime, you're doing nothing other than lolling about cos you're all dosed up. Couple of years of that mate, and that's what you get. Fat. And by the way, the light's hurting you cos … whatchamacallit – photosensitivity is another "side,"' he said, accentuating the word bitterly, '"effect."'

'Christ,' said Dan. 'Can I refuse the medication?'

'You can, in theory, but it won't help your case.'

All this was threatening to spoil this sacred time outside in the real world. Dan was well into his new body. He pictured himself as Elvis in his last days. He looked at the Elf. She was borderline skinny. Come to think of it, Jack was hardly fat either. What did this mean? Were they on different drugs? Or had they just arrived, like him? Jack seemed to be an old hand. He was so clued up – he must have been here for ages.

'It's not natural,' was all he could think of to say.

'Natural! Natural! Next to Love, that must be the most overused word in the English language! Just cos you don't like it you can't say it isn't natural! Is this natural?' Jack was starting to rant, holding up Dan's Walkman.

'You don't mind the fact that that's not natural, cos it entertains you. It's no more or less natural than the medication. The fact is that it is natural for human beings to invent Walkmans, and drugs, and bombs, the lot!' he sighed, then went on, 'Humans are just naturally stupid, and most of them pretty nasty as well. But that's natural too. It's not survival of the nicest, is it? The whole world's designed to look out for itself. That includes us losers being locked up and kept quiet. Do you think that that,' he pointed to a dandelion clock, 'cares if it puts something else in the shade, or strangles the life out of the next thing? No.'

He picked the stem. Dan observed the microcosmic Big Bang as Jack played his unwitting part in nature's grand plan. The mind-bogglingly delicate engineering of the head fractured and the obliging breeze carried the tiny seed bearing parachutes this way and that. He squinted at Jack.

'Where do nice people fit in then?' Jack's dim view seemed all wrong. He actually felt sorry for him, he obviously hadn't seen the light like he had.

'Nice people? Like who?'

'Like you.'

'Me! How d'you know I'm a nice person? You don't know anything about me. I don't believe in niceness. People don't do good for good's sake, however much they kid themselves. If people really did do things for others without wanting anything in return, now that really would be unnatural.'

Dan was too tired to protest. Just as Jack was about to launch into the next chapter, Dave stuck his head out the door and called him over.

'Looks like it's time for me to go. You behave yourself and I'll be seeing you sooner than you think,' he said, clasping both of Dan's hands and looking into his eyes with what could easily be mistaken for the genuine concern of a nice person.

Dan lay back and began to contemplate the tree. Its overlaid leaves floated against the sky as if they were on a pond. Where the large, hand-like arrangement of leaves overlapped there were segments of darker greens. They reminded him of diagrams in school maths lessons, of sets and subsets. Then again, if he made a telescope of his cupped hands, what he saw was a stained-glass window with light pouring through its cracks and holes, dancing around, highlighting the colour like a magic marker.

The trunk was purple in the dark shadows. The idea that colour was totally dependent on light struck him as too bizarre for words. He remembered his physics teacher telling the class this as if it was just any old fact. That it was merely a question of the wavelength of a given substance had such huge implications – the way we saw things was just a façade then, to do with our brains, not with the way things actually were. Did that mean that without light everything would be in black and white ... or that the flashing greens and golds were real, as real as so-called reality? Were they actually there, all the time, just unseen, or were they in his brain, or was that the same thing?

'Hey, Dreamer! Come and meet my mum!' Alec was gesturing to him to join them where they were sitting on a wooden bench.

'Go get a cup! Go get a cup!'

'Pleased to meet you.' Dan extended his hand towards

Alec's mum, then pushed it back casually into his pocket when it wasn't taken.

'I'm not going back in there until I absolutely have to,' he said. 'What's that you got there – champagne?'

'Nope, but it's the next best thing – Coca-Cola! All the way from The Land of the Free! Here you go fella, you can share my cup,' said Alec with an American twang.

'Thanks, don't mind if I do.' Dan took the plastic toothmug and Alec filled it up with the fizzy brown liquid.

'Cheers!'

They clunked receptacles, Alec drinking out of the bottle. Dan's first mouthful burst all over his tongue like Spacedust.

'Hey Alec, d'you remember Spacedust? It was around when I was at school – it came in little sachets... I wonder why they don't sell it any more...'

'Yeah, yeah... Shpaishdusht. I remember it well.' Now he was playing private dick.

'Back in the old days we used to give it to the dog for laughs. I dunno what happened sonny, maybe we ate up the whole goddamn planet ... or maybe you just got in-terested in other things in the sweet shop ... like these, shmoke?' He held out a new packet of Marlboro. The gen-erosity with the Coke was guilt. Those fags smelt of Mat.

'Are they mine?'

'No,' he said, Londoner again and as transparent as clingfilm. 'My mum just brought them.' He tried to elbow his taciturn parent without Dan noticing.

'Didn't you mum?' She nodded.

Dan remembered a song with the lyric, *'Mother hides the murderer, mother hides the madman.'* Huh, not my mother, he thought. He took a fag anyway. With the Coke, a Marlboro, the sunshine, and the Elf in his sights, it seemed silly to make an issue of it.

4

The elf

All too quickly they were ushered back indoors. Why did time insist on behaving like this? He wondered if that was what relativity was all about. He knew it had something to do with the possibility of the landscape whizzing past the train instead of vice versa. Was it anything to do with sad hours seeming long, as Juliet had said, he recalled, as she longed for Romeo? It was so unfair, why couldn't happy hours seem long? Instead they sped past like an Intercity 125.

He slumped back into a sticky chair to watch TV. Even though it was up full blast, he couldn't seem to make sense of anything.

'Why is the colour turned up so bright?' he asked the Elf, who, happily, had just come over and sat down beside him. What appeared to be some sort of news programme had taken on the gay hues of a cartoon.

'All the tellies in this place are like this, I don't know why,' she said. 'Nurse, can you do something about the colour? It's way too bright. It's making me feel sick.'

'Looks OK to me,' said someone who Dan had never seen before. They looked at each other in puzzlement, then shrugged.

'What have you got in there?' said Dan, anxious to engage her before she fluttered off again. She was constantly on the move, busy, a girl with a mission. She didn't seem to be as laid out by the drugs as everyone else. Maybe elves were impervious to pernicious substances. He pointed to her little rectangular wicker suitcase.

'You mean my basket case?' she said, eyebrows raised prettily. He laughed.

'Yeah.'

'Everything a girl could possibly need.'

'Oh, right.' How disappointing. That meant make-up and Tampax – girls' things.

She opened it and proudly held it out under his nose, then proceeded to unpack it and lay the contents out on the floor in front of them.

'You must be very good at packing,' he said, as an implausible amount of what at first sight appeared to be rubbish materialised.

'I've done a lot of it in my time,' she said with an inscrutable sigh.

He pictured her, all alone, traversing the globe in a flowery dress clutching her little case. She gave him a guided tour of her curios. He supposed that women were even more uncomfortable without their stuff than men, being used to lugging handbags full of it around all the time. She'd recreated this habit with whatever she could find and was perfectly able to justify the possession of each object, be it plastic knife, sachet of sugar, old tube ticket, empty lighter or whatever. She did pause when it came to the empty lighter, then stuck the nib-and-inkless Bic biro in her mouth, saying, 'It's for lighting these!'

Dan was captivated. He wanted to give her something for her collection. Of course! He fished in his pocket, found the Smartie lid and held it out to her.

'I'd like you to have this.'

She gave a little gasp, then asked if he was sure, as if

he'd just offered her his granny's engagement ring.

Just then, all heads able to react turned to a fracas in the other room. Someone new was being admitted. They went over and joined Alec who'd perked up, as if watching a tedious piece of theatre that suddenly had the potential to redeem itself.

'CAN'T WE EVER GET ANY SODDING PEACE?' yelled Krish, in a most unholy way, as he threw down his bat, ran to the wall and headbutted it. There was a loud crack, making everyone wince.

'Shameela's back again,' said Alec.

Dan was fascinated. Shameela was a small middle-aged Asian woman who, like himself and the Elf, had been kitted out in 'Emergency Clothing'. She was being carried into the isolation, observation, or whatever it was room by four security guards, face up, each one holding a limb.

She appeared to be in some sort of catatonic state, rigid, with her mouth wide open, saliva bubbling at the corners. Dan rushed back into the TV room to watch through the hatch. They dumped her on the floor with their usual degree of customer care and left, locking the door behind them. She lay there motionless for a while, then rolled over onto her front and Dan watched as her whole body convulsed with huge sobs.

In a flash he understood compassion. Actually felt it physically, rather than just trying to. The only comfort that he could give, from his side of the hatch, was to suffer with her. He almost felt he was her at that moment. Did it, could it help? Why not? Didn't everyone say that a problem shared is a problem halved? Poor her, he thought, poor all of us. He prayed hopefully, with any prayer-like words that came to mind. 'Save and comfort those who suffer... Oh hear us when we cry to Thee, for those in peril on the sea...'

It was working. After a few minutes, she looked up, then over to the hatch where she saw him. She stood up and approached it, tears still wet on her face. She dried her eyes. He put his outstretched hands onto the glass, and she did the same. She was saying something that he couldn't hear and gazing at him in raptures. He gestured that she should lie down and relax, putting his two hands under his cheek and shutting his eyes in the universal signal for sleep. Obediently, she did the same, lay down, smiled, and seemed to nod off. Feeling strangely drained, Dan sat down, rubbing his eyes. The Elf joined him and said, 'Wow! By now she's usually climbing the walls.'

Shameela appeared the next morning at breakfast. On seeing Dan slump down in front of his rubbery toast, she ran over and prostrated herself at his feet. He felt her greasy hair brush against his exposed shins and his mind flipped instantly to biblical references. Who was it that had washed Jesus' feet with ointment on her hair? He couldn't remember. He wasn't even sure whether he was making it up.

'You have cured me! Oh, God is good, God is good!'

She stroked his face, patted his head and made a general of fuss of him.

'There's no cure for what you've got, love,' said Alec, who'd appeared, wearing an inside-out gabardine raincoat. He sat down next to Dan with a bowl of porridge into which he had added so much jam that it looked positively visceral.

With that Shameela sprang up like a cat whose tail had been trodden on, clambered over Dan, lunged at Alec, put her hands round his neck and started to throttle him. The blood and guts of the porridge flew through the air, pausing in suspended animation before splattering all over Alec like a special effect in a low budget movie. His eyes bulged as he wrenched Shameela's hands away from his neck.

Dan wanted to get out of the way, but was trapped in

24

his chair that was attached to the table. Obviously they were like that to prevent people from throwing them around. Funny how these were the only sort of chairs that had ever given him that urge.

Meanwhile, Alec, incandescent with fury, rugby-tackled his fleeing assailant, bringing her thumping to the ground, where he pinned her down and raised his fist above her face, holding it cocked like a pistol. Pink goo was dripping onto her dress. The rest of the cast looked on, slurping their tea, as if waiting for the snap of a clapboard and the director to call, 'Cut!'

Security rushed over, but just in time Alec regained his poise. As he was walking away the usually monosyllabic Spide called out, 'Just as well you were wearing your Mac mate!'

Everyone laughed, except Dan. As if she could read his mind, the Elf went over and put her arm round him.

'It's not your fault sweetie,' she said, rubbing his back with her hand. She had the magic touch for sure. He felt better instantly.

'I wonder why he had it on inside out.'

'Maybe it's raining on the inside,' she said, with her impeccable logic.

5

The family

Later that day, lost in a Brazilian love song, its rhythms coursing through him till they reached his toes, which couldn't help but wiggle gleefully, he felt a tap on his arm. He looked up, reluctantly dragging himself away from the carnival.

The nurse that he didn't know was telling him he had visitors. Looking round he saw six family members. At least two of them were the sort that you didn't see from one year to the next, so to see them now was a bit much. The others, well, about fucking time too. Bloody cheek, he thought, do they really expect me to be pleased to see them?

He scanned their faces. He'd never seen the resemblance between those tied by blood so clearly. He picked out similarities in bone structure as if he had X-ray eyes. Everyone looked pale green as if suffering a bilious attack. Various emotions were expressed on their faces. Pity, bewilderment, there but for the grace of God go I-ness, anger... Anger, for God's sake! And would you believe it, fear!

'Don't worry, I won't bite,' he said, realising that the ice-breaking was down to him, unfairly, he thought.

His brother was the first to speak.

'I'm really sorry Dan, I blame myself, I should've known that things weren't right when you came to borrow that money...'

Hadn't Mat also blamed himself? How come everyone wanted to make this their fault? Was it some sort of warped egomania?

He looked at his Dad. He was bound to think it was his fault. He'd always said he was a borderline case himself. He probably thought he'd passed on a gene for insanity, one which, unlike his indulgent son, he'd managed to keep under control. Dan watched as a thousand emotions passed over his face like speeded up weather patterns, before he turned away to wipe his eyes.

'Hey, Dad, Dad, don't worry, I'm OK.' He went over and they embraced in the awkward way of two men who don't know quite where to put their arms. He felt his father slump gratefully against him in an uncomfortable parent/child role-reversal.

The nurse led them into another unknown room, with tables, chairs and a blackboard. Dan felt him relax a bit. He was a teacher, for him the presence of a blackboard was as comforting as a teddy.

No one knew what to do next. Communicating with Dan was as tricky as flying a kite. He swooped around the room wildly, stimulated by the sight of these strange and familiar faces. Memories abounded, but before he had time to complete the reminiscence, another one had pushed in, altering the course of his speeding thoughts, while the nonplussed family desperately clung to the thread. When they asked how he was, he replied that he was fine, never better, his only complaint being the lack of fresh air and the side effects of the medication, but typically, they chose not to manifest themselves when he would have liked them to.

Instead he told them how they were feeling. It wasn't

difficult. It was as blatantly obvious as if they were telling him with words. He didn't know why they were all so freaked out. The more he tried to convince them that he was perfectly well, the more strained the atmosphere became.

He remembered Jack's speech about mental illness. Perhaps he should have been telling them that he was ill, so that they'd think that he wasn't or something. It was all getting confusing again. The medication was pulling his body down by its peculiar gravity. He sat down. He wanted to sleep.

'I think Dan's getting tired now. We'd better go,' said his mother. The relief in the room was palpable.

They filed back into the ward. Shameela threw her cup of tea at his Auntie Veronica, saying, as she was led away, that God had told her to. Auntie Veronica said it didn't matter, although she looked as if it did. His mum said, 'Thank goodness it wasn't very hot.'

With much kissing and hugging, they left, after handing over a plastic bag containing drinks and sweets, as if he'd been locked up for regressing to childhood. Another had in it some of his own clothes, a jacket and a pair of trainers, at last!

He knew that whatever he had said, whatever he'd done, it had been wrong. The visit had been a disaster. They hadn't gone away happy, and he wanted everyone to be happy, especially them. He rummaged in the plastic bags seeking solace. He found it in a box of chocolates, but by the time he'd handed it round, all that remained was the strawberry cream, his least favourite. He knew he should have taken the caramel before anyone else got to it, but that would have been wrong. This was the last straw. He went over to the window, gazing out on its medicinal greenery and bit his lip, trying to force back tears. He looked around for the Elf. If anyone could cheer him up, she could. He couldn't see her anywhere.

'Hey, Alec, have you seen the Elf-girl anywhere?'

'Yeah,' said Alec, with a finger in his mouth, excavating excess toffee from between his teeth, 'she's gone mate, while you were entertaining. Dunno where.'

The wind dropped, the already struggling kite nose-dived.

The next morning the absence of entertaining company gave him the time to do some prolonged contemplation of himself, in front of a mirror in the communal loos. He too was green, translucent. His whole face pointing forwards like Pinocchio after his first few fibs. His pupils were huge, making his eyes look bigger and darker. He could live with that. He needed a shave badly, but he could just concentrate it away until the smooth face of his mother as a young woman looked back at him. His dark mop of hair was happily doing its own thing, so no change there.

He went to the loo, and as he was standing there looking up at the brilliant white square of frosted glass, he noticed that someone had drawn tiny crosses about a centimetre long, all over the place, in pencil. Strange, he thought. It gave the place the look of a prehistoric cave. His eyes then fell upon a bevy of what were either huge mosquitoes or teenage daddy-long-legs. As if startled by something imperceptible to him, they all took off at once, buzzed around a bit, then settled down again.

Just then a shaft of light illuminated the little room and wow! Each insect was casting a shadow in the shape of a little cross! He wondered who else had noticed this phenomenon and taken the time to trace all the little shadows. Sentimentally, he supposed it was the Elf. Was it true that Beelzebub meant Lord of the Flies? Maybe flies were fallen angels. Come to think of it, anything with wings would cast a cross-shaped shadow. Was the cross actually a plane? Maybe if the given mythology had been different, if his religious education had filled his imagination with scenes from the life of an elephant God or something, it would be trunks that he saw wherever he looked, and not the crucifixes that were rife, jumping out of every angle. Perhaps then in the glimpses of himself that he saw in every reflective surface he'd see Dumbo.

He thought of his dad, with heart-swelling fondness, and the particular family holiday spent arguing about Erich Von Däniken's book, 'The Chariots of the Gods'. His dad had been into it at the time (even though he'd staunchly denied it later), brother thought it was a load of tosh, mother was sick of hearing about it, and he'd reserved judgement, since he couldn't be bothered to read it.

Pondering celestial beings and considering the strong possibility that he was one, he wandered back into the TV room. Dave was waiting for him.

'Get your stuff together mate, you're out of here!'

6

Manic depression

Having hardly any stuff to get together, very soon he was following Dave, stopping and waiting every two minutes while he fumbled with keys, unlocked another door and locked it behind them. Eventually the final door was opened onto the outside world. Light and space hit him in the face. Space isn't usually so surprising, the breadth of the sky not usually so striking, so vast. He breathed in deeply, feeling himself expand and relax, as if he'd just been released from a vacuum pack. He looked back at his former prison, seeing it for the first time. It looked as innocuous as a Victorian red-brick schoolhouse-type building could look.

Dave was leading him through a labyrinth of such buildings into what appeared to be a central one, and then into a weird tunnel-like corridor. After a while, Dan noticed that they were going round in a circle, passing doors with the names of trees on them. Larch, Elm, Oak... Maybe the corridor was circular so that you couldn't get lost. If you kept going for long enough, and concentrated, you would eventually find the right exit, like a roundabout.

'Where are we going?' Not since he was a child had he had to ask this question so often.

'Birch, if we haven't gone past it. I haven't been here that long myself, this place is a bit confusing.'

'Am I going to get the cane now or what?' Dave looked at him blankly.

They went past doors with signs that read Art Therapy, Dance Therapy, Electro-Convulsive Therapy Suite...

'Hey Dave, which one do you think is the odd one out?' He was trying to make a joke of it, but the thought of what went on behind that door made his blood run cold. He wondered why the 'suite', as if it was the best room in a posh hotel. They passed a dining room that looked like the nave of a church, with a high timbered ceiling and paintings on the walls, overtaking a couple of shuffling people who were still in their nightclothes.

'I think this is where we came in,' said Dan. His legs were starting to ache. He was sure he'd seen that pay-phone before.

'You're right, Birch is just here. We must have missed it.' Dave pushed the swing door open, the noticeably un-locked swing door, and led him into his new abode.

'My boy, I knew you'd be joining us soon!' It was Jack. He leapt up and threw his arms around Dan, squashing his nose against his stale, stiff lapel. Dan tried to look over his shoulder and scan the room for the Elf but he couldn't see her.

Jack told him that he was waiting to go into the office to register his complaint for the day. He wanted to bring to the staff's attention the poor caged budgie in the cor-ner. He considered its presence to be offensive, not only to the poor bird, but to all those held under the Mental Health Act. If they didn't see him soon, he was going to let it out and be done with it.

After standing back to make room for the embrace, Dave led Dan into the office.

'Oi!' said Jack, barging in front of them, 'I think you'll find that I was before you!'

A wiry grey-haired man was sitting behind a desk. He reminded Dan of a spruced up Catweazle. He stood up, and with one hand on his hip pointed to the door and said, in a BBC voice, 'Not now Jack! Out!'

Jack copied his gesture, letting the pointing hand droop, and minced out of the office with the words, 'Up yours Teapot!'

Unperturbed, the man behind the desk gestured for the new ward member to sit down. Dave said his goodbyes and left.

Dan felt like it was his first day in big school. As if to remind him that it wasn't, the man offered him a cigarette.

'Welcome to Birch Ward, Dan. My name's Colin. I think you'll find things a bit easier here. You'll be part of this ward until you're better. You're free to walk in the hospital grounds, but don't go any further. You are being held on a Section, so if you did we'd have to bring you straight back in. Is that clear?'

'Yeah, I mean Yes, thanks.'

It seemed like a surprisingly large amount of freedom, after last week.

'You seem to be suffering quite considerably from side-effects of your medication, is that right?'

'Em, yeah, I think so.'

It was hard to tell what they considered suffering. Any suffering paled into insignificance when held up against The Feeling. Not that it was pleasant, the mad tongue, the rolling eyes, the cracking lips, the shakes, the constipation, the sudden crippling ache of his legs, the jerking gait... He was pretty sure that the constant desire for nicotine was something he'd been feeling before but he couldn't remember when his memory had started playing games with him... Why did people keep going on about getting better? It wasn't possible for him to be feeling any better. Why medicate him at all? They should be bottling his fabulous sensations and handing them out liberally to just about everyone. Instead, they should talk about the day when you re-enter a grey, humdrum reality where magic belongs in storybooks. That's hardly 'better'.

'In that case I'll speak to the Doctor about it. It's quite normal to have to modify the drug therapy, I'm sure we can sort something out. It's often the way with hypomania,' said the man. What did he say his name was?

'Hypomania? What's that?'

'That's what you've got luvvy. Hasn't anyone explained that to you?'

'No.'

He tutted with annoyance.

'Dan, it says in your notes that earlier in the year you were clinically depressed. Do you remember?'

He nodded. Of course he fucking remembered. You don't forget a stay with the Lord of Darkness in a hurry.

'Well, what's happening to you now is the opposite of that, a sort of clinical happiness, if you like.'

Clinical happiness? It sounded like something a dentist might feel, looking round a sparkling new surgery. There was nothing clinical about the mind-blowing sensuality that was his new life. In fact the depression hadn't been clinical either. His world had been sterile, but he himself had been something toxic, repulsive, decomposing, fit for incineration. He wouldn't have been let anywhere near a clinic.

'Hasn't anyone explained to you what manic depression is Dan?' Dan shook his head.

Jimi Hendrix cropped up in Dan's mind, *'Manic depression ... something, something ... my soul...'* He couldn't recall the lyric. Was it something, something ... *my veins?* Or was that cocaine? He'd always thought that manic depression was something in itself, i.e., a depressed maniac. From his experience of depression, a maniac is the last thing you could be. An incapacitated slug, perhaps. An actively crazy psychopath, not. Obviously he, and half the world, had got it wrong.

The nurse then gave him a short lecture on mood swings and what he said was also called bipolar disorder. That sounded more like it. After all, he did feel as if he'd been round the world and back, but didn't like the implication that he'd be visiting the ice caps again.

'I'll show you your bed and locker now, if you'll just follow me. We'll be moving to a temporary home in the next couple of days, but not to worry about that now.'

They went into a large room to see a crowd gathered at the window. Colin pushed through to see what was going on. Everyone was watching with horror as a green and blue budgie stood idiotically on the grass, lost in space without its perch, mirror and cuttlefish bone. One of the several hospital cats was poised, ready to pounce.

Jack was yelling, 'STOP IT! PLEASE, SOMEONE, STOP THAT BLEEDIN' MOGGY!' whilst trying to squeeze himself out of the window. It was too late. Oblivious to the dangers of predators, the obliging budgie remained motionless as the cat, playing to its audience, seized its prey with dramatic panache, and loped off to toy with it in peace. Colin put a hand up to his face and shook his head despairingly.

'Well thank you very much Jack, you've just given me a fine illustration of the pitfalls of care in the community,' he said, leading Dan towards the 'Male Area'.

Pandemonium ensued. People were shouting at Jack, who'd backed into a corner, weeping with bitter regret. Some of the younger members of the ward seemed to find it hilarious. The nurse hastily showed Dan to his bed in the men's dormitory and hurried back to try to settle everyone down.

Dan sat down, lay back, closed his eyes and tried to convince himself that the five minutes of freedom followed by a swift death (not that cats are known for their merciful swiftness), was preferable to a life sentence. The words 'manic depression' wouldn't leave him alone – was that it? Was that what all this was about? No, no, the summer hadn't been about illness – it had been about recovery from an illness, hadn't it? He thought back to what he considered to be the happiest time of his life and felt himself rise to defend it, in a courtroom, the European Court of Human Rights if necessary, to defend the right to pure, unblemished, complete and utter happiness. When had it begun? He decided it dated from the first day he met Mat. He'd tell him that one day.

7

Bedsit land

He was living on the seventh floor of a tower block in a bedsit, or the more glamorous 'studio flat'. Maybe the architect, from the leafy comfort of his spacious home, had imagined that living in such close proximity would promote a marvellous community spirit, but deadlocks and stickers of Rottweillers hardly inspire the confidence to ask for a cup of sugar.

Even after a year, he still came across people on his floor that he'd never seen before. The closest thing to togetherness was the sound of soap operas sounding out from open windows on hot days. The virtual community with its distilled drama was a safer bet.

One day, he was waiting for the lift, kicking at chewing gum on the floor, when his next door neighbour joined him. It arrived empty, the rush hour having long since passed. A few moments into its shaky descent, it stopped. It wasn't unusual. After some irrational button pushing and cursing, they leant back against the graffiti and looked at each other. Mat pulled his headset down around his neck.

'I'm Mat. Hello.'

'Dan.' They shook hands. Dan felt awkward. Mat seemed

to be everything that he wasn't. Good-looking, fit, trendy, cool and black. He could hear something interesting coming from his headphones.

'What are you listening to?' Mat took them off and handed them to him, telling him a name that went in one ear and out the other. It was some sort of jazzy stuff, exciting and loud.

'If you like it, I'll do you a tape.'

At that moment, the lift, its matchmaking done, came shuddering back to life and they went their separate ways.

Dan felt ridiculously cheerful. In fact, it had made getting up worthwhile. He'd been struggling to keep the spring of optimism inside him from drying up. Everyone kept telling him how well he was doing. He'd had a 'bad patch'. That was all. So they said.

He'd actually gone out with the intention of buying food, before meeting Mat. Instead he set off to find the best blank tape money could buy. Back home again, the cupboard was bare, save for an old box of cereal and some bread. Although man couldn't live on bread alone, he could, he mused, live on toast.

As he ate, he looked out of the wall of windows that made up one side of the flat, scattering crumbs on the windowsill for the pigeons. It was May. Summer was elbowing spring out of the way. Not that it was easy to tell on this estate. Here the year seemed to be split in two: winter, which was cold and grey, and summer, which was hot and grey. The landscaping around the so-called play area amounted to a patchy green space, much beloved of local dogs. Recently the council had planted a few trees, one of which had been snapped in half since the last time he'd seen it. The block opposite was identical to theirs – a high-rise human hutch. From his window he could see the station, miniaturised into a train set with its ever-busy railway lines snaking into the distance while plane after plane thundered overhead.

Since his return to London, he'd been working in his Uncle Paul's garage, a bus ride away, forcing himself to face the necessity for cash. He lied to all his friends about what he'd been doing before that, giving them a cock-and-bull story about a weird virus, careful to tell the same story to those who knew each other. His mum's brother had always liked him. With no children himself he over-flowed with avuncular love, never mentioning the 'bad patch'. He paid him over the odds to valet his cars. Looking at the smeary windscreens at the end of the day, he'd thrust cash into his grubby paw with a wink saying, 'Yep, well done! That's them ready for the carwash!'

He'd given Dan some holiday pay and told him to go away and make some bloody decisions about his future. He was closing the place down for a while, taking Auntie Pat on a once-in-a-lifetime cruise, because she was suffering from 'the change'. For a week Dan drifted about, doing nothing. The only decision he made about the future was that he wasn't going to think about it for now. The recent past was not a place he cared to revisit, so he concentrated on the here and now, finding that it didn't have much to recommend itself either. Maybe some new music would help.

He finished his toast and brushed the crumbs off his T-shirt. Blank tape in hand, and pretty sure that a decent enough interval had elapsed, he took a deep breath and knocked on his neighbour's door.

'Enter! Enter!' said Mat, smiling.

In a back to front version of his flat, this man had arranged his life. One side of the room was a wall of records, arranged in sections and neatly labelled. Under the windows was an arrangement of machines, stacked on top of each other, linked by a spaghetti-like mass of wires.

Mat gestured for his guest to sit down on his bed, as he unwrapped the tape and sat down in front of the controls like the pilot of the block. In a fluid movement, he spun across the bare floor on his chair on wheels, put the tape in one machine, the original into another and pressed 're-cord'. Dan watched him. He seemed to be the epitome of cool, totally at home in his skin, his life. They didn't talk much, just sat listening and smoking. Every now and then Mat would say, 'Check out the bass!' or 'This tune's doin' it!' Job done, Dan thanked him and got up to leave. To his surprise, Mat said he'd drop some more round and maybe they could have a drink sometime.

Back in his flat Dan lay on his bed, smoking, listening to his tape, looking out at the purple haze that hung over the London night, inspired. The spring inside had swelled into a babbling brook, effervescent, surging, as if it had just found its way past a boulder.

8

The feeling

Like trees coming into leaf, it's hard to pinpoint exactly when change begins. Once established, it's too late, you can't imagine the possibility of bare branches. Dan was feeling really good. Something weird had happened to the world around him. He knew it had begun with the altered colours, but he couldn't have said when. In fact, by the time traffic lights began to leave their normal confines, radiating diffuse mists of red, amber and green, mingling with the air in watercolour washes, he was past the point of no return.

Mat's tapes had transformed his solitary state into a communion with musicians. He would sit with his headphones on, watching the outside world as it changed and remained the same, then, transported by a particular passage or solo, he'd close his eyes and sink back onto his bed as high as an opium eater. What had been a track, a song, a tune, words, was now a picture in sound. Suddenly it all made perfect sense. Rhythm sections were the root, foundations for a mathematical construction. Each player's part separate, a coloured thread in a tapestry. He could pick one out and follow it, sometimes loose, sometimes tight, always connected.

His mind began an elaborate improvisation on this theme. As he gazed outside, buildings became the drum and bass. The trains played percussion. Wailing planes were guitars. Horns, well, obviously they were the horns. Shouting, barking and chirping provided vocal harmonies whilst the breeze sent a plastic bag tumbling and soaring in the sky like a clarinet, or a flute.

It seemed to him that the whole world was a sort of symphony. He felt that he had just stumbled upon a mighty truth. If nature, music, the workings of his body, the paths of the planets, everything, was interwoven in some simple yet complex way, governed by patterns which, if you could get far away enough you would see, then ... then what? It was as frustrating as trying to remember a dream – he just couldn't put his finger on it. Whatever it was all about, he was happy. The point was that if all things were connected then he wasn't alone after all. Or at least not all of the time. Occasional unison was as inevitable as the long, nerve-racking solos.

Nerve-wrecking solos more like. This must be payback time, he thought, as he breathed in the air, now as intoxicating as an Arabian night. The exact inverse of the way he'd been feeling a couple of months back, when the possibility of suicide had been the only thing that had kept him going. At that point he'd been a mistake. An unadvised, misplaced incidental. Something to be edited out. So alone, it took solitude into a new dimension. Without even himself for comfort. A worm on concrete on a hot day, a broken down vehicle on the hard shoulder, a spider in a bathtub, the sole, sickly survivor of a nuclear holocaust... Anything awful, anything bleak. So unlovable, so incapable of love, devoid of humanity. Sick. Ill. A waste of space. Without feeling, untouchable, unreachable. Seeing no worth in anything, thus unworthy, worthless. Meaningless. An unpleasant taste, an ache, a pain. A pain in the arse.

He shivered, picturing as he did several times a day the ransacked medicine cabinet and his hand, blurred by tears. Once capable, useful, now full of pills, which he'd expected to be the last thing he'd ever see. If only he'd known that this sort of happiness was possible. After all, what had he suffered? His life hadn't been hard. Maybe it hadn't been hard enough. It was pathetic. The loss of a lover, not through death, but to someone else. It's hardly uncommon. But now, in the face of his new-found, all-encompassing, cosmically connected, (if semi-clad) truth, it dawned on him that what he'd lost wasn't love, but a poor imitation of it. He'd been in love with her like a tightrope walker loves his rope.

To happiness then! Joie de vivre! It was more than just feeling good now. It had become an exquisite and protracted high. It stayed with him night and day. People started to comment on how well he looked. Mat was convinced he'd got a girl tucked away somewhere.

'You look like you're getting it good an' proper, mate!' he said winking at Dan, who was happy for him to think so. His energy levels were rising. His need for sleep was falling. He was up with the lark, and still up with the birds that remained twittering incongruously under streetlights in the wee small hours. He liked to position himself in front of the wall of windows, watching the squares of coloured light that were the windows of the opposite block. As more and more of its inhabitants went to bed, the building would dim, like a huge machine shutting down for the night. Gazing outwards, his stereo by his side, he'd peruse the FM dial, considering the possibility that external forces were programming estate dwellers to transmit information to the heavens by means of light switches.

What was happening? He knew that it was out of the ordinary, this boundless energy that found him walking from south London to the city to borrow fifty quid from his perplexed brother. Spurred on by the music from his headset, he wove his way through the busy jostling mass of, he decided, mostly miserable faces, seeing new and profound meaning in every signpost and advert. It was as if the world up until then had been in code, and he had just found the key. God, the colours! So bright, so cunning. Luring, implying, seducing, warning. And numbers! He wished he'd been good at maths. A computer whizz-kid. Then he could decode all these patterns, all the waves, all the geometry inside. He saw himself in front of a computer, tapping furiously at a keyboard, a modern day Einstein, winning the Nobel Prize for his Theory of Absolutely Everything.

Back in his flat, garish and unlikely garments that had inexplicably found their way into his possession were now his favourite clothes, as if they'd been lurking there at the back of the cupboard just waiting for his reinvention. He was fun to be with. Soon he was the life and soul. Friends started to hang around. He and Mat threw impromptu parties that took place in their two flats, annoying the neighbours when they started to spill out into the corridor. He found that his disinterest in the opposite sex had, like everything else, turned upside down. Suddenly he was brimming with confidence. He seemed to be able to have anyone he pleased. It was all part of the general excess, never lasting longer, or even as long as, a night. But it was great not to care. Not to be thinking about Her. When had he become attractive? He wasn't complaining. He could have taken on the entire female population, and taught it a thing or two.

Mat decided that with their combined talents they could start organising bigger parties. The success of these would guarantee club nights, leading inevitably to their own clubs, record label, company, empire. It may have been just another dream for Mat, but the idea mushroomed in Dan's mind until it became destiny. The theme would be, well what else? Saving the world from the destruction wreaked on it by capitalism. Well, somebody had to. Hadn't he always known he was different? The depression must have been some sort of test, some sort of interview, which he'd passed. After all, it wasn't going to be easy to save the world, there was going to be resistance, there always was, wasn't there? Obviously the clubs and the merchandising would kick-start the movement... A whole new system of economics and everything had to be conceived of and put into practise, and all by him. Jesus, it was quite daunting.

Alas, all this was to fall by the wayside, if it hadn't already, the day the light changed. Dawn was breaking. He and Mat were on their way home after a night out. They'd decided to walk, Mat was speeding, Dan may as well have been. Both of them assumed that the energy of the other was down to the same thing as their own. They climbed over the railings to cut through the park. To Dan's surprise it had transformed into the Garden of Eden. The landscape was trembling as the intensifying daylight pushed away the darkness. Everything was glowing, as if embarrassed to reveal its nakedness. He stopped, allowing the geese, illicitly grazing on the sports fields, to waddle back to the safety of the lake. Throwing himself onto the damp grass, he looked up at the sky, dug his fingernails into the earth, rolled over and breathed in the ancient, homely smell of it. Rich, resinous, spicy and as sweet as an exotic cake mix. The sponge, the base, the envy of all planets – God, he could have eaten it, it was so good.

Mat was laughing at him.

'C'mon man, get up!'

'But it's so beautiful!'

'You're tripping mate. Let's get home.'

On the other side of the fence, he saw colour seeping from the traffic lights.

'Mat, look at the light!' He stopped dead in his tracks, tugging on his friend's sleeve.

'What are you on?' said Mat, urging him homewards. They parted at their respective doorways.

'Get some sleep. Laters.'

Dan knew that there was not even the remotest possibility of sleep.

A few days, or maybe even a week later he knocked on Mat's door, at a time when most of the block was sleeping. Mat opened it with a towel wrapped round his waist.

'Listen man, I'm busy right now,' he said, winking at his neighbour.

'Can't you just come round for a minute? I haven't seen you for ages. I need to talk to you...'

Mat wasn't listening. He was looking at Dan strangely.

'You look thinner... You're looking good though...' From inside they heard a girl calling him back to bed.

'Gotta go mate. Check you tomorrow.' He leant towards Dan's cheek and gave him a kiss. This seemed quite normal to them both. Then he whispered in his ear, 'It's taking over this town, you know about it already don't you? That's what you were on, wasn't it... Remember, the other night?'

Dan remembered, in fact it wasn't really a case of remembering, since the feeling had only intensified since then.

'What's taking over?' he said, alarmed. They looked at each other, saucer-eyed and excited. Luminous green shimmered around Mat like phosphorescence, and when their eyes met there was a flash of white light.

'Ecstasy mate, Ecstasy,' whispered Mat. With that he went back to the waiting girl. As far as Dan was concerned, this confirmed everything. But he hadn't needed to take a tablet. He'd been chosen. There was no doubt about it. He went back to his flat and catching sight of himself in his bathroom mirror, saw that he was lit up like a standard lamp, tall and thin, his face a glowing porcelain shade.

He switched on his ancient telly. He discovered that if he turned the contrast, colour and brightness right down and fiddled with the channel knob, very interesting patterns appeared, dancing across his screen like Bridget Riley paintings come to life. When he grew tired of this, he blackened the screen further, until it became a window onto deep space, with the odd distant glimmer here and there.

He remembered someone telling him that space was as empty as a cathedral containing three grains of sand, and looking out at the strange orangey-yellow night sky, it looked even emptier than that. Once that would have freaked him out – the terrible enormity of the universe and, worse, the inversely proportionate terrible insignificance of self – but now it didn't bother him in the least. Other dimensions, nothing scary about that. If there were three, then why not six, seven, nine, ten? He looked at his fingers. Ten of them. His digits. People were saying that digital technology was going to change the world forever, and for better, in the next, significantly, ten years. Did they mean like digital watches? He'd always liked the neat way that all ten numerals fitted into the little upright rectangle. He turned to the silent television. The jumping dots had become a tightly knit crowd of dancing human beings, all fitting in to the rectangular screen, a synchronised tribe, a living jigsaw. It looked so real, God, he was going crazy! He blinked and rubbed his eyes, but it didn't go away. Was digitalis the name of a medical condition? If so, he'd got it.

It was almost dawn. This time of day was becoming familiar. Why didn't anyone have the time for him at the moment? No one seemed interested in his plans. The parties had stopped as soon as their novelty had worn off. Raves somewhere off the M25 were the thing now, but the last place he wanted to be was in a crowd. He didn't need it. He was having a wild time, all by himself. With his head as light as a feather, his physical self was turning over so fast that it seemed slow, a spinning wheel of a machine. Or a rocket that had just been launched into space, getting lighter and higher as redundant sections of himself were jettisoned, falling away into deep space, paring him down to the essential. It was pure pleasure, languorous, abandoned, decadent, delicious. He was transparent, porous, perforated. He could feel wind and light rushing through his cell walls. He was plugged into the main source, lit up. He could live on light. He could feel it, taste its liquid gold running through his veins. It was love, love... Love that he couldn't see. Or touch. That could never be taken away... What was going on? For want of anything better, he christened this concoction of sensation The Feeling. It had to last forever.

He lit a cigarette, dragged on it once or twice, then put it down in one of the ashtrays that were filled to overflowing with perfect tubes of grey ash where many had burnt away unsmoked. He seemed unable to remember trivia such as the fact that there was already one lit, dying a slow death, three feet away. Who cares? It seemed funny to him. Everything was funny. Funny and serious in that somehow even a joke had more meaning than you'd once thought. God must be a joker. God must be a boogie man...

He looked around the room. He was pleased with what he had done. That's why he kept asking Mat to come round. He'd transformed the place. It started with a few party decorations, before becoming the prototype club, venue, whatever, for the entertainment conglomerate that was soon to be Mat's and his. Paper and pencil had quickly been abandoned. The walls were now a psychedelic jumble of colour. His mind was constantly playing the word association game, one leading to another, the association having more significance than ever. If not linked by meaning, then related by rhyme ... or shape, or ... anything. He was trying his best to concentrate on the grand plan... It wasn't easy... But then it wouldn't be, would it? Coincidence abounded. Everything that caught his eye, every cover of every book or tape was just what he'd been thinking about, looking for, was about him, was the writing on the wall... Not for nothing was there a cockerel on a cornflakes box, oh no, it wasn't just marketing, it was a sign. The herald of the morning, a new day, a new life. The colours telling you something very important indeed. In fact, he decided that if you were to eat one thing the colour of every colour of the rainbow then that would be enough, whatever it was. One cherry tomato, one cornflake, one banana, one pea, one blueberry (if you could get hold of one), one... What was indigo? A glass of Ribena maybe, violet – God, it was outrageous that he wasn't sure of the difference between indigo and violet. He really must go to the shops, he thought, chewing on a stale cornflake. Maybe he had a picture of a rainbow somewhere in the flat. He hunted around feverishly, thinking about how funny it was that he'd always thought that it was a fine toothcomb, not a fine-tooth comb. A fine-tooth comb was something like a nit comb, whereas a fine toothcomb was something that someone like Marie Antoinette would have used as an eighteenth century equivalent of dental floss. Very ornate, with a long handle of silver or gold ... inlaid with gems with a tiny ivory comb at the end for picking bits of wild boar from between the royal teeth, or what was left of them...

He gave up looking for a rainbow and turned his attention to the rising sun. The city was stretching and yawning. His friend, the bravest pigeon of the lot, seemed to see him from a way off and flew towards the open window. Graceful and confident on the wing, the bird landed unsteadily, scrabbling and flapping on the hostile windowsill. He held out a few cornflakes in his cupped hand to the bird, who cocked his head and turned his orange eye on him with suspicion. All in good time, he thought, dropping them before the shy creature. It seemed wrong to offer something and then only give it on his terms.

The sun was well and truly up now. It was going to be a beautiful day. The sky was pink seeping into blue and the scrubby grass and little trees seemed to be dancing, swaying, with one gentle motion. Everything that lived – tree, dog, bird or man – was surrounded by the snap, crackle and popping green light that had danced around Mat the other night. The sun was blaring out its rays like a child's drawing. He found that he could reach out to it and take a golden thread, pulling off more and more, a sunshine candyfloss man, or write in the air with sparklers for fingers, scattering electric confetti wherever he pleased. He anointed Pidge with a smattering of sunshine, and he was transfigured into the Holy Dove, or something suspiciously like it.

He turned away from the window reluctantly. He wanted to lie down but there was to be no respite from the work he had to do. The sense of urgency was overwhelming. It had to be done today. If he didn't get it together today, something was going to happen, something bad. All he had to do was finish the business plan, sort out his paperwork and get to the bank. Get the loan and get started. Hang on, what about a bit of publicity first? Why hadn't he thought of it before? The newspaper building on the other side of the park! He'd go in there, maybe dress up a bit first, and tell them about it... Something told him they'd be waiting for him. His time had come.

He sat on the floor in front of his pile of notebooks to take yet more dictation from who knows what, his jumbled thoughts tumbling onto the page as the night flights made their descents into the London morning from who knows where.

9

There must be some mistake

Later that day, Mat knocked on his door.

'Who is it?'

'It's me, who you got in there with you?'

Dan opened the door. 'No one.'

Mat came in and then jumped back as if he'd walked into an electric fence.

'What the fuck have you been up to?!' He looked round at the painted walls, candles, brimming ashtrays and piles of papers covered with indecipherable scribblings and diagrams. Dan paced around, muttering to himself. Mat grabbed his shoulders and sat him down, knelt in front of him and looked into his eyes.

'Listen man, tell me, what are you on?'

Dan started to laugh.

'Nothing! Nothing at all, except nicotine!' He reached for another fag. 'I've done all this for us Mat! Don't you see? The thing is that I can't concentrate on it properly at the moment, but...' He sat down on the floor and began to hunt through the mountains of paper. 'I want to show you the business plan, I've done it... It's to take to the bank ... and the papers... What's the time? We could do that to-day... I'm ready.'

In the midst of the chaos, miraculously, a little black address book stood out. Did he see Mat picking it up and slipping it into his pocket, or was he just being paranoid?

'Got any smoke?' he asked, still lost in his paperchase.

'Er ... yeah, I think so mate, I'll just go next door and have a look.' Mat looked back as he left, saying that he'd leave the door on the latch. Dan gazed out of the wall of windows, open to their fullest extent, a doorway onto the warm oceanic sky.

He barely noticed that Mat had gone, or come back. He sat down cross-legged on the bed, transfixed by the sun. Mat sat down next to him and rolled a joint. House music pulsed faintly from the stereo, and as they smoked, clouds of swirling blue and brown smoke got caught in the sunbeams, filling the room with a heavy haze. Dan told him that he had never been so happy in his entire life, now that he knew what it was all about.

'That's good man, that's good.' Mat nodded, the last of the spliff billowing from his nostrils.

When his brother arrived at his door, out of the blue, Dan greeted him with delight. It wasn't so often that he came down his end. One minute he was there, the next he'd gone off somewhere with Mat, saying something about having to make some calls. Dan wondered why he hadn't just used his phone – maybe he was trying to save him some money.

He tried to find something to offer his dear sibling by way of hospitality. Tap water would have to do. He really must go and get some supplies today. He didn't need food any longer, but he might just treat himself to something, in honour of his visitor. Suddenly, his brother was back in his flat, looking at the walls with furrowed brows.

It's good, isn't it, you see, when Mat and I get our club... But that's not all... Did you know all along?' said Dan. His brother looked at him oddly.

'Know what all along?'

Dan didn't reply and proceeded to show him page after page of what could have been mistaken for meaningless scrawl. There was no way that his hand could keep up with his brain so he'd resorted to his own version of shorthand, absolutely sure that he'd be able to read it when the time came. Not that he had any sense of time. Without the desire for sleep, or food, the clock was redundant.

In what was for him therefore no time at all, a crowd materialised at his door. His parents were there, giving him very strange looks indeed. They almost seemed to be cross with him about something. Had he forgotten about a family reunion or something? Anyway, once he'd had an opportunity to explain his plans to them, he knew that they'd be proud of him. It would make up for what he'd put them through earlier in the year.

But what was this? There were suddenly more people in the corridor, one of whom was a policeman. Had there been some sort of incident on his floor? He was worried about Mat. Where was he anyway? He was sure that he'd been there earlier.

Hang on, the policeman was coming in, asking him to go with him. Not bloody likely. But before he could do anything about it he was being led out the door, the policeman holding his arm in a vice-like grip. He looked round frantically for something essential to take with him, saw his Walkman and grabbed it, hoping that there was a tape inside. He needed to block out as many of these bad vibes as possible. They were hurting him, as if he'd been caught in the eye of an electrical storm.

In the corridor he shook off the man and made a run for it. Obviously the lift couldn't be relied upon as a getaway vehicle, so he headed for the only alternative. Much clattering ensued as the policeman, followed by the rest of the crowd, made after him down the never-ending stairwell.

Dan took them steps three at a time, dodging past two Rastas sweating profusely under the weight of a giant leather sofa. They were ordered out of the way. Dan could hear their voices receding as he descended, saying, 'Take it easy man! Cha, ya wan' us to take it back down again eh? Serious?' They were laughing. 'You just have to breathe in deep Officer, innit?'

By this time Dan was outside, heading down the short-cut to the station, where he felt sure he could lose them. Suddenly a police car appeared at the end of the alleyway, blocking his escape route. Another policeman jumped out and held up his hand as if to stop the traffic. He stopped. In any case, he'd trodden on something sharp in his bare feet and couldn't run anymore. Whatever the game was, it was up.

'Get into the car please... Sir,' ordered the policeman.

Really, the shame of it, being taken away in a bloody Mini Metro. A Mini Metro for the Mini Metropolitan Police. No wonder people had lost their respect for the law.

He was ushered discourteously into the back seat. Next to him on the seat was a bag of weed. He picked it up.

'Is this yours?' he asked, holding it up. Looking round the officer said, 'No, it's yours.'

'I'd hardly be showing it to you if it was, would I?' The guy must think I'm an idiot, he thought.

'That's what they all say,' came the reply.

Strange. Ah well, he thought, never look a gift horse in the mouth, slipping it into his pocket.

The first policeman had caught up, and got into the passenger seat.

'Where are we going?'

'Never you mind,' he said. Even stranger.

'What am I supposed to have done?' asked Dan, but was given no answer. As if he didn't know. God, the bastards had found out about the plan... But how?

They drove along at a disappointingly slow pace

through the familiar streets. He wasn't sure what he'd do if he saw anyone he knew. Would he shout for help? Wave? Or duck down with embarrassment? The latter, he decided. But he didn't, so he needn't have worried.

Before long, they arrived at the local cop shop. They drove round the back and he was led inside and made to stand before another uniformed man at a desk. He barely looked up as he asked him his name, address etc, and then told him to empty his pockets. Dan obliged, protesting vainly as he wrote down, 1 Small bag of marijuana, 1 Personal stereo. Formalities complete, he was led in the direction of a cell.

'Please can I keep my Walkman? I'll go mad in there without it...' he pleaded. For some reason everyone seemed to find this very amusing.

'Don't suppose you can do much harm with it,' said the laughing policeman, whose laughter was, under the circumstances, not quite so infectious as that of the eponymous hero of the now sinister song.

He needed air, but there was nothing but a vent, high up on the wall. Banging on the door he demanded release, or a cigarette at the very least, but there didn't seem to be anyone about. Either that or they were ignoring him. Defeated, he sat down on the hard bed. Feeling strangely exposed, he pulled its meagre blue blanket around him like a shawl. Still inhabiting a time-free zone, he tried to keep count of the number of times he turned his tape over. He opened the battery compartment and touched the batteries, sure that he could sustain their fading power with his live fingertips.

Eventually, the door was opened. Relieved that the claustrophobic's nightmare was over, he asked if he could go home. There had obviously been some horrendous cock-up. He'd been mistaken for a notorious local ganja peddler – that was all, the plan was safe, and now they were going to apologise. Not so. Instead, he was bundled into the back of a van, which drove off, and judging by the length of the journey, they weren't giving him a lift home.

10

Smoke and mirrors

Well, he supposed it was inevitable. After all, he'd known that there was going to be resistance. But how had they found out, so soon? Was Mat some sort of double agent?

After lurching around for what seemed like ages, suddenly he was sent flying as the van stopped sharply. When the doors opened he tried to make a dash for it but a swarm of blokes in uniform appeared out of nowhere, grabbing at his flailing arms until he was lifted off the ground. They carried him, kicking like a naughty child, through at least three doors which had to be unlocked and locked again, past a blur of people who seemed to be queuing for food and into a large, bright, colourful room.

Everything was primary coloured – brash, like a children's play area in a shopping centre, or perhaps a fast food joint. An enclosure full of foam balls wouldn't have gone amiss – or even the appearance of Ronald McDonald, wondering where all his customers had gone. On one wall gigantic poisonous-looking toadstools loomed ominously out of a Disneyesque landscape. The others glittered as if inlaid with chips of diamond. The carpet was littered with fag ends, plastic cutlery and paper plates, some of which had bits of food on them. Coleslaw, by the looks of it.

As he was taking all this in, he heard the door being locked behind him. He ran back to it, somehow knowing that there wasn't much point. The smell of school dinners was permeating the stale heat. God it was boiling! He looked around for a window, but the nearest thing to it was a glass hatch looking into a similar room, empty, despite a flickering television.

He scurried around frantically in search of a source of fresh air, found a door and pushed it open. A big black girl was lying face down on a thin blue mattress, apparently lifeless, her hair in high bunches like a schoolgirl, a wiggly parting snaking down the back of her head. Her dress had ridden up revealing red lacy knickers. Dan knelt down beside her, to feel for a pulse or something, when the one visible eye opened, swollen and piggy. She heaved herself over onto her back and gazed up at him, asking in a lisping, babyish voice if he'd come to get her. When he said that he hadn't, and that he didn't even know where he was, she got to her feet in that lurching way of large beasts of the field, raised her fists and made for him as he backed away, pulling the door shut behind him. Jesus! Hiding from her was suddenly his top priority.

He made himself a safe house out of the furniture, piling the featherweight armchairs on top of one another into a sort of foam igloo. He crawled inside, and as time passed started to feel a bit calmer, especially when he found his Walkman still in his trouser pocket. The funny thing was that he wasn't frightened. Affronted, definitely. Indignant, yes. But quite certain that something very important was happening, to him, to the world... Something hugely significant that he was at the very centre of – was responsible for even. Where he was or why he was here may have been unclear, but that he was meant to be here, for some very important reason indeed, was brilliantly clear, dazzling in fact. The thought was so powerful that it almost blew the lid off his den.

After a while, he stuck his head out and looked around. There was no movement coming from the side room, so he tiptoed across to the door that said 'Toilet'. He was dying of thirst. He grabbed a tap before it vanished like a mirage and put his mouth under the warm dribble, cupping his hands, splashing water on his face and running his fingers through his hair. Looking up he confronted a hazy image in a scoured piece of metal that was, he supposed, some sort of a mirror. Rubbing it with his sleeve didn't help. He was a blur. The image mesmerised him. His skin seemed to be dissolving. The barrier between him and the outside world was melting. If he looked for long enough he was pretty sure the image would fade to nothing.

He was distracted by knocking coming from the direction of the hatch. Looking over, he saw a young black guy in a yellow waterproof waving cheerfully from the other room before sitting down and lighting a cigarette. He bounded over to the glass and watched in despair as the smoker blew a stream of perfect smoke-rings that bounced off the glass, bigger and thinner, before twisting, sliding downwards and disappearing. As he was turning away from the torture the guy pointed to the door. Moments later, a stream of smoke flowed through the keyhole. He tried to breathe it in, banged on the door for more, this time ready, his lips pressed to the keyhole, stopping the gaps with his fingers, but a voice was telling his new friend to get out of the way.

Hearing the rattle of keys, he stood aside as the door opened. Two casually dressed men walked past him, each carrying a tray of food. Bringing up the rear, a woman in a white coat followed by one of the guys in uniform. Spotting an open window in the next room, he seized his chance, pushed past them and ran towards it.

It was too high up for him to feel the benefit, if he could

just get his nose close enough... Springing onto the window ledge, he gulped as much of the cool air as he could, catching sight of a huge moon as he heard someone shout, 'He's trying to get out!'

He almost laughed – the window was open three inches at the most, and barred. Just as he was about to say something witty about Houdini, he was grabbed and slammed to the floor, flipped over onto his front and pinned to the ground with his arms bent behind his back. His only weapon was his teeth, and he used them on the first bit of flesh that came close enough.

A man yelped. His trousers and pants were ripped from his backside. Pulling his head up he saw the woman in the white coat coming towards him with the biggest needle he'd ever seen in his life, holding it pointing upwards and tapping it, checking it with slightly cross-eyes like he'd seen on TV. Only this time it was destined for him. She disappeared from view. He shut his eyes and braced himself as what felt like a sword was thrust into his tensed muscle. Powerless to resist, he was lifted up by his limbs and carried horizontally towards a flight of stairs, hooked, squirming and wriggling. The bareness of bum was the worst thing, no contest. He'd liked those trousers too – his brother had brought them back from India...

'Don't break my Walkman...' he squawked. Funny thing was that one of the guys picked it up and wrapped the headphones round it with a care that seemed totally perverse.

With his arms being wrenched out of their sockets, he was bumped up a flight of stairs like a suitcase, then dumped in a little airless room. Being locked in the big room was one thing. This was something else.

Then the air-pressure changed. He was being compressed by some sort of G force. His head started a slow spin, he couldn't think straight. He needed to pee. No choice, it had to be in the corner. Trousers already round his ankles. He tried to mop up with a pillowcase, suddenly all fingers and thumbs. The heat was suffocating. The little frosted window terminally shut. Moonlight shimmered on the watery glass. A small, round, blue light in the ceiling faded with each heartbeat. Fuck! He remembered this feeling. Then he'd wanted it and it didn't work. This time he didn't want it and it was working.

11

Room service

Surprised to find himself alive, he tried to piece together the night before. Had it been the night before? What was that thing called? Cryonics? It could have been 2525 for all he knew. He could hear voices, the rattle of keys. He pulled himself up onto his elbows to greet whatever was coming.

The door opened. The same crowd was there. One of them had a bandaged hand. So it wasn't a dream, he had bitten someone... He made a mental note to apologise to him at some point, but as yet it wouldn't have been entirely sincere. They all seemed tense, as if they were waiting for him to spring at them and rip their throats out. He decided to employ that old school method of bamboozlement, i.e., to deliver the exact opposite of the behaviour expected. From behind the wall of guards stepped a bloke in jeans and a T-shirt, carrying a tray containing what appeared to be breakfast.

'G'day Dan,' he said, avoiding eye contact. 'Are you hungry?'

Tempting as it was to say, 'Fuck off you bastards,' he flipped into ultra-polite mode.

'Yes, I am, thanks. Are you from Australia?' He wished

the guy didn't look so pitiful, squirming before him.

'Yeah, I am, as it goes... We'll leave you to it for now,' he said, as if he couldn't get out of the stuffy little room fast enough.

'Any chance of a bath?' asked Dan. The palms of his hands were filthy.

'Yeah, yeah, sure thing mate, I'll send someone up to get you.'

The door was locked and he was left alone. The porridge was cold and glutinous, the tea was stewed but at least it was sweet. Anything was better than the horrible taste in his mouth.

He must have crashed out again, because next thing he was looking up at a colossal bosom. A pendant of transparent coloured glass was dangling above him, throwing out little darts of light, swinging to and fro as if dousing for his heart.

'Hello there my love, how are you feeling now, hmmm?'

A matronly black woman wearing a white apron was leaning over the bed, smiling at him, her eyes sparkling. He hadn't heard her come in. How come she wasn't surrounded by the security blokes? She leant back and put her hands on her hips.

'Are you ready for a nice hot bath, my darlin'?'

She helped him out of the bed, and onto his feet. Feeling severely wobbly, he gestured apologetically towards the soggy pillowcase in the corner. She nodded as she led him out into the corridor and back down the staircase. With her arm around him, he realised gratefully that she was covering his backside with a handful of his ripped trousers. Still holding him, she unlocked a door.

They entered an old-fashioned laundry room as hot as a furnace. It had a high ceiling with a pulley suspended from it, draped with items of misshapen clothing, grey towels, and underwear. In the centre of the room was a large bath. He sank onto a chair in the corner and watched as the woman turned on the taps.

'Is there a law here preventing the entry of air from the outside world, or something?' he asked, blowing air down the neck of his shirt and fanning it in and out.

'Better than being too cold, sweetheart.'

'True, true,' he conceded, although, thinking about it he wasn't so sure. He couldn't imagine being anything other than sweltering. It was like trying to imagine the need for an overcoat, hat, scarf and gloves, on the hottest day of the year. Still, he was looking forward to the bath. When they'd come to take him away, he hadn't stopped to put on socks and shoes, and no one had suggested it to him. As if everyone had wanted him to conform to their idea of the dangerous wild man. Give a dog a bad name and all that. It was weird not to have anything but the clothes that he was wearing. Where was all the paraphernalia of normality – his keys, travelcard, wallet, fags? Was his flat locked? Was his stuff safe?

The woman was busy, pulling damp bundles of washing out of antiquated machines and transferring them into laundrette-size tumble dryers mercilessly pumping out a fiery sirocco. Clearing his throat, he suggested that the bath might be ready by now.

'So it is,' she said, turning off the taps and checking the temperature of the water with her hand.

'Well, jump in then.' She turned back to the burgeoning piles of sheets. He coughed again.

'Ahem. You can leave me alone now, thanks very much for your help.' The woman giggled.

'I can't leave you alone my darlin', but don't be shy, I won't look. I've got plenty to be getting on with. I got to find you something nice to put on afterwards.'

Resignedly, he took off his bedraggled clothes and climbed in, concentrating on keeping his balance. He'd never understood why people talked about jumping into baths. It conjured up ludicrous images of naked bathers approaching the tub as if a swimming pool, hurling themselves into the water with abandon, which, in the bathroom, would be suicidal.

He immersed his head, first staying as still as he could, then listening to the whirring of himself as he swayed from side to side, his hair helpless as pondweed. He pulled himself up again, and asked if there was any shampoo. The bath attendant went to a cupboard.

'You're in luck,' she said, approaching the bath with a dusty bottle of Vosene.

'Thank you ma'am.' He took the green teardrop-shaped bottle and opened it, the smell whisking him back to childhood. He half-expected her to start washing his hair for him as he pressed a flannel to his face, but she left him to it and went back to her work.

Even in the presence of this stranger, he felt deliciously free in his nakedness. Recently, his body had transformed. It wasn't that old rag, tag and bobtail of spare parts thrown together for a laugh. No, now he was the proud possessor of a sleek unified form, delicate yet strong, an eggshell, perfect. Not skinny, but lithe. Not bony, but sculptural. Like his mind, his body had just fulfilled its potential. He was beautiful, simple as that.

As the water cooled he watched himself wrinkle. He was travelling happily up and down the tiny hills and dales of his fingertips when the woman said that it was time to get out. He let the water out reluctantly, watching as it swirled down the plughole. There was a black rim round the bath and what looked like tealeaves left on the bottom in a pattern so random and yet so familiar that it must, he was sure, resound throughout the universe. Probably could have told his fortune too.

The woman was taking a break. Leaning against a washing machine, she was flapping at her face with a tea towel, tipping Smarties from the tube into her mouth. Dan concentrated on her giving him one, at the very least.

'What's your name?' he asked.

'Gloria, and you?'

'Dan,' he replied.

'Bingo!' she grinned. Holding up the orange lid she said, 'The letter is D. Must be your lucky day!' She came over to the side of the still steaming bath.

'Open wide!'

He tipped his head back like a baby bird as she poured in a mouthful. She held up a pair of silky black boxer shorts.

'These'll suit a good-looking young man like you.'

They'd come from a cupboard overflowing with cast-offs labelled, 'Emergency Clothing'. Dan laughed out loud at the thought of people in peril, fighting over crimplene trousers and musty jumpers as if their lives depended on it.

'What's so funny?' asked Gloria.

"Emergency Clothing'. Dunno, it's just funny.'

'Well, this is an emergency, isn't it?' she said, her eyebrows raised knowingly.

'Is it?' His heart started to thump. She knew something. Something about him, about what was going to happen...

She steadied him as he got out of the bath and handed him a rough towel. When dry, she helped him dress. By the time she was finished with him he'd turned into a mannequin in an Oxfam shop window, sporting maroon trousers with rock-solid seams and a shrunken T-shirt, the words 'FRANKIE SAYS RELAX' faded and misshapen across his chest. He squeezed his feet into an old pair of tartan carpet slippers, wondering about the previous owner.

'There you are now.' She stood back to admire him, smiling.

'Oh! Mustn't forget,' she said, slipping the plastic talisman into his pocket, 'Your lucky charm.'

She led him into the television room, sat him down and patted him on the head.

'See ya later alligator,' she said, blowing him a kiss. Another woman approached, holding out a small plastic beaker of the orange liquid.

'Dan, would you drink this for me?' She said, enunciating each word very slowly and carefully. He took it, not bothering to ask what it was – any lip may have resulted in another needle. Before he knew it, the G force feeling was back. Curling up on the squeaky plastic sofa, he prepared for another journey to the outer limits.

12

Jack

He opened his eyes. Birch ward. The open ward. Looking around his new quarters, it appeared at first that he had the large dormitory to himself. He got up, put his things into his locker, rubbed his aching legs and decided to have a snoop around. Some of the beds had curtains drawn around them, but most were on view, strewn with rumpled sheets and dirty clothes. Lockers were covered with sweet wrappers and Lucozade bottles, photos and old magazines. On a few of them stood clear plastic vases of drooping flowers, festering in green water. The colour scheme was pastel, in two tones, dirty and peeling. The whole place could do with, as his mum would have said, a jolly good airing.

There was a whimpering sound coming from behind the closed curtains of the end bed. It was Jack – he could smell him.

'Jack, are you OK? It's me, Dan, can I come in?'

'Leave me alone. I just want to be on my own, comprendez?'

'OK, OK.' Dan backed off. He knew the feeling. However, before he'd turned away, Jack's disembodied face appeared from between the curtains, red-eyed and wet

71

with tears.

'Apologies, apologies, I didn't mean...' He looked at Dan dolefully.

'Don't worry about it. You don't have to apologise to me.'

'What, you mean I should be apologising to a dead bird, is that it?'

'No! Anyway, I'm sure you did the right thing...' said Dan, trying to sound sure. He pulled back the curtain and sat down next to him on the bed. They both stared ahead, with nothing more to say on the subject.

'Let's go somewhere where we can smoke,' said Jack eventually. They walked back out into the dayroom. Someone had taped a piece of paper to the empty bird-cage with the words, 'GERALD, GONE, NOT FORGOT-TEN. R.I.P.' in thick black felt-tip. Dan felt all eyes on them as they walked towards the door. He considered changing it later to, 'GERALD, FREE AT LAST,' then decided against it, thinking that Jack might think he was joining in with his tormentors and not actually suggesting that the bird had gratefully fluttered off his mortal coil.

Jack led him back into the corridor and out into the sun-shine. They sat down on the nearest bench and sparked up. After about two minutes, Dan's skin began to tingle and burn. He told Jack that he'd have to go and sit in the shade. It was a bummer, because he'd always loved soak-ing up the sun, and now that its light had revealed the truth of all things to him, he felt even more inclined to-wards its worship.

'Just imagine when it's like this all the time, for every-one,' said Jack, leading him to a wooden shelter like the ones in the park. 'Welcome to the bus-stop!' he said, let-ting Dan go before him with a bow.

Dan looked around at the graffiti and the debris of much dope smoking at his feet.

'What do you mean, like this for everyone, all of the

time?' Maybe Jack knew something about a secret state plan to silence everyone with tranquillisers.

'The sky, mate. It's there to protect us, but it's getting thinner and thinner. Full of holes it is. And they don't help.' He pointed up at a passing 747. Dan looked up at the sky, seeing it as a piece of wood with planes burrowing through it like death-watch beetle.

Try as he might to stay focused on one of his pet topics, Jack sighed and said that he couldn't stop thinking about that wretched bird. Dan didn't know what to suggest. He hunted half-heartedly through the butts, broken fags and Rizla packets with his foot, in the hope that someone might have dropped their stash.

'It's not the first time I've killed something you know.'

'I guess it's pretty hard not to,' said Dan, thinking of squashed insects, small furry pets and baby animals killed with enthusiastic kindness.

'I dunno about that mate, most people seem to get by without doing away with someone.'

'What, you mean you've killed a person?! Fucking hell, Jack!' Dan felt fear fizz up and down his spine. He was hanging out with a murderer. This was what his life had come to. He looked at the unhappy man next to him and relented, with his greying hair sticking up in peaks and his blue eyes framed with the wrinkly evidence of laughter – or maybe too much squinting at the sky. This was Jack, not some cold-blooded killer.

'Told you you didn't know anything about me,' said Jack. Had he? He couldn't remember.

'I was even younger than you, still at school.' He looked at Dan and smiled sadly. 'Yeah, that's right, way back in pre-history. In the sort of place where everyone knows your business, not like here, London, I mean. That can be a good thing, but only if you're on the right side of it. Capisce?'

Dan nodded sagely, trying to exhibit more worldly wisdom than he considered he actually possessed.

'My ma brought me up. Used to call me her war baby. Dunno what happened to my dad, she never spoke about him. She did a good job, mind, I didn't miss what I'd never had. She was a looker, my ma. A lot of blokes were after her. I was too young to know what was going on, but the story goes that she had an affair with my teacher, then dumped him using me as the reason. I don't think I was the reason, I think she'd just gone off him. She was probably just trying to soften the blow, as you do. Anyway, he always hated me for it. Any opportunity to lay into me. One day he went too far. It wasn't the first time he'd caned me for nothing, but this time he was really going for it. I turned on him and punched him. Just once, that was all. The bastard dropped down dead.'

'Bloody hell!' said Dan.

Jack went on. 'It turned out later that he'd had a heart attack, but as far as the world and his wife were concerned I'd killed him. The funeral parade went right past our house. Ma and me were the only people in the whole village that didn't go. She hit the bottle, and if there was ever any left over, I'd polish it off. Soon got a taste for it. It killed her in the end... So I came to London to escape, and this is where I've ended up. And I feel a lot sorrier about that bird than I ever will about that bastard.'

'But you didn't kill him. He was most probably going to have that heart attack anyway,' said Dan. Jack shook his head.

'Oh, but I did. Jack the teacher slayer. That's me. That's how people saw me, that's what I was. And still am, in my head. It's too late to change now. It would be like telling you that you were really... I dunno, a girl or something... And when I've had a few, sometimes I just lose it ... my temper, you know.'

He pulled back his cuffs and showed Dan the insides of his wrists, scored with pale scars.

'I never really wanted to kill myself, I just wanted to... I shouldn't be telling you all this mate,' he said, tears starting to flow down his face in a seamless, sobless stream. 'Me soul was sick mate, sick. Know what I mean?'

Dan nodded again. Oh yes, soul-sickness was something he knew all about.

If only he could swallow up everyone's pain like Pacman. Why did it have to keep trying to spoil his fun? He modified the thought to everyone's fun, and, still at a loss for words, moved closer to Jack, and put his arm tentatively around his shoulders.

'I've been high like you before,' said Jack. 'You enjoy it while it lasts. It's the only real holiday you'll ever get in your life. But anyway,' he breathed in deeply, then out noisily, 'I've got a good feeling about you, you're going to be OK.'

They walked back through the maze of buildings towards Birch. Dan was thinking about what Jack had said. He'd wanted to refute the possibility that he, or anyone for that matter, had been high like him before. The Feeling was his – his alone. As exclusively his as the colossal downer had been, whether Jack had been there or not.

It was lunchtime. The circular corridor was filling up. Hungry hordes were emerging from doorways. Dan followed the flow. The tube – that's what it reminded him of. He lost Jack in the crowd and felt a twinge of disloyalty at his relief.

Everyone filed into the cavernous dining room and formed a noisy queue at the counter. There was a choice of casserole or salad, apple pie and custard or fruit to follow. Plates towering with stodge were piled precariously onto trays, cups of tea or coffee sloshed over saucers loaded with sachets of sugar. Or Sweet 'n' Lo, for the huddle of bony folk who, whilst the others tucked in, tried to hide lettuce leaves under their knives.

He found a space, sat down and looked around him.

God, the place must be gigantic. He wasn't very good at judging numbers, but there must have been hundreds of people by his reckoning. Some of them were leaving as the next sitting was arriving.

It could almost have been a school, no, college. One that took a lot of mature students and with an unorthodox admissions policy at that. Then again, it could be mistaken for a soup kitchen, he thought, as another group of what almost looked like down-and-outs trooped in.

Suddenly, through the sparkling green sea of faces, he caught a glimpse of a girl walking out the door talking to some bloke. It was the Elf, he was sure of it. He struggled out of his chair, abandoned his now even less interesting tray and raced after her. Shit! His legs were killing him. He tried his best to dodge past the replete diners, sauntering back to their wards four abreast, but it was too late, he'd lost her. Damn! He kicked himself for not finding out her name. How thick can you get? Maybe if he ran round in the opposite direction he'd find her, and then it would look casual at the same time. He tried it, but found that in this rush hour traffic he was as welcome as someone going round the wrong way on an ice rink.

He noticed that there were stairways leading off the corridor, twisting upwards with arrows pointing the way to further tree-titled wards. May as well try one, he thought and found himself heading up towards Willow, which seemed like an appropriate place for her, even though willowy meant tall and she was fairly short.

No one seemed surprised to see him burst through the doors. A long-haired guy with glasses sitting in front of a chessboard asked him, without looking up, who he was looking for.

'Er, I don't know, I mean, I don't know her name.'

'Hmm, interesting…' said the guy, rubbing his chin and frowning. Dan guessed that they were about the same age. It wasn't clear whether he was referring to the state of play on the board, or the stranger's predicament.

'What's she in here for, do you know?'

'No idea.' She didn't seem in the slightest bit ill to him, but he was starting to realise that this sort of malady defied the usual definitions.

'Well, this is OCD, if that's any help.'

'Sorry?' Dan's brain failed to recognise these three sounds.

'Obsessive-Compulsive. Two months ago I wouldn't have laid a finger on this chess set. Now I can touch it, without even thinking about it ... almost. Without disinfecting it first, I mean. Good news, isn't it? It started when I was a little kid, one day I saw my dad just as he was about to....'

'Yeah, brilliant. Well done mate, bye...' Dan was backing out the door. Seemed like a nice enough bloke, but he didn't feel like listening to his life story, especially when there was such a pressing matter at hand.

Oh well, he thought, he was bound to run into her soon, as long as she didn't go anywhere else. He was getting tired anyway. He found his way back to Birch, and collapsed in front of the telly. Again it seemed too bright, too loud. Adverts and more adverts screamed their insidious messages. Jack walked past and pointed at the screen.

'That's the devil's own work that is!' he proclaimed, stomping off.

13

Milk and lime

He turned his chair away from the sensory onslaught and surveyed the room. It was so much more normal than the other place. The furniture had wooden arms and legs. Plants throbbed with life, soaking up sunlight on the windowsill. He wondered if some insects could actually hear photosynthesis, rumbling like distant engines. Without regular doses of green vibes, he decided he became deficient in some vital vitamin. Greenery and wooden furniture. It must be a sort of indoor substitute for the woods.

Just as he was drifting off, the doors flew open. A girl and a boy came spinning into the ward, singing at the tops of their voices. Colin came out of the smoke-filled office and clapped his hands together loudly.

'Let's see if we can't have some peace and quiet you two! Pipe down!' he said, then went back to his crossword.

'Alright, let's see if we can't!' said the girl, suddenly on her back spinning around, her energy ricocheting round the room like a silver pinball.

'BA-BOOM-CHA, BA-BOOM-BOOM-CHA, BA-BOOM-CHA, BA-BOOM-BOOM, CHA-CHA...' Her partner was accompanying her on an imaginary kit, marching around her like an automaton. They were heading in Dan's direction. They stopped in front of him, bowed, and the girl introduced them as Jo-Jo and the Human Drum Machine.

Dan clapped enthusiastically. This seemed to give them further inspiration. They took centre stage and the Human Drum Machine proceeded to run through his repertoire, sixteen bars of each pattern, whilst Jo-Jo gyrated around him, occasionally jumping up and (almost) doing the splits as she landed.

Dan tapped his feet and looked around to see how the show was going down with everyone else. It was as if it wasn't happening at all. Colin had had enough.

'Right you two, in here, NOW!' They traipsed into the office, pretending to be scared, leaving the door open behind them.

'Now look,' said Colin, sternly, 'there are people in this ward who would appreciate some rest, I know that you're having difficulty with this concept, but I would urge you to behave with a little more decorum. Especially you, Joanne, since your case is up for review next week. As for you, Julian, it's a shame you can't apply yourself to something a little more constructive with the same degree of enthusiasm.'

Blimey, it really was more like a school than a college, thought Dan.

'Look, Mr High-and-Mighty, we're just having a bit of a laugh, a bit of exercise! I'll be going, don't you worry. What are you going to do about it? Tell the doctors that I'm not fit to be released into the community because I like dancing?' The HDM, as he was known for short, was nodding in agreement.

'Go on babe!' he said, heartily.

The minute they were dismissed, they burst into a grand finale, Jo-Jo whirling and twirling ecstatically, while the HDM let loose a solo that no drum machine could ever reproduce, digital revolution or not. With that, they quit the ward in much the same way as they had entered.

Dan waited for the next act in excited anticipation like a child at the circus. Looking around he was disappointed to see that he was the only one there under the age of, well, old. He couldn't imagine any of them delivering the goods. Still, the ward was filling up again, so he remained hopeful. If only he wasn't so tired, he would continue his quest for the Elf. He nodded off in his chair, imagining he was wooing her with his witty repartee.

He awoke to find himself open-mouthed and dribbling, like a sleeping drunk on a bus. Hastily wiping his mouth and hoping she hadn't popped into Birch for some reason, he got up and went in search of water.

He stumbled into what looked like a kitchen and asked the cleaner, who was wearing a see-through, pink, plastic apron, if it was OK to get a drink.

'Course it is love, there's tea or coffee in the cupboard. There might even be some squash somewhere.' With that she finished mopping up some spilt milk and said, 'No point in crying over it, is there love?'

'No. No, there isn't,' said Dan, forgetting to laugh at her joke, revelling in the luxury of making himself a drink when he felt like it, instead of having to wait for the over-due tinkling trundle of that infernal tea trolley. The cleaning lady went to a cupboard and took out one of those orange and white cones that warn of hazards on the public highway and placed it in front of the wet patch.

'Wouldn't want you to slip, love. There's a jug of milk in the fridge. If it's getting empty you can fill it up from there,' she said, pointing to a large, canteen-type dispenser with a tap sticking out of it. On closer inspection, Dan could make out a faded and scrubbed drawing of a pair of breasts. Was this place meant to be so hilarious? He started giggling to himself, spooning instant coffee clumsily into a cup, thinking about Jo-Jo and The Human Drum Machine and remembering a time at school when they'd nicked one of those witch's hat things. One more look at the half-deleted graffiti on the milk machine and he was laughing out loud.

'What's so funny?' said a familiar voice. He spun round to see the Elf perched on top of the cone. He thought he was going to faint. Gone was the prepared speech. He just about managed a weak, 'Oh! It's you!'

'Expecting someone else?'

'No, no ... I'm really glad to see you. I looked for you earlier ... but...' He was blushing, sure that she'd seen him laughing at the drawing of the tits, and now she thought he was a sexist bastard.

'I'm in Lime. It's not in this building. Do you want me to show you where it is? Then you can come and visit me.'

'Yeah, definitely.' He was unable to conceal his eagerness. Still, who cares? He was a lunatic – lunatics probably didn't bother with all that playing hard to get stuff.

So she was in Lime, he should have guessed, would have guessed if he'd seen the sign leading to it. It was her colour, for sure. OK, so everyone had the radioactive Ready Brek glow, but it suited her more than most. Lime, fresh, refreshing, tart... No, that was the wrong word, sharp was better. Much more interesting than lemon, but you don't get lemon trees in England, or do you? Were wards only named after native species?

'Do you get lime trees in England?' Probably not, he thought, the most obvious chat-up line she'd ever heard. The coffee making was abandoned and he followed her out of the ward, the pain in his legs miraculously gone.

'Yes you do, they're the ones that get pruned so that they look all knobbly and crippled.'

'Do they ever have limes?'

'Well, they might, if they were left to their own devices.'

She led him out into the grounds, which were glowing with the warm yellow light of the late afternoon. He felt his energy return with a rush. Quite a few people were wandering about. She seemed to know everyone, and greeted them affectionately as they passed. He was glad to be seen with her, apparently it would be good for his cred.

A vehicle that belonged on a golf course was making its snail-like way up the road. The driver leant out and waved at her.

'Hey Domingo, you're breaking the speed limit again!' she called out, laughing. As if it was top secret, she whispered, 'He's such a sweet guy, I think he's from Portugal.' She looked at Dan as he tried to hide his face.

'What's the matter with you?'

'Oh, nothing, it's just the sun, it's a bit bright, that's all.' Fuck! That was the security bloke that he'd bitten! Trust him to be a mate of hers. It was too late – he'd been rumbled. The man was waving at him and gesticulating, pointing to his hand and feigning agony.

'What's he doing?' asked the Elf. Dan thought it best to come clean.

'Er, I bit him, when I first got here. I didn't mean to, it was just a sort of reflex action...' She looked at him, open-mouthed. Desperate not to scupper his chances, he took a deep breath, and strode purposefully towards the buggy.

'Um, I'm really sorry about biting you. I've never done it before... I don't know what got into me,' he said, envisioning the giant needle entering the flesh of his bare behind. 'Is your hand OK?'

'Ay, eeza no problaim, eez OK. Donta worry. I stilla leeve!' Hopeful of his redemption, he turned back to the Elf, half-expecting her to have vanished. He followed her into another building and up the dark stairwell to Lime. There was not much to distinguish it from Birch, apart from her lovely presence.

'You can have a cup of coffee here if you like. I'll make it.' They went into the kitchen. The door of their milk dispenser was open, revealing an empty plastic bag. To his surprise, she took it out and blew into the valve that fitted the tap. When it was fully inflated she stepped out into the dayroom and called to another girl.

'Another one for the collection Anna,' she said, throwing it over to her. As is the way with balloons, the doubled effort sent it only half the distance required. Dan picked it up and took it to the girl, who was curled up on a chair, staring at him.

'Thanks, Nice Boy,' she said. 'What do you think of our Love Substitutes?'

'What do you mean?' She and the Elf were giggling. They beckoned to him to follow them through a door that said, 'Female Area'. This was obviously their dormitory. Girls' things were all over the place. They both bent down and from under their beds pulled out two more balloons, still holding little droplets of milk that rolled around inside them like white mercury. They passed him one. On it had been written, 'The Miraculous Milk-filled Cushion for when you are missing your Mum'.

'We give them to people when they're upset,' said the Elf. Anna nodded. Dan wasn't sure how to respond.

'Good idea,' he said. They burst out laughing.

'God, don't be so serious!' said Anna. He tried to protest that he wasn't, but that never works. The door flying open saved him.

'Oh-oh, it's the Bitch. Quick, under the bed.' The Elf tried to stall the nurse as Dan dived down.

'There's a boy in here, isn't there Kate?'

Kate! That was her name! He could see her slight ankles with their opalescent flesh from his new viewpoint. One of them sported an Indian silver chain, partly obscured by her clumpy trainers, laced up in an extraordinarily complex way. For some reason he saw himself sinking his teeth into it, in much the way you find yourself imagining dropping a newborn baby from a balcony when someone had just entrusted you with it for a moment – even when there isn't a balcony. His brain reeled in horror at the scene that would follow, he'd be straight back in acute, as he'd come to know the other place, and known to all as 'the biter' for ever more. Suddenly the trailing bedcover was pulled up and the upside-down face of an annoyed woman appeared, thick varnishes of hairspray making her hair hang down in strange, rigid, wing-like shapes.

'You, OUT!'

He emerged, and all three of them tried to suppress laughter. The angrier she looked, the more difficult it was. They were marched out of the dormitory and Dan was asked to leave. He'd really been hoping to spend some time alone with... Kate.

He made his way back across the warm grass. The sun was no longer so fierce. Where it touched him he felt its warmth sink into the muscles of his legs and the bones beneath. My God, the strength of it! Just how powerful must it be, to send this heat all the way from however far away it was? Billions of miles away, light years away. Was there such a thing as the speed of warmth? What an act of faith it was to create something dependent on a burning star! Maybe he was solar powered. Or maybe his suicide had been partly successful and he'd been trapped somewhere between life and death. A delightfully dizzy limbo, when all the endorphins flood into the bloodstream making death the best thing that ever happened to you. That was one of those supposed facts that make out that ultimately, nature is good and kind. That death is bearable. If it wasn't, which of course it's not really, then why bother with life at all?

His mind was racing again, away with, in his case, the elves. He looked up and saw swifts high in the sky and he felt happy, as if he was up there with them, surfing thermals. He realised that he needn't fear trouble here. It wasn't school, you might get told off but so what? It wasn't like they were going to expel you.

He was late for supper. People were already returning to the ward. He went to the dining room, got his hard lump of scrambled egg on soggy toast swimming in an unappealing milky fluid, and sat down on his own. The clinking of cutlery was deafening. People brushing past set his teeth on edge. The crowd was too much.

He hurried back to the ward where the medication trolley was waiting, brimming with its poisons like a mobile overdose van. There were two nurses, one reading out the different dosages while the other tipped pills and potions into the Lilliputian beakers, careful not to touch anything with her fingers. Then, after holding it up to the other nurse to check, she'd pour the contents into yet another beaker held out by the patient. Another queue was forming. This was all new to him.

In the other place medication had been brought to you, possibly because you were unable to move. Here, the younger ward members stayed away until summoned, the old ones stood, if capable, obediently, thanking the nurses with pitiful deference. One by one the youths came forward sulkily, and were made to stick their tongues out afterwards and show underneath, in case they were thinking about spitting out their pills. Or saving them up. Spitting out seemed to be a matter of principle, of honour. Dan discovered that it wasn't easy. If you didn't get them out quickly enough, the sugar coating would wear away and what tasted like the contents of a cyanide capsule would seep around the mouth.

When it came to Jack's turn he raised his beaker and smacked it against the one that the nurse was holding.

'Cheers me dears!' he said, knocking it back.

Dan swallowed his and limped off to the dormitory, to the chagrin of Jack who looked as if he'd been hoping to regale him with more of his tales of woe, now that the floodgates had been opened.

He sought out his bed and pulled the curtains around

it. He looked in his locker for the wash stuff that his mum had brought him, found the bathroom, and once again became a captive of his mirror image. He began to brush his teeth, contemplated shaving, but couldn't be bothered. It suited the general look, he decided. His hair was sticking out all over the place. He could have been a hippie, an escaped convict, John the Baptist, even the Lord Jesus himself. Were halos artists' interpretations of auras? Maybe something got lost in translation. Was this what those Bible stories about seeing the light were all about? Surely a man who fasted in the wild for forty days and forty nights would be eligible for sectioning under the Mental Heath Act?

With this interesting thought, he rinsed his mouth and spat into the sink. He had a horrible metallic taste in his mouth, which was refusing to go away. Maybe a final fag of the day would help. He went and got one from his locker, stuck his headphones on and went into the loos, ignoring the No Smoking signs. After not having listened to his Walkman for a day or so, the music burst into his brain like another narcotic, fusing with the nicotine and the dastardly prescribed concoction, which was beginning to do its worst. Carried by the sound he was soon back on his bed, too hot to get in, but feeling too exposed to undress. He wished he had his own room where he could think about the Elf in peace. He shut his eyes and drifted off with images of the day capering around his mind.

He woke in the night to find his headphones askew on his head, the tape long since finished. He couldn't bear the grunts and snores that filled the room, so he fiddled with the radio dial, stumbling upon the BBC World Service like a homesick traveller. It was a request show. Some far-flung Reverend wanted to hear Fingal's Cave, followed by Bob Marley singing Stir It Up, for somebody Aziz in Doha, wherever that was. The comforting thought of someone, somewhere, dancing around a crackling wireless sent him back into a dreamless sleep.

14

Riders on the storm

He was getting used to waking up with a sort of hangover. This morning it was particularly bad. The last thing you need when feeling like that is the scraping of a hundred spoons around a hundred plates, accompanied by the demented percussion of teaspoons rattling furiously against teacups. It was like some sort of torture. Jamming screwed-up bits of paper napkin into his ears helped muffle the sound a bit. When he could stand it no longer, he stomped back to the ward in the first bad mood he'd been in for ages. He wanted to go back to bed but was told that there was to be a ward round any minute.

Before too long he found himself in the office facing Sherlock and a junior sidekick with blond hair in a little bunch.

'Do you have any objection to the presence of a student, Dan? This is a teaching hospital, you see.'

He looked at the guy, who under different circumstances might have been one of his mates. He wasn't sure how he felt about it. If they thought he was mental, then why did they think he was in a fit state to make that sort of decision?

'Suppose not,' he said. The student gave a quick smile

that didn't quite reach the eyes behind his John Lennon specs.

'So, how are you feeling today?' Dr Holmes looked at him with her eyebrows raised. Dan noticed that she'd plucked them away to the width of a pencil line.

'Like I've had one too many, I mean, I've got a terrible headache,' he said, still wishing he could block out all the extraneous racket. The supersleuth and her Watson exchanged glances, as if this were a sure sign of something. Then to his amazement she asked him exactly the same things as she had done last time.

'Do you think that you are ill?'

'Definitely,' he replied, reeling off the list of side-effects that he was experiencing, some of which were quite personal. Still, she was a doctor after all. More knowing glances were exchanged. He wished that he had objected to the presence of this student, who was obviously a total creep, ponytail or not.

'Do you think you could take seven away from one hundred today, Dan?' He stared at her. Hadn't he just told her that his head felt as if it had been fastened to a pneumatic drill?

'Are you serious?' He looked from one to the other. Well fuck this, he thought, getting up, the grating of his chair on the floor ripping through his aching head like machine-gunfire.

'Where are you going, Dan?' It was the student's turn to speak.

'I'm going to lie down on my bed, away from you. I don't suppose I could have an aspirin, doctor?' Without waiting for a reply he stormed out of the office, with tears welling up again. Bastards! The HDM, waiting outside gave him the thumbs up as he passed. Suddenly Jack was by his side.

'That won't have done you any favours, mate!' he barked.

'I don't give a toss. Jack, do us a favour, and go and ask Colin, or whatever his name is, for a painkiller. I've got to lie down, I'm not joking, my head's about to explode.'

Suddenly a man on a mission, Jack told him to wait there, strode across the dayroom and stood before the seated nurse.

'Is this a hospital, or what? There's a young lad over there in a really bad way. He wants something for his headache. Not too much to ask, is it?' Colin put down his paper.

'Jack, you know as well as I do that I can't go around giving out drugs that haven't been prescribed. I'll speak to the doctor about it shortly. She's seeing someone else now.'

'Look, you useless ponce, he's not asking for morphine! There's a bottle of aspirin in your office, just go and get it will ya?' Colin ignored him, picking up his newspaper again.

Jack marched towards the office, banged on the door and walked in. The HDM was in there, getting his grilling. Apparently his latest percussive achievement had just gone down like a lead balloon.

'Sorry mate,' he said, patting him on the shoulder. The whole of Birch could hear Jack shouting at the irritated psychiatrist.

'Who do you think you are love, Dr Mengele? There's a poor lad back there in agony. DO SOMETHING!' He slammed his fist down on the desk.

It worked. The doctor excused herself and accompanied Dan to his bedside, pulling the curtains behind her. He sat down, held his head in his hands and started shaking. She went away, came back with a couple of pills, which were added to the walking pharmacy that was his body, and said that from then on his medication would be adjusted.

Eyes shut, Dan lay on his bed for the rest of the morning with the lyrics of a Pink Floyd tune going backwards and forwards in his mind. *'When I was a child, I had a fever, My hands felt just like two balloons...'* Balloons. He saw his hands as two Miraculous Milk-filled Cushions, and hoped that the Elf didn't think he was being unsociable. *'...Now I've got that feeling once again, I can't explain, you would not understand, This is not how I am...'*

He wondered if Mat had a copy of that album. It wasn't really his cup of tea, but he'd ask him anyway. He tried to replay the entire work in his head, remembering family holidays, sitting in the back seat of the car as his dad sped down some autoroute or other to show his ungrateful kids some wonderful part of their European heritage.

'...OK, just a little pin-prick, there'll be no more Aaaaaah, but you may feel a little sick...'

How offended the parents had been when the twofold raging mass of hormones grunted and went off in search of frites, as they swooned before Le Pont d'Avignon, or some such place. If the hateful brats even bothered to get out of the car, that was. How offended he'd been that his dad refused to accept, without even giving it a chance, that 'The Wall' was as much a masterpiece as the piece of Beethoven that they were listening to. It was, he decided, quite likely that Mr Sony had invented the personal stereo in an attempt to make family holidays bearable.

'...I can ease the pain, get you on your feet again... There is no pain you are receding... A distant ship's smoke on the horizon, you are only coming through in waves...' Waves, of course! *'...I ...I ...I have become comfortably numb...'*

At some point someone brought him some highly suspect lunch, which he ignored, turning his head away from the fetid smell of boiled cabbage. Someone else brought some more pills, which he swallowed, before sinking into sleep again.

He awoke to the sound of the curtain being drawn back. There was a group of people silhouetted against the light that was streaming through the high window. The image reminded him of a scene from a science fiction film, the approaching aliens indistinguishable, backlit by the dazzling beam of the headlights of their interplanetary craft.

'Hello darling.' It was his mum's voice. 'How are you feeling?'

'Mum!' he whimpered, reaching up to her with arms outstretched like a baby. She held him, patted his head and stroked his hair, while his dad and brother sat on the bed and made a sort of anxious small talk.

His aches and pains were gone, lost in a medicated fog. His head felt better, but woolly in the aftermath of the sort of headache he never wanted to experience again. Colin came in to see how he was, and said that if they were hungry they could go to the hospital canteen.

They followed his directions and found their way to the surprisingly normal-looking place. As they went in his dad seemed pleased. He said it looked quite nice, rubbing his hands together as if it was an unexpected find on the side of the motorway. The food looked a whole lot better than the slops in the dining room, so Dan piled his tray high with goodies, everyone else just having coffee.

The first mouthful of what was only averagely hot lasagne hit his sore mouth like molten lava. He leapt up, yelped, spitting it out and pouring water into his burning mouth, surprised not to be lost in a steam cloud. His family looked at him in amazement, coffee cups poised between table and lips.

'Too hot?' said his brother.

'Nah, too cold,' said Dan, and they both started giggling like kids who found it amusing to behave badly in a restaurant.

'Boys, stop it!' said their Dad. 'You're upsetting your mother.'

It was true. She asked Dan if his mouth was OK. His lips looked like victims of the hosepipe ban, so badly chapped that they were split at the sides. She said that unless he kept his mouth shut for a week, she couldn't imagine how they were going to heal.

Just as he was demolishing the last mouthful of his not-bad-at-all lemon meringue pie, who should walk in but the Elf, with the bloke he'd seen her with the other day in the dining room. He wondered if he should be jealous of this character. He was quite attractive. But then again, everything looked attractive. He wasn't sure if he wanted to be seen with his family or not, but it was too late, she was coming over.

'Hi!' she said, smiling round at his entourage.

'I came to see you earlier, but they said you were in bed with a headache. Are you OK?' She was wearing bright green eyeshadow and red lipstick. Dan saw his Mum purse her lips in disapproval.

'Mum, Dad, Bruv, this is the El … Kate.'

She shook hands politely with them all. The unknown bloke was coming over with hot chocolate and dough-nuts.

'This is Ray,' she said. 'But we call him IRA.'

'Hullo,' said Ray in an Irish accent, before sinking his teeth into a doughnut, the thick icing oozing out of the gaps between his teeth in tiny sausages.

'Get it?' she laughed, 'I-R-Ray! He's just got out of prison, isn't that great!'

'Yeah!' Dan enthused. The rest of the family nodded and smiled uncomfortably, exchanging more anxious glances. His dad announced that it was time for their appointment with the doctor. His family trooped out after him. His mum watched as Dan tried to pull down the sleeves of his T-shirt.

'It's just the sun, mum, it hurts.'

She said she'd have a word with the doctor about it. They went back into Birch, where the doctor was waiting for them. They followed her into a side room.

'You wait in the dayroom Dan, I just want to have a word with your family,' and with that the door was shut in his face. Bloody cheek! he thought, but actually felt quite relieved to get away from all the distress signals he was receiving, from his mum in particular.

Jack was dozing by the open window. Suddenly a head appeared on the other side, waved at Dan and leant in, singing softly, *'Grocer Jack, Grocer Jack...'* It was Alec, he must have been let out of acute. Jack came to life, shook hands vigorously with his friend and scuttled out of the ward to join him. Dan watched them as they strolled off together, arms slung around each other's shoulders. What a strange pair they made, Alec, despite the heat of the afternoon, wearing his bright yellow anorak, and Jack in his cardboard-look suit. They came from such different worlds. It was as if this distance allowed them a closeness that would otherwise be unlikely, like diverse fauna that could inhabit the same space because they were not vying for prey.

He went and sat down in the chair that Jack had vacated. He wanted to catch up with the Elf, and talk to her properly. Why was she here? She seemed happy enough, but, then again, he thought, no one was here without a tale to tell. The woman sitting across from him, for example. Who was she? Where did she come from? She looked so sad. In fact the more he contemplated her, with her swollen legs protruding beneath her old summer dress, the sadder he felt. Whoever she was, she can't have imagined that she'd be spending her late middle age in here. She was flicking through an ancient, crumpled Woman's Weekly. She could have been deciding whether to make scones or a Victoria sponge for her grandchildren's tea. Maybe she had no grandchildren, and the chances were her parents were either dead, or too ancient to visit, or maybe...

The woman became aware of his gaze upon her and

obligingly held out what looked like a rectangular table tennis bat. It was in fact one of those plastic chopping boards with a hole in the handle, so it could be hung up tidily on the kitchen wall. Onto this she had stuck a typed précis of her life story, plastered with yellowing Sellotape, as if she were a Saxon church somewhere in the country-side, still brave enough to remain unlocked. He thanked her, and began to read.

```
My name is Joan. I got married to a saleman when
I was seventeen after I got pregnant. My husband
went to work one day and never came back. My
dad died so my mum and I lived together with
my baby son. On my 21st birthday I went out
dancing with my girlfriends. On my way home I
got raped by four men who I had grown up with.
I never told anyone because no one would have
believed me. They left me pregnant again and I
had a little girl. My mother never forgave me
and said that if that was what I was like no
wonder Dennis left me. My mother died of cancer
the next year. I was too upset too look after my
babies and they were taken into care and adopted
and I have never seen them again. I was put in a
hospital when I was 23 years old where I stayed
for nearly 10 years. I was given a lot of ECT to
make me better. My Auntie Alice visited me once
a month, and then I was well enough to go into a
Therapeutic Community, which was a nice place.
After that the council gave me a flat. It had a
little balcony where I could sit out and watch
the trains going past. I got a little cat called
Lucky because that's what I was. My next door
neighbour used to come in and bring me cakes
and things and I thought he was kind. Then one
day he raped me and beat me so that I thought I
would die. Auntie Alice found me and brought me
here. I'm better now but I only speak to ladies.
```

Horrified, Dan handed back the potted history to the woman who was sitting back with an inscrutable expression on her wizened face. My God, a whole life! Since before he was born! It was unthinkable, unbearable... Unreal... He wanted to apologise to her on behalf of fate, who when confronted by the likes of Joan, must surely cover its face in shame. She altered her gaze to one of dispassion.

The consultation was over. Hearing the door open, he looked over to see his dad shaking the doctor's hand and thanking her as if she'd just had his boy over for a pyjama party. Suddenly they noticed him, snivelling by the window. His mum rushed over.

'What's the matter, darling?'

'I'm OK, mum, it's just Joan, she's just shown me her life story and it's really awful, she was raped five times... And...'

She looked round at Joan and said, 'Please don't upset him. He's very sensitive at the moment.'

'I like your scarf,' replied Joan, heaving herself out of her chair and heading for the female dormitory, life story tucked inside her magazine. She pushed past Dan's dad and brother, pausing to give them both in turn a withering look.

'What on earth did she say to you?' asked his dad.

'Nothing,' said Dan, truthfully.

The family parted. Dan was in the dark as to what the doctor had said, but it didn't make any difference anyway, it looked like he was here for the duration. He went outside wearing the huge sunglasses that his mum had lent him. They weren't what he'd have chosen for himself, but needs must. The atmosphere was heavy and close. In the distance, dark grey clouds were gathering. It was going to rain. Rain! He'd almost forgotten what it was like. He scanned the grounds for the Elf, but instead spotted the beacon of Alec's anorak over by the bus stop, with four or five others. Company, that's what he needed. He headed over to join them.

'Cool shades man!' jeered Alec. Dan hastily removed them, glad of the band of rolling cloud that had eclipsed the sun. Jack came forward to greet him, thumping him on the back.

'Good to see you up and about again, old chum! Family gone now?'

One of the lads waiting for the bus that never came had a bit of gear, which he skinned up and passed around. Everyone except Alec fell upon it like starving men, holding onto it for longer than the dope smoker's book of etiquette would have advised, till it was snatched away with a desperate, 'Gis anovva lug, mate!' Alec seemed content with his joint of pure tobacco, beautifully crafted by his long fingers, which was passed round as well and seemed to be just as effective.

'It's magic, see?' he said. Dan considered that magic could be a result of the suspension of disbelief, but that seemed like a very boring idea, so he dismissed it. He watched as the guy introduced as Tim drew a caricature of him with huge sun specs obscuring the larger portion of his face on the shelter wall.

Alec was now lying on the grass, arms outstretched, with his anorak done up and his hood on. A few seconds later there was an almighty crack as the heavens split open and the rain came down in a waterfall. Huge drops bombarded the hard, unready ground and ran in rivulets into the miniature canyons in the desiccated earth. He lay stock-still and unblinking, sparkling with little rainbows like the horse chestnut in acute. The bunch of stoners danced around him like tribesmen on the savannah worshipping the magic man whose premature donning of a waterproof had heralded the cloudburst.

They laughed, voices weak against the downpour, heads back and mouths open, letting the rain plop onto their extended tongues until they were drenched. All of a sudden it stopped and the sun broke through. A near perfect rainbow appeared, spanning the sky in a grand finale. Steam started to rise from the ground and from their clothes. Alec sat up and wiped his eyes. They looked at each other, not knowing quite what to do next, until the collective munchies sent them back to their various wards for tea.

With his trainers squelching, Dan headed back towards Birch, hungry for the bag of tuck his family had brought. He saw a female figure approaching. He rubbed his eyes, I must be hallucinating, he thought, she looks just like Fran. He felt his guts liquefy, it was Fran! Standing before him as if she'd just ridden in on the storm.

'Dan!' she said, flinging herself against his damp body, 'God! This is all my fault!'

15

Fran

As the saying goes, you could have knocked him down with a feather. After a few moments of paralysis, he diffidently returned her embrace, feeling his body's memory of her return, as if he'd just slipped on an old pair of shoes that once he used to live in. She stood back and looked at him, her face contorted with concern.

'How are you?' she said.

'Funnily enough, I'm stoned.' He suddenly had the urge to laugh.

'Yes, I spoke to the nurse in your ward, he said you were on medication.'

'No, what I meant was I've just had a smoke over there.'

'Dan!' she sounded disapproving, 'Do you think that's sensible?'

'Yes I bloody do! What's it to you anyway? Do me a favour, don't say it's because you care.'

He was feeling uncharacteristically bold. Ironically, he felt he had the advantage for once, strangely liberated by his situation. The temptation to give her a really hard time was almost too powerful to resist. She looked back at him, positively grief-stricken. He softened immediately, he couldn't endure anyone else's pain today, and less charitably, he decided that she probably wanted to do penance and then leave with a lightened load, and he didn't necessarily want that either.

'And by the way, it's not.'

'Not what?'

'Your fault – you're in a queue for that particular accolade.'

Blimey, he thought cockily, this is going well, he didn't think he'd ever used the word 'accolade' in his life. Dan the ventriloquist's dummy – a mouthpiece for the Great Heartbroken.

She was looking at him oddly, as if this were not what she'd expected at all. He looked back at her. Was this person really the one-time love of his life? She looked so ... so normal, unremarkable, incapable of inspiring the emotion ... the passion that she used to... He noticed that she wasn't glowing green, and hoped that it was just the shock of seeing her that had temporarily banished the light show. It would be typical if she managed to stamp that out as well. They stood before each other as awkwardly as strangers thrust together at a party.

'I...' 'Do you...' Their words clashed.

'Go on,' she said.

'No you,' he said.

'I was just going to say that I'd brought you some things. I spoke to your neighbour, he said that you'd probably need cigarettes and batteries.'

'Thanks, yeah I do, but how come you spoke to Mat?' For some reason the thought of them talking made him go hot with, not exactly anger, but one of its close relatives.

'I got his number from your brother, when he rang to tell me what had happened. I just wanted to talk to someone that wasn't in your family, since I'm not exactly their favourite person.'

It was true. They'd all been wary of this woman, too old

for him, a cradle-snatcher. They'd told him it was doomed, but he hadn't listened. His mum had said that she'd soon want to settle down and have children and the last thing they wanted was to see him as a father when he was still a child himself. How sickening that they'd been right.

He peered into the plastic bag that she held out to him, the gap between them made plain by the batteries that were one size too small and the Silk Cut that were too weak.

'Thanks Fran. Do you want a cup of tea or something?'

'Yeah, whatever.' They walked back to the ward in a strained silence.

She followed him into the kitchen. Weak black tea with no sugar for her, he remembered. Strong milky tea with two large sugars for him.

'So, how's the self-made man?' he enquired sarcastically. He remembered this dewy-eyed description of her new love with bitterness. He'd imagined him making himself out of a kit, usurping God and nature with his phenomenal self-possession.

'Don't Dan, please.' She was looking at the floor.

'Still together, I assume?' He couldn't help himself, even though the thought of them still made him want to vomit.

She took a deep breath.

'Yes we are. You'd like him, you know. Anyway I didn't come here to talk about him.'

'So why did you come? Curious to see what the inside of a nuthouse was like?'

'No, I heard that you were in hospital and I wanted to visit you. Is that a crime? One day you'll understand why I did what I did, I know I hurt you and I'm sorry, but everyone gets hurt you know.'

'Don't patronise me Fran. Spare me that 'One day you'll understand' crap. I'm not an infant. You met someone else. Full stop.'

'OK, I've made a mistake, I shouldn't have come, I'm going.' She picked up her handbag and made to leave.

Games, games, games. Still, he knew the rules, even though he'd have rather that she did go. She seemed so out of place in his new life. He didn't even want her any more, not today at least. He wanted chocolate, and the Elf.

'Don't go, I'm sorry, it's just so weird to see you here, I mean, it's weird to see you at all, after all this time.'

They took their drinks and went to sit down in the day-room. He introduced her to Jack and Joan, and pointed out the HDM. He moaned about his medication, because it seemed like a relatively easy topic. He wanted to explain to her the wondrous gift of joy and energy that he'd been given, but didn't want to give her the credit for anything good that had happened to him in the intervening months since she dumped him in favour of that dickhead.

Suppertime came and the exodus from wards to dining room began.

'I think I'd better get going.' She stood up.

'Yeah,' he said, trying to sound sad about it.

'Shall I come and see you again?' she asked.

'I dunno. Maybe it's better if you don't, I mean, not that it hasn't been good to see you, but it's a bit upsetting for me you know...'

'Yes, I understand.' She took his hands and squeezed them, and they embraced, Dan still damp from the rain. He hung a suitably sober expression on his face till she was out of sight.

He set off for the dining room feeling vaguely guilty. It seemed unfair to make her feel bad about something that he didn't care about anymore, or at least was beginning to stop caring about. Jack came up behind him, curious to know more about his visitor.

'Who was that lovely lady, then? You're a dark horse aren't you matey-boy!'

'That was my ex, if you must know.'

Actually he felt quite proud, pleased that Jack had seen

him with someone who was obviously not mad, proving that he still had one foot in the other world. Still, he wasn't averse to this one. It was OK here, in the asylum. He was a member of a secret society. Interesting word, asylum. Asylum seekers were people who needed a safe haven, away from evil regimes where they were tortured for what they knew and wouldn't say, not the embarrassment to the world that the asylum dweller feels himself to be. The fact that these places were called lunatic asylums, did, he thought, imply an original concern that was reassuring. Loony bin, however, seemed more appropriate. He was in the bin, with all the other rubbish, but, like Stig of the Dump, it suited him for the moment.

'I had a woman not so long ago,' said Jack bitterly. 'Totally cleaned me out, she did. Lost my flat cos of 'er. We got it together, see. When she went she took all my money and I couldn't pay the rent by myself.'

They picked up their trays and waited in the queue. Dan wondered if anything good had ever happened to Jack, and just why that was. It was as if one early disaster laid the foundation for a disastrous life. It seemed so unfair. Maybe it was Jack's karma, but that didn't fit in with forgiveness, but then it was from a totally different religion ... so why should it? Anyway if God was that forgiving, why did people go to hell? Or were heaven and hell actually something to experience whilst alive? If that was the case then he was certainly in a privileged position, because he'd been to hell but somehow he'd managed to escape. Now he was in heaven, which was not a place after all, but a feeling, The Feeling, not in the least bit dependent on actual circumstances. If he'd told Fran that he considered himself very lucky to be here, she would have thought he was nuts. But of course she thought that already.

Memories of her, of them, were repeating in his mind like a slide-show. He wished she hadn't come. She'd fucked up his head. If there were a blood test for jealousy, he'd still test positive. He'd been in remission, that was all, and now he was on the verge of a relapse. He imagined her driving away, possibly in his flash car, calling him on his flashy carphone, telling him she was on her way home. No doubt Mr Right would be getting a simple yet delicious supper together, opening the wine, ready to listen to her and understand, before making love to her with the consummate skill of a master.

Tortured by these thoughts, he ate his supper, barely noticing what it was except that it was good in the way anything is after a smoke. He felt unsociable. He didn't even want to see the Elf whilst Fran was on his mind. Since there seemed to be a reason for everything, he decided that she had come in order to give him the opportunity to sort out what he felt, then to file it away in some dark recess of his memory once and for all.

He finished his meal and went to his bed, pulling the curtains around it. Putting his headphones on to further discourage any visitor, he lay down and closed his eyes. He didn't turn his Walkman on because he didn't want to taint any of his new music with associations of her.

He felt himself being sucked back into the past. Hurtling down a tunnel on a kamikaze tube train, speeding past illuminated spaces in the darkness which weren't stations, but blasts of colourful reminiscence, billboards flashing past, half recognised then gone. Too fast, too fast... He couldn't do any real contemplation at this speed. He had to be logical about it, to start at the beginning.

College, the day he first saw her, in the library, dropping a huge pile of books that he helped her pick up. He was looking for a soulmate, preferably in female form, and in the flustered blush of the mysterious mature student he saw a part of himself reflected and promptly fell for her. Why French? She'd asked. Il ne savait pas, but it had been something he'd been OK at in school, and he liked the lit. As for her, she had wound up in the South of France doing the markets with what seemed to him to be more than her fair share of men, before deciding to come home and do something worthwhile with her fluency.

It all sounded incredibly romantic to him. It also made him feel desperately insecure. He had no idea why he felt compelled to put himself through the agony of imagining her past, with Jean, or Thierry, or Pascal. After all, she was here now, with him, she'd walked away from all that, but this intangible thing that was her history inspired in him a voracious jealousy. In that it could never be seen, it assumed mammoth proportions in his imagination, and the fact that it had all taken place in another country, in another language, and, what's more, while he was still at school, made it a thousand times worse.

He knew that it was starting to annoy her, the fact that no amount of reassurance was enough, so he bit his lip and concentrated on the good times. He took them out and looked at them one by one as if they were faded photographs. A place, a raised glass, a sleepless night, a meal, a visit to a gallery, a day trip... Lying in bed in her groovy mum's flat, in the wrong capital city in the wrong century, reciting Baudelaire, translating, trying to find a better way to convey the luxury of a lover's hair than, *'Oh fleece that to the very shoulder foams.'* He remembered how they'd cracked up, imagining someone proclaiming his desire for a sheep. Dan and Fran – even their names rhymed.

He'd been living in halls, sharing a room with a studious type for whom he had no feeling, ignoring the various entertainments on offer, blinkered. When she said she had a mate who had a flat to rent he'd jumped at it. He pictured the day when he'd got the keys. They'd had champagne with their fish and chips and, save for trips to the corner shop for supplies, they didn't go out for a week. He stuck two fingers up to the green-eyed monster and was blissfully happy. Women lived longer than men, so by his reckoning they'd die at about the same time.

The end of the summer term had arrived and the prospect of a year in France loomed. Everyone was thrilled. They were going to Paris. Why couldn't he see it as the fabulous opportunity that everyone kept telling him it was? All he could envisage was a land littered with Fran's ex-lovers. By now the barrow boys would have made good and descended en masse on Paris, ready to jump out from behind every bouquiniste and off every bateau mouche to lure her back to the South for a weekend of peculiarly French passion.

He began to detect something hovering in the air between them. She'd been distanced lately, busier than usual. They'd spent less time together, but it was probably just down to the exams. He tried to ignore it – maybe it was just hormones or something. Finally she'd come round to the flat, and whereas once they'd dived into each other's eyes, this time she kept averting her gaze. He'd tried to be flippant.

'Centime for your thoughts, Mademoiselle?'

'Dan, I'm not coming,' she said gently, taking his hand.

'Didn't think you were!' he said trying to kiss her. She pulled away.

'To Paris. In fact I'm thinking of leaving college altogether. I don't know how to tell you this but...'

She was ill, that must be it, she was dying, it was just like Love Story, well, he wouldn't go either in that case, fuck college, nothing was more important than her...

'...I've been seeing someone else.'

He groaned, rolling over on his bed as he relived the ensuing scene. The tears, the rage, the disbelief, the pleading, the begging, the total loss of cool, of dignity, life-plan, of everything, everything... No, no he wouldn't have it! She was making a big mistake. Who is he? Who is the bastard? Yes it fucking does matter! Was it that bloke at the party? Think about it, think for a minute, please, please Fran, don't leave me, I love you, you said you loved me! Jacques Brel's rusty voice rasping *'Ne me quitte pas'* in his ears. Bloody hell, she had given him that sodding record!

But it was done, and she went, leaving her key. What a cliché. Why was every word French? Even her name almost spelt France. He looked at himself in the mirror. No wonder she wanted rid of the snotty-nosed wretch he saw before him. He tried to swallow it, feeling pain explode somewhere deep inside, scattering emotional shrapnel, which just like the metal variety, would turn up in unexpected places in years to come. He ran to the wall of windows, and watched her walk across the car park. Did he detect a certain lightness in her step? Yes, he bloody well did! The bitch was almost dancing with relief, he almost expected her to kick her heels in the air. Suddenly France beckoned. He was going to find a Jeanne, a Pascale, a Thérèse, and maybe a Françoise too, and he would never fucking come back.

Suddenly he heard the rustle of curtains. It was Colin, telling him to come and get his medication. Ah, medication! What an excellent idea. He almost asked for a double helping. He plonked himself down in front of the telly. It was Top of the Pops. Black Box was Number One and Jo-Jo and the HDM were going ape, as if they were at a rave. They were yelling at the tops of their voices, *'YOU JUST WALK RIGHT IN, WALK, WALK, WALK RIGHT IN!... WHOA-OH, WHOA-OH, WHO-OH-OH-OH-OH!'* Dan looked round to see the Elf doing just that, right on cue. *'LET ME TELL YOU WHAT YOU DO, WHAT YOU DO, WHAT YOU DO TO ME! YOU'RE SUCH A HOT TEMPTATION!...'*

She was too. He felt the medication kick in, in what was now its not unpleasant way, and the green light came back on. Mmm, he thought, breathing in the sight of her, happy to be back in the present, with The Feeling, where there was music, light, and no pain.

Colin came over and turned down the volume to much protestation, then clapped his hands and announced to the assembly, 'Right Ladies and Gentlemen, Boys and Girls, tomorrow morning after breakfast we'll be moving to our new home whilst this place gets a much needed lick of paint. We'll be going to Ash, in the old building, so if you could be so kind as to get your things together this evening, it'll make things a lot easier in the morning, OK?'

Good, thought Dan. He would leave behind all thoughts of Fran in this place, where they could be papered over and forgotten. He went over to the Elf who was sharing a joke with Joanne.

'Do you want to go for a walk?' he asked. He suddenly needed to be outdoors, where the air was still fresh after the rain.

'OK,' she said, smiling. They walked out into the garden, into the colour saturated by the sun's varnish. He resolved to be brave. He led her into the privacy of what once had been a walled garden and took her hand. She didn't resist, and they exchanged knowing sidelong smiles, an inevitable melody stretching into tomorrow. He left her at the foot of the stairs that led to Lime, kissing her little hand goodnight. If the pain in his legs hadn't been so great, he would have skipped all the way back to Birch. Mat would have been proud of him, he always said heartache was like a hangover. All you needed to get over it was another drink.

16

Ash

After breakfast the next morning, if it wasn't already, the scene was pure Bedlam. Bags were packed, things were lost, dropped, broken and trodden on. The able-bodied were piled high with pillows and blankets, whilst the chair-bound waited to be helped across the grounds to the old building. Colin directed proceedings with supreme patience, breaking up pillow fights and arguments over packets of biscuits and cigarettes.

After much to-ing and fro-ing the place stood empty. With nothing but the odd plant, a few old magazines scattered about and a couple of jam jars of dead flowers on the windowsill, it had the sad air of a derelict house. Dan asked if he should bring the plants, but Colin shook his head as he unplugged the phone and tucked it under his arm, hooking his mug that declared, 'You don't have to be mad to work here, but it helps!' over a free finger.

'Don't worry, someone will look after them,' he said, locking the door behind them.

Dan joined the line of refugees with their lives stuffed hurriedly into plastic bags as it made its way across the grounds and into the old building, which, Jack told him, contained the administrative headquarters of Woodland

Park Hospital. They shuffled into the foyer with its hundred signposts and pathetic trickling water feature. There was one sign pointing up the stairs that read 'Patients' Affairs', and he felt a tingling in his lower body, imagining leading the Elf up to where, in a perfect world, the powers that be would have considerately equipped private rooms for medicated afternoons of inter-ward passion.

Colin pushed through to the front and led the way down a stuffy corridor. They passed another payphone, reminding Dan that if only he could get hold of some change, there were lots of people he wanted to ring. It seemed that his friends didn't know what had happened to him, otherwise they would have come to see him by now, surely? Soon they came to a door that said, 'Ash'.

'Here we are!' said Colin. 'Try not to disturb anyone too much whilst you settle in.'

Dan didn't like the look of it. It was the mental hospital of his imagination. The sort of place you never get out of. He was looking down another tunnel, straight this time, with little rooms running down each side. At the end of the corridor was large, dark, dayroom, which looked as if it was in far more need of renovation than Birch. Its inhabitants were engaged in the standard occupations of gawping at the telly, staring vacantly into space, playing board games and chain-smoking.

Playing draughts with Tim, the graffiti artist, was Alec, who for some reason chose to ignore Dan's greeting. Maybe he was just on the verge of one of those sickeningly good moves, hop-scotching across the board, building a triumphant column of his opponent's pieces as he went.

Another middle-aged man, who introduced himself as Steve, came out of the office. He informed everyone that their name had been stuck on the door of one of the small rooms. Dan found his round the corner. His own room! Not dissimilar to the one in acute, but with one very important difference – an open window. A window you could just, if needs be, squeeze out of. Maybe this ward wasn't so bad after all.

He put his belongings in his locker and went back into the corridor. At the far end there was a dining room. He hoped they'd still be eating with the others in the main building. He liked the huge space, the paintings on the walls, the chance to see new faces, the chance to see her.

The newcomers were left to their own devices. Dan sat down in the dayroom and lit a cigarette, hoping that someone would come and visit him soon, as supplies were getting precariously low. Jack came over.

'Thinking about your girlfriend are you? Forget 'er mate, you're better off without 'em, believe me!'

He had been thinking about his girlfriend, but not the one that Jack meant.

'Hey Jack, I think Alec blanked me a minute ago. D'you know what that's all about, or was I imagining it?'

'You weren't imagining it, but don't worry I've sorted him out on that score.'

'What score?'

'He thought you were after the apple of his eye, that little girl called Kate. I told him that your girlfriend had been to see you, so no worries.'

'Jack, that was my ex, I told you so.' Typical. Where was it written that if ever there was the least opportunity for complication, a complication there must be? The last thing he wanted was to be Alec's rival.

'Did ya? Sorry mate, I must have missed that.'

They went over to the draught players. Tim was grinning. He'd won.

'You wait till I'm not so drugged up,' growled Alec.

'It's Blake's 7!' he said, greeting Dan coldly. Not knowing how to reply, Dan offered him one of his few remaining fags instead. Looking around the room he noticed that an old lady sitting next to the window was crying.

'What's the matter with her?' he asked, immediately upset.

'The goats just got her flowers... DIDN'T THEY GRACE?' Alec called across to her. She looked up and waved back, sadly.

'Her daughter only brought them in yesterday... DIDN'T SHE GRACE?'

Another wave. There was something about Alec that he didn't like, but then questioned his objectivity given the new information about Alec's feelings for the Elf. Perhaps Mat had been right, maybe he was dodgy after all.

He assumed that The Goats was a collective noun for over-zealous cleaning ladies or flower thieves, when, as if to put him right, there was a clattering of hooves as two real live ones pogoed onto the window ledge and stuck their heads through the window. He couldn't believe it. Even goats knew that if ever there was a place where they could let themselves go, then this was it. They looked round mischievously at their audience before extending their upper lips and snapping at the dying flowers on the windowsill. They seemed to prefer the fresher ones, and shook the bunches sending stagnant water drops flying whilst they made their selection. Jack ran to the nearest vase and picked out a carnation.

'Here's a nice one for you, mate!' he said, stroking the pot-bellied creature tenderly.

'Oi! You there!' A dapper little man came rushing over.

'What do you think you're doing? Those flowers happen to be mine!'

'What do you mean, they "happen to be" yours?' said Jack. 'D'you think that flowers were put on this Earth for you? What bloody good are they doing sitting dying in a poxy vase?'

The man was as red as a tomato but his voice remained calm.

'Now you just listen to me. No, I wouldn't be so foolish as to imagine that they were mine in that sense of the word, but in that a dear lady friend of mine just gave them to me, they are, at this point in time, mine. So kindly desist in giving them to our cloven-hoofed friends. I can assure you that they do very well out of this ward as it is.'

Jack was stumped. For a moment he looked like a schoolboy in trouble, before clicking his heels and saluting.

'Aye, aye, captain!' he said, smartly.

Colin came out of the office just in time to catch the end of Malcolm's speech.

'Jack, I might have guessed it would be you who'd manage to upset someone in the first five minutes. Apologise to Malcolm, and leave other people's things alone.'

Jack did so, sheepishly. Malcolm introduced himself to Dan, shaking his hand firmly and saying that if he had any questions whatsoever, he shouldn't hesitate to ask. Dan asked Jack if Malcolm was a member of staff.

'No mate, ex-army. And for God's sake don't ask 'im about it, or he'll never stop going on. D-day landings, Japanese prisoner of war camp, you name it, he was there.'

To Dan's disappointment, a cavalcade of large trolleys was advancing down the long corridor, in a cloud of warm, unappetising aroma. Everyone trooped to the dining room. He sat down at a table and was soon joined by... what had the Elf called him? IRA? Was he after her as well?

'Hullo there, mind if I join you?' He sat down without waiting for an answer. 'How're you doing?' he asked, as he sandwiched the entire contents of his plate between two slices of bread.

'Not bad, thanks, and yourself?' replied Dan.

'Not bad at all. Look, this is what I did in OT yesterday.' Out of his pocket he brought a tiny carved wooden bird. He passed it to Dan, who wiped his hands on his jeans respectfully before taking it. It was beautiful, delicate, made with a loving care that seemed to make his terrorist proclivities less probable.

'It's amazing, you must be really talented.' He turned it over in his hand, admiring it for what he considered long enough, before handing it back.

'Cheers.' Ray put it back in his pocket before turning his attention to his jumbo sandwich.

'What's OT?'

'Occupational Therapy,' he said, through his mouthful, showering Dan with bits of food. 'You know, art and stuff. It's good. When I get out of here I'm going to get a job as a wood carver.'

'Yeah, you should.' Dan experienced a tremor of anxiety at the mention of the future. Ray rammed in the last of his meal, said, 'See y'around' and was off. Hopefully not for a date with a certain person.

After lunch the ward fell quiet in the stultifying heat of the afternoon. Was it Sunday? It certainly felt like it, then he remembered Top of the Pops yesterday evening, and knew it couldn't be.

In the distance he could hear an ice cream van cranking out a laborious version of *'Popeye the Sailor Man'*, stopping and starting like an antique barrel organ, its song almost plaintive as it tried not to melt away in the blistering stillness. He'd always found the sound vaguely depressing, reminding him of hot, empty days when the summer holidays had lost their charm, stretching into an endless void of deathly boredom.

He decided to explore the building. He daren't go out in this sunshine. He'd have had to put on those naff sunglasses. He thought of his mum, always losing them, and how he and his brother would pretend to help her look, when all the time they were on her head. How she couldn't have been aware of them, he didn't know – they were hardly lightweight.

He walked up the corridor, which was deserted, except for an old black guy sitting in front of a window, glowing in the full sunshine. He was rocking gently back and forth on his chair, wearing a white baseball cap from which two little red plastic cones protruded. When he got closer, Dan saw that on it was written 'Horny Little Devil'. The sight of this lone human seemed so sad, so hopeless. Somehow the young didn't seem so pitiful. It was like a dogs' home. All the puppies would get another chance, even if they were a bit fucked up, but the old ones... What would happen to the old ones?

He just could not walk past this person. He went closer and stuck out his hand.

'Hi, I'm Dan.'

Slowly, the man extended a hand, as gnarled as an old piece of driftwood, and smiled. He didn't say what his name was, but pointed at Dan's headphones.

'Do you want to listen to some music?' He held them out to him. After some negotiation with the horns they were in place. Dan switched it on. The old man's eyes lit up, and he nodded and smiled, before lifting himself out of his seat and beginning to dance with the very slightest movement of his feet and hips. Still holding the machine, Dan moved around with him as if he had the old man on a lead.

Suddenly there was the sound of footsteps running up the corridor towards them.

'What the hell do you think you're doing?' It was a butch female nurse. He'd seen her help serve lunch. She snatched the headphones from the baseball cap and thrust them into Dan's hands.

'Mr Atkinson! What were you thinking of? You know you've got to relax!' She led him back to his chair and sat him down. He looked as if he were about to say something, but she wouldn't give him a chance.

'It's Dan, isn't it?'

'Yeah ... look, he was enjoying that. It wasn't doing him any harm was it?'

'I think we can be the judge of that,' she said imperiously. 'Just let Mr Atkinson have his rest. He mustn't get over-excited.'

Not much chance of that, thought Dan, astonished by her reaction. He walked self-consciously up the corridor, listening to his echoing footsteps, half-expecting her to lasso him as he approached the door.

When he was safely on the other side, he put on his headphones and turned the music up full blast – he needed to get back on his buzz again after that encounter with the Beast of Belsen. The music urged him on, as if every lyric was written for him, for that precise moment. He retraced the way back to the foyer, then turned down the unexplored corridor.

Around the corner he was stopped in his tracks by the sight of a counter, over which there was a sign that said, 'SHOP'. Why hadn't anyone told him about this? It was laden with an abundance of sweets, the sort he hadn't bothered with for years. The 1p variety of pink spongy prawns, Black Jacks, Rhubarb and Custards, Milk Bottles, and behind them, the more expensive selection of Sherbet Dib-dabs, Sherbet fountains and Chalk lollies. Further back, for the filthy rich, yet more icons of confectionery culture, Mars Bars, Kit-Kats and the like. Turning off his Walkman was almost an act of respect.

Inside was an assortment of items arranged on shelves: lip salve, tissues, shampoo, combs and, its necessity less obvious, shoe polish. Just out of reach was an empty Fruit and Nut box filled with single cigarettes. His mind did a double take as he remembered that subterfuge would be unnecessary. He was after all, several years over the legal age for smoking.

Suddenly the curly-haired head of a woman popped up from behind the counter like a jack-in-the-box.

'What can I get you my love?' Dan surveyed the goodies with longing. He was sure those prawns used to be double the size.

'I haven't got any money,' he said mournfully.

'Run out has it?' she said.

'I didn't have any to run out.'

'Your benefit not come through yet then?' Benefit? No one had mentioned that either. She explained to him that he'd have to go up to Patients' Affairs and fill in some forms, but that the office was closed now and wouldn't be open again till Monday. Having some experience of the dole office, he didn't hold out much hope of seeing any money by this means much before Christmas. He dawdled in front of the counter, preying on the woman's sympathy.

'OK,' she said finally, 'You can owe me.'

It was a happy man who walked away, with a paper bag full of primary school drugs and three single cigarettes, the cheapo extra-long sort, which he used to hate, but which had suddenly come into their own. He carried on down the corridor, reliving boyhood as each puffy pink prawn dissolved on his tongue.

He turned another corner and seemed to walk through an invisible beam, activating a skinny little man, perched on a windowsill like an old London sparrow, in a dusty brown and grey suit. As Dan got closer he could see his ankles and wrists sticking out from the trousers and sleeves, which made him look more like a child whose mother had decided that he could ruddy well make do with the uniform he'd got, whether it was getting too small or not. The man grinned, revealing a virtually empty gumline. That's what he reminded him of, an aged boy, how a character from a long-running comic would look if real time were to impinge on its world. Dan pulled down his headphones to hear what he was saying.

'Gotta cigarette? Gotta cigarette? Gotta cigarette? Gotta cigarette?'

Bloody hell, Nick O'Teen would be pleased with the way things were going in here, he thought, handing over yet another.

'Gotta light? Gotta light? Gotta light? Gotta light?' asked the boy-sparrow-cum-parrot. Dan gave him one, and walked away, with the little man repeating, 'Much obliged! Much obliged! Much obliged! Much obliged!'

On again, till he came to an open door on his left that said 'Games Room'. He tried the door and found it open. He had the strong feeling that he shouldn't be anywhere that sounded as if it might offer fun. The place reminded him of his old youth club, with its pool table and table football. An upright piano stood against the far wall. He crept up to it like a criminal and saw on its music stand a tattered book of sheet music. On the front it boasted the title 'Songs That Will Live Forever' with the last three words crossed out and replaced with 'Have Died'. He turned off his Walkman again and sat down in front of the keyboard. He depressed middle C with his index finger. The sound cut through the thick silence, round, complete and important.

'I'm sorry. We're not open for another half an hour,' said a voice from behind him. He jumped, then looked round to see a balding man in corduroys with a pile of LPs under his arm.

'Oh, OK, I'll come back later.' He got up to leave.

'Do you play?' said the man as he was walking away.

'What, you mean the piano? Yeah, I mean no... I had some lessons as a kid ... but I'm no good.'

The man seemed delighted, like a retired piano teacher nostalgic for an enthusiastic pupil.

'Out of practice, you mean!'

God, the guy was making him feel guilty for neglecting his scales for the last five years.

'Come and play for us later, the others would love it!' He beamed.

Back in the corridor Dan wondered how he could engineer a game of pool without having to endure total public humiliation.

He passed through a curious gateway made of two huge flaps of transparent yellow rubber, past a door that said 'Library', thinking that to go in there would probably be asking for more trouble. He turned a final corner and lo and behold, he was looking through glass doors into a built-in church.

Its effect was spectacular. The modest rose window cast hazy beams of coloured light through an opaque, internal dusk. The whole place was a chorus of red and green, deep violet shadows and brilliant golden highlights. It was empty, apart from a solitary figure sitting in one of the front pews.

His eyes were drawn to the stained glass. It looked as if it had been designed using one of those weird spyrograph things he'd had when he was small. He remembered his biro going round and round, creating a pattern not unlike that which he saw before him. It could have been a representation of a flower, atomic structure, even the dimensions of the entire cosmos. Was creation's geometry created in the same way, by the general whizzing round and round of everything?

His mouth had gone dry with the sheer visual thrill, so he popped in another Rhubarb and Custard, remembering guiltily that you shouldn't really eat in church, before pushing open the door on which was written, 'Quiet Please. This Is A Church'. In case you hadn't noticed.

He sat down on a pew at the back and breathed in the smell of flowers and furniture polish. If he half closed his eyes the special effects were magnified, the light suffused, shedding its multicoloured glow more and more wantonly, penetrating him with a force that threatened to send him rocketing skywards. He had to hold onto the back of the pew in front of him as he experienced an explosive rush. He was either going to be blasted directly to Seventh Heaven or, if he had been that way inclined, leap up with his arms outstretched and holler, 'Hallelujah!' before prostrating himself in the aisle.

He tried to quieten his heart, which was beating at an alarming rate by contemplation of the number seven. Was there anything more to the phrase Seventh Heaven, other than the fact that the words rhymed, sort of? He focused on the number, trying to outdo himself. Seven deadly sins, seven brides for seven brothers, the seventh son, the seventh day of a seven day week, the seven wonders of the world, give me a child of seven – I give you the man, the cells of the body are regenerated every seven years, one year is seven to a dog... Blake's 7 for God's sake. This trick seemed to work. He let go of the pew. The white-knuckle ride was over.

He'd never been a churchgoer. That wasn't how he'd been brought up. His parents had been given quite considerable grief due to the fact that mum was a catholic and dad a protestant, so he and his brother were nothings. Baptised catholic to avoid the eternal shame of a grandmother, and sent to a C of E school. It occurred to him that this may have given him a balanced view of things like, say, Northern Ireland, if he could work it all out in the first place. Instead, religious education amounted to parrot-style memorising of chunks of the gospels to be regurgitated at exam time, and his housemaster's protracted lectures, which would begin with, 'You know lad, God said...'

Anyhow, he suddenly saw the attraction and resolved to come on Sunday. He'd never been able to get his head round the God idea. It was just too cosy. Some sort of Father Christmas type character, a great idea, handy when in trouble – sad but typical that it wasn't true. But now all that had changed. What a fool he'd been! Suddenly he felt the urge to go tell it on the mountain. He rubbed his eyes and looked up again. His dad was standing before him in white robes with golden trim, saying, 'Yes, my child.'

He rubbed them some more and saw that actually, it was Anna, the Elf's friend. Christ! Spooky or what? His palms were wet with sweat.

'Didn't you see me? I was sitting at the front. Kate's gone home for the weekend,' she said, pouting. She sat down next to him and sidled up close, giving off a strong damsel in distress vibe. She was holding a packet of tissues, crumpled in her tight fist – she must have been having a good cry along with her prayers.

To his surprise, she began to hitch up her skirt. Now things were in danger of becoming sacrilegious. He pretended not to notice.

'Look,' she said seductively. He couldn't help it, he looked sideways and down, expecting to see an extraordinary tattoo, or maybe even no knickers.

'Jesus!' he gasped, seeing instead a sticky red mess of fresh blood. Was she haemorrhaging, or experiencing some other strange female condition gone wrong?

She smiled a satisfied smile, took out one of her tissues and proceeded to dab at the blood. As she did so, she revealed a network of scars, some old and pale, some newer and pinker, some with scabs, and now these open wounds. There was barely any unmarked flesh between her knees and the tops of her thighs. Dan felt sick, he reached out to steady himself again. He'd never seen anything like it in his life.

'What on earth have you done to yourself?' he asked, unable to conceal his horror.

'I just cut up,' she said, 'It's my thing, you know.'

No, he didn't know.

'But why?' He looked at the massacred flesh incredulously. She opened her other fist to reveal a razor blade.

'It makes me feel better.'

'How?' He'd heard about pinching yourself to divert the mind from a stubbed toe, but this was something else.

'Put it this way, it's better than feeling nothing. You

should try it.' She waved her viciously glinting little analgesic in front of his face. He tried to snatch it away from her, but she quickly wrapped it in the bloody tissue and stuffed it into her bum-bag. Patting her thighs to see if they were dry, she pulled down her skirt as casually as if she had just showed him a particularly impressive insect bite.

'This is the only place I get any peace.'

This was too much. Sufficient unto the afternoon is the headfuck thereof. He felt it would hardly be Christian to leave it at that, so he offered to walk her back to her ward. She declined, saying she was going to visit Krish, who was now a resident of Oak. They stood up and on the way to the door she turned round and genuflected dramatically, crossing herself several times. She stood before him expectantly before they went their separate ways. He knew what she wanted, but instead gave her a hug that he hoped would feel brotherly. As he pulled away he saw that her face was wet with tears. She took out another tissue and wiped her eyes, then, smiling too brightly, blew him a kiss and was off.

He was dragged back to Ash ward by a dark undertow, chewing on a Milk Bottle that he wished he'd offered her by way of an edible Love Substitute.

17

Insomniac

Back in the ward, he thought it best to keep himself to himself, so he went to his room and shut out the world. He tried to dismiss the macabre image of Anna's thighs by replacing them with how he imagined the Elf's might look, hoping to God that she wasn't into the same thing.

The ice cream van's jangling Popeye theme was replaying in his head, now a menacing soundtrack to the afternoon's events, spiralling in his mind's eye like the special effects of an old pop video. He couldn't relax with all that going on so he went back into the dayroom.

There was no sign of Jack, or Alec or anyone that he knew. He went over to the open window and watched the goats in their paddock. One was dozing under the shady canopy of a majestic plane tree, while his partner in crime was indolently munching an old newspaper. He wondered if anyone had ever considered the use of goats as a means of recycling waste.

He remembered an evening with Fran spent watching yet another apocalyptic documentary about landfill sites and the apparently insurmountable problem of the zillions of tons of rubbish which the average household promptly forgets about after putting it out tidily for the bin men. As if this action alone dealt with it once and for all. Perhaps one day, when human beings are as dead as dinosaurs, a new breed of geologists would wonder at the colourful striations of plastic detritus in rock formations, which, despite leaching noxious substances into the surrounding matter, would have remained totally unchanged by time. Now, goats could reduce some of it surely, if not the plastics. Maybe the resulting matter could fuel power stations. But then why should they eat newspapers when they could have carnations?

The outside world beckoned, so he climbed out of the window, deciding that there was no need to be so conventional as to find a door. The dappled light on the earth gave the effect of looking through shallow water, the magic touch of the sun turning the daisies into glittering flecks of panner's gold. He approached the goats, who eyed him disinterestedly, nonchalantly accepting his attentions, pushing their necks against him to maximise the effect of behind-the-ear scratching.

He sat down under the tree and smoked his last cigarette – someone had to turn up soon with more. With the serendipity that he was coming to expect of life he watched as two fine naked limbs appeared from out of the window. The complete Mat followed suit, looking cooler than a frozen cucumber in cycling shorts, T-shirt, baseball cap and shades.

'Wha'appen! Are you going to introduce me to your new girlfriends?' he said, not coming any further. Mat and goats didn't really go together. Dan leapt up and bounded over to him. Mat greeted him by giving him five, a salutation that Dan always found a bit embarrassing. He could never quite get enough confident gusto behind him, so he gave in return the fives equivalent of a limp handshake, but today it didn't matter. His benefactor had arrived.

Visitors are like buses. You wait for one for hours and then a whole lot turns up at once. He and Mat were just about to go for a walk when who should walk in but Vicky, his old neighbour, childhood sweetheart, object of fantasy and sister that he'd never had. She was one of life's constants. Their friendship had endured where others had fallen away, the knowledge of each other as children bringing to it a particular quality that those conceived in adulthood could never reproduce. Maybe they were bound by the fact that they had shared their first ever snog, one hot afternoon, when the parents were too busy at the barbecue to notice them topping up their lemonade with martini and sneaking off towards the bushes.

She was with a bloke who looked scared to death and as if he were wondering why the hell he'd let her persuade him to come along. He was obviously her latest, and although not wishing for anything other than her happiness, Dan still didn't really relish seeing her with anyone else. Vicky hugged him for a long time whilst Mat and the spare part, who was called John, said, 'Hello,' and then stood awkwardly, waiting for the public private moment to be over.

Dan danced around his little group of guests like a host that had been at the bottle before they'd arrived, and now regretted it. He tried desperately to get their orders for tea or coffee straight in his mind, but found he kept having to go back and check. He kept calling John Chris, which was unfortunate, as Chris was the name of Vicky's ex, a fact of which, by the look on his face, John was painfully aware. Mat wasn't helping to ease the atmosphere, as he insisted on keeping his sunglasses on, even though the dayroom, in contrast to the brilliance through the window, had an almost stygian gloom about it. Not that Dan noticed.

Despite his insistence that he could manage, Vicky came into the kitchen and got it all together with frightening efficiency. Before she picked up the tray she asked, 'How are you really?'

'Good thanks, yeah, honest I'm OK. How's life with

you?' She ignored his question.

'But you're not really OK are you?' she said, taking his hand. 'Otherwise you wouldn't be in here, would you?'

'I dunno.' He didn't want to go down this particular avenue. He wanted to talk and laugh with his friends and not stray too far from The Feeling. They rejoined the others. They sat together drinking their tea, Vicky pointing out to him the fact that he already had one fag on the go, and that it was probably better to finish the Crunchy before proceeding with the Double Decker.

Before too long Jack and Alec sauntered in. On seeing Mat, Alec piped up, '*The future's so bright, I gotta wear shades...*'

'That's right,' said Mat unflinchingly. Jack looked Vicky up and down and said, 'Right little Casanova aren't you mate!' John shifted uncomfortably in his chair. He gave her a look that said, 'Let's go for Christ's sake,' and before too long they stood up and said their goodbyes.

Dan relaxed a bit after they left. It was far easier being with Mat, whose knowledge of him was limited to what he had gleaned over the last couple of months. With him he could be his present self, instead of disappointing everyone. Soon it was his turn to leave. Dan walked him to the gates, thinking how easy it would be to go with him, but for some highly complex reason that he couldn't be bothered to wrangle with, he didn't really want to.

He ambled back to the ward, stopping to pass the time of day with an audacious squirrel. It made a strange clucking sound. He did the same. The squirrel replied politely, as if that was all there was to talking to the animals.

The rest of the day came and went with what was becoming a predictable routine. He skipped supper. He wasn't in the least bit hungry, being stuffed full with more confectionery than he'd eaten in the last year.

Despite the delightful privacy of his new room, he couldn't sleep. Maybe it was due to his unfeasibly high blood sugar level, or because he'd managed to spit a couple of his tablets into his hand, then thrown them out of the dayroom window. He hoped the goats hadn't got them. As he tossed and turned, he started to wish he'd swallowed the lot. The air was still and the temperature too high for comfort. He must have drifted off at some point, because he'd woken up, tangled in his sheet and drenched in sweat. After that, sleep had eluded him again. He got up to open his door, thinking that it might create a draught. He looked up and down the corridor. To his right, up by the dayroom, the night nurse was slumped in her chair, having no trouble sleeping. That was probably because she was meant to be awake.

He'd suffered from what had seemed like years of sleeplessness. Smoking furtive fags out of his bedroom window, thinking about his future with anxiety which would sometimes turn into exhilarated optimism, longing for adventure, even alien abduction, whilst the town slept snug and smug. He used to reassure himself that he wasn't the only person in Britain still awake, with the thought of long-distance lorry drivers and night nurses (which he now realised had been a bad choice), when his solitude was intensified by the closedown of Radio Luxembourg.

He had to find a strategy for dealing with what was becoming a neurosis. He discovered that the only way to beat insomnia was to pull the wool over its eyes. Night after night he would kid himself that it was imperative that he remained wide-awake. He appointed himself nightwatchman to the nation, one slipshod drooping eyelid spelling disaster that only his wakefulness could avert. It had done the trick. Trying to stay awake was a highly effective sedative. It had worked back then, and had gone on working well into the following day's lessons, but nothing seemed to work tonight.

He draped his crumpled sheet around him and emerged from his room looking as if he'd just got lucky at a toga party. A light was on at the other end of the corridor and he made for it on unsteady legs, zigzagging like a moth. Tim was sitting in the corner of the empty dining room in his pyjamas, bent over a sketchbook. He had headphones on and was lost in his endeavour, tongue protruding from his mouth as his fat felt-tip moved over the page, oblivious to Dan who stood watching him at work. He was nodding his head happily when he suddenly broke the silence with a loud *'ACI-I-I-D!'*, threatening to wake the nurse. Dan glanced back down the corridor. She didn't stir. The nocturnal artist gave a long, post-concentration sigh and rocked back on his chair to admire his creation. At that moment he caught sight of the tousled apparition that was Dan. He lost his balance and tumbled backwards, grabbing at another chair as he fell, adding to the clatter that had to wake the sleeping giant down the hall.

Dan rushed over. Tim was wide-eyed with fright, with his legs still bent over the chair in a horizontal sitting position.

'Jesus man! You nearly gave me a heart attack!'

'God! I'm really sorry, I didn't mean to freak you out!' He put out his hand and helped him up. He was a mixed-race guy of about nineteen, who thankfully seemed to take it with good humour, and even more thankfully, was not paralysed from the neck down because of him.

'Wot are you like?' he said looking Dan up and down.

'Ssshh! Ssshh!' They clutched their stomachs and barred their lips as they cracked up.

'I thought I was tripping!' said Tim. They were convulsed, bent double, when they heard the rustling approach of an unyielding female garment. They turned to see the huge nurse, who looked old enough to have been around to attend to Malcolm on one of the many occasions when he narrowly escaped death on the battlefield. She was still bleary-eyed, but assumed a suitably stern stance with her hands bearing down on her mammoth hips.

'You know what I'm going to say to you don't you?' she said, stringing it out.

'Get back to your rooms at once!' Tim gathered up his things and they were chaperoned back to their respective rooms, snorting with laughter.

Back on his bed, Dan made a mental note to ask Tim if he could have a look at his drawings. He eventually fell asleep wondering why he was here.

The next morning he was rudely awoken by loud banging on his door.

'Time to get up Dan!' Thinking that it must be very late, he pulled on his clothes and went out to see what was going on. There was a pervasive smell of porridge floating up the corridor, making him feel sick.

It was Steve who was on duty that morning. Dan asked him the time and he was told that it was seven o'clock. What on earth was the point of getting everyone up at that time of day? Especially that time of day? It wasn't as if anyone had to get ready to go anywhere. He went obediently to the dining room and sat down before a cup of brown liquid, masquerading as coffee. Suddenly he felt himself being tipped back on his chair and then forward again, sending his drink flying out of the cup and slopping over the table. He looked round to see Tim grinning at him, indecently bright-eyed and bushy-tailed.

They spent the rest of the day together. Tim said he'd been at art college when all of a sudden the postcards of his favourite paintings on the walls of his room had started to come to life and speak to him. Speak to him with proper voices that he could hear as if people were there in the room with him. They had told him that it was his mission in life to cover the walls of his neighbourhood with graffiti, which was a hidden language that only the chosen few could read. That made sense. Dan had always wondered about the unintelligible hieroglyphics that he saw all over the place. He'd always assumed it was Arabic or something, until someone had told him that graffiti artists each had a signature that their peers recognised. It was a sort of jazzy improvisation on the 'I woz ere' theme.

Anyway, Tim had obeyed his orders, sneaking around with his spray cans, until one day he became convinced that all red cars contained secret graffiti police that were out to get him. When they did, they were going to kill him, knowing that he was privy to some very dangerous information indeed.

He told Dan all this in a secretive fashion, all the while looking around furtively. He was obviously still convinced of the plot to silence him forever. He was as edgy as the guy in 1984.

'What do the doctors say you've got?' asked Dan. Whatever it was, it didn't sound like a whole lot of fun. The poor bloke seemed to be trapped in some sort of waking nightmare.

'Paranoid schizophrenia, so they tell me.' He was starting to look upset. He told him that the medication he was on was lethal and that the people here were probably in on the plot as well.

Dan had always thought that schizophrenics had split personalities. In the daytime, say, the manager of a small provincial branch of a Building Society, who turned homicidal transvestite at night. It could be that the word 'paranoid' made it a totally different condition. Whatever the case, the topic of conversation had to be changed, that was for sure.

'D'you play pool?'

As soon as the Games Room was open they were there, first in the queue for the table. Never had the mathematical poetry of this game, an ability for which his dad had always maintained was the sign of a misspent youth, been so crystal clear. As much as he would have liked to misspend his youth, he hadn't been allowed to, a fact to which his game usually testified. Today however, he was surpassing himself. It was purely a question of confidence, as if belief alone could turn the pockets into magnetic fields into which the ball was irresistibly drawn, time after time. Tim wasn't bad either, and they whiled away several happy hours before others demanded their turn.

Just when he thought he'd got away with it the man in the cords appeared.

'Ah!' he enthused, 'It's the musician! I hope you're not going to disappoint us today!' He went over to the piano stool and patted it.

There was no escaping it, he tried to shy away, but all present were cheering him on, making it impossible for him to refuse. He knew he was incapable of sight-reading one of the Songs That Had Died, so he launched into a tune from Grade 3 piano that had lodged stubbornly in his memory, from whence any good tune had fled. Tim was right by his side. To Dan's surprise, he seemed to be impressed.

'Wicked man, wicked!' he said.

This stoked up the rekindling fire that the piano had once lit in Dan's soul. Said fire had unfortunately been dampened and finally all but extinguished by an overbearing piano teacher suffering from a particularly pungent body odour that had made the forty minutes in the tiny soundproofed music room a positive torture. She'd stood behind him, tapping her foot to keep time, whilst doing something that he couldn't quite make out in the polished gleam above the keyboard. It looked like she was pulling up her pants, he wasn't sure, and didn't want to find out.

But it wasn't just that. The keyboard had remained a total enigma, as he tried to co-ordinate the dots on the page with the black and white puzzle before him. The tunes were by and large as dull as ditchwater, or at least they were when Mrs Wilde, a name that didn't suit her at all, played them.

After his triumph on the pool table, Dan felt that a world of unknown talents was now his oyster. A mate of his had once shown him a few bluesy chords, which suddenly came back to him. He moved these boastfully up and down the keyboard, which seemed to have just let him in on a secret. He was enjoying himself. Having exhausted the possibilities of his limited knowledge, he stood up, trembling as if he'd just done his bit at the school concert.

'Bravo!' said the ever-smiling man, clapping heartily. It made up for a million of Mrs Wilde's despairing tuts.

Later on, Tim showed him his sketchbook, gave him a piece of paper and lent him a few colours. Dan drew round and round in circles, then filled in all the little sections, thinking about leaves upon leaves, Venn diagrams and stained-glass windows, remembering that the next day was Sunday and he was going to check out church.

18

Neverland

When he told him where he was going the next morning, Jack said that he'd come along as well, even though he was not what he called 'a God botherer'. When Alec asked where they were going, he decided to join in for a laugh. When Tim saw them sauntering off together, he felt sure that there was something going on, so he said 'C'mon' to Joanne, who bounced after them, and whatever she did, the HDM did. IRA, however, said he wasn't going anywhere near a 'focking church'.

They passed Sparrowman on his customary perch, bringing him to life as they passed. He made his usual demand, which prompted everyone to reach out towards Dan's fags. A pre-worship smoke seemed to be in order, so he offered them round, watching his packet dwindle yet again. When they'd finished, he looked round to see the little man, carefully picking up all the butts off the floor and pocketing them, grinning his gummy grin as if they were manna. Jack told him his name was Percy and that he'd been there since the war, and didn't look like he was joking.

They were late, of course. Red-hot faces turned round to glare at the disrespectful gang that was shuffling in

135

noisily. They filed into a pew at the back.

'Sorry we're late, Father!' Jack called out, waving to the priest.

'That's quite alright. We're very happy that you've all come to join us here today,' he said in mellifluous tones. 'If you'd all like to pick up the blue book in front of you and turn to page six, we can continue.'

Much page turning and coughing ensued.

Dan looked around. Congregations throughout the country may well have been diminishing, but you would have never thought it judging from the turnout here this morning. He wondered if it was due to the lack of anything else to do, or because, like him, they truly believed that they had something to be thankful for. There were in fact more people crying de profundis than experiencing religious ecstasy, but the ecstatic ones over-compensated for the introversion of the depressed. They sang out with cheerful voice, punctuating the priest's words with whoops and applause. Someone ran out into the aisle and seemed to collapse, limbs twitching, as if still attached to the ECT electrodes. It was Shameela. Security rushed over and carted her off. The service continued.

Dan was disappointed with it. He had been hoping for something a bit whacky and progressive, but it was the same old one that he'd endured on the few occasions when he'd been forced to go to church for some reason or another. Suddenly the little blue book seemed interminably long. As the sermon droned on, its narrative far too ambitious for a medicated congregation, he started giggling to himself, imagining how it might be if 'Songs of Praise' was broadcast 'From the church of Woodland Park Hospital, set in charming parkland, a true haven in the teeming city.'

The camera would pan round, taking in the remarkable cross-section of society that he saw before him. There were African ladies in their Sunday finery, with extravagant turban-like headdress, next to prim white ladies in country casuals. Old people abounded, some in wheelchairs attended by nurses in sports wear. There were young people, middle-aged people, an assortment of angry apostles, south London sibyls and quite a few characters in kaftan-like robes as if they were acting in a Passion play. One old man with a long white beard stood out from the crowd as if God himself had fallen victim to the Mental Health Act. There seemed to be considerable competition on the chosen one front, making Dan feel slightly uncomfortable. Maybe he hadn't been singled out by the universe after all. He spotted Anna, near the front, next to Krish, in his baggy orange trousers, giving it an 'All Faiths Welcome' feel. The priest was leading the unsynchronised muttering of the creed.

'...I believe ... and in all things visible and invisible...'

Jack elbowed Dan in the ribs. 'See!' he spat into Dan's ear, 'Visible and invisible! Even they know about the invisible things!'

The master of ceremonies was reading out a long list of people for whom all must pray. The names sounded totally fictitious and some people appeared to know them off by heart, 'Nancy Newell, Nellie Poppell, Florence Grey, Bessie Conway, Annie-Lavinia Wright, Kitty Mags, Walter Woodcock, Humphrey England, Harold Cox...'

Who were these people? And where were they? Did anyone know, or care?

It was time for another hymn. All turned to number 223 in their tatty hymnbooks. The organ huffed and puffed its way through the introduction, before the crowd joined in, in an approximation of unison, some high and reedy, some low and croaky, some embarrassingly loud, some feeble.

'God is working his purpose out as year succeeds to year...'

'Well if he's still working it out, what bloody chance 'ave

we got? I've had enough of this rubbish,' said Jack, elbowing his way out. Alec followed him.

'We'll leave you to your prayers,' he hissed at Dan, 'Peace be with you brother.'

The congregation's collective head swivelled round again, grimacing at the disturbance. Dan would have liked to go with them, but guilt and his inner wimp were in cahoots, gluing him to his pew.

After the predictably gross Sunday lunch, it was just a matter of passing the time before the Elf got back, but no doubt that wouldn't be for ages. In his younger days Sundays had been rescued from total oblivion by the impending Top 40, but that all seemed like kids' stuff, now that he was into greater things.

It was cooler and breezier than it had been of late, so he set off for a walk. Mr Atkinson was sitting in the corridor next to a man, a relation – it was in the cheekbones, reading to him from a Bible. The old man looked up as Dan approached. He pointed to his ears and started to sway back and forth, smiling.

'Looks like he likes you,' said the younger man.

'I gave him a listen of my Walkman the other day, but apparently I shouldn't have.'

'Who says so?' The bloke seemed annoyed.

'That nurse, the young one with the short hair.'

'Gerry, I expect. I'll have a word with her,' he said, massaging his forehead.

Dan could feel his fatigue. He'd become very aware of other people's aches and pains lately, physical or otherwise. Every time he walked past Joan with her swollen legs, his legs, which were a lot better, started to hurt again, feeling taut and hot, as if they were going to burst. He'd mentioned this phenomenon to Steve, who dismissed it with, 'You're imagining it.' If that were the case then he must have a very good imagination indeed, he'd thought, pulling up the legs of his jeans expecting them to look like Joan's, which, granted, they did not.

'So, you've met Eustace then?'

'Eustace? I heard someone call him Nelson,' said Dan.

'That's because he's been in here longer than Nelson Mandela's been on Robben Island. He's my uncle.'

Eustace was trying to say something, struggling to get his mouth into gear.

'Nn-n-n...'

'What's that?' Dan bent closer to him.

'Nn-n-n ... n ... Neverland!' he said, looking out of the window wistfully, as if at a distant horizon.

'That's just about all he ever says,' said the man.

'What does he mean?' Dan remembered Peter Pan, flashing back to a family outing. The pantomime, a girl dressed as a boy 'flying' over the stage on a disappointingly visible wire...

'I'm not sure really. Dad says it's what he called England. Neverland. Where you could never catch up with the never-never, and you'd never get home and you'd never be at home, and you'd never get a decent job... And now it looks like he'll never get out of here. I can't look after him. So anyway,' he paused, taking his Uncle's hand and squeezing it, 'I think he's entitled to listen to a bit of music now and again. In fact, I think I'll get him a Walkman of his own. It's his birthday today you know.'

'Many Happy Returns,' said Dan, although he never knew quite what that meant. Happy Returns to where? From where...? He remembered Mat telling him about the time he went to visit his family in Jamaica. He said he'd expected to feel like he'd come home, but felt more of an alien there than he did in London.

The Blake signal started to come over the airwaves.

'My family are here now,' said Dan. Several moments later as he was kneeling beside the old man, showing him the way around the controls of his stereo, the doors at the end of the corridor swung open and in walked his mum, dad and brother. Dan looked up and waved. They waved back. For some reason he could feel their fears and suspicions dissolving, as if he'd just been acquitted of the charge of malignant naughtiness.

It was a good visit. The atmosphere in the dayroom was cheerful. Most people seemed to have a visitor or two. Before long the family was absorbed into the throng. His brother had a game of draughts with Tim, while his dad, oblivious to his folly, said to Malcolm, 'So, Dan tells me that you were in the army...'

Benny, released from acute, had joined Ash that morning. He was now sitting close to his wife, who had brought their newborn baby into the ward, to much cooing and clucking from the sorority, and Dan's mum was soon engaged in conversation with the new mother with that instant intimacy that leaves men flummoxed.

Dan watched as the outsize man picked up his golden baby girl as if she were made of bone china and cradled her in his branch-like arms. The infant stirred, looked up at her father with eyes that struggled to focus, before deciding there was no real need, yawned, dribbled, then went back to sleep. Benny looked around, swollen with as much pride as if she'd just delivered a speech at the Albert Hall.

Looking over to his dad, Dan saw that he needed rescuing. He was making desperate eye signals, as if to say that he'd had more than his fill of Malcolm's far-fetched autobiography.

'Dad! Come and see this!' he beckoned to him to come over to the window. He could hear Malcolm saying, '... Yes, they all said it was a miracle. If I hadn't been so fit, I wouldn't be here today. Important to keep yourself in trim you know,' as he patted his portly midriff. 'Healthy body, healthy mind!'

'Excuse me, I must go and talk to my son,' said the reluctant audience of one, prising himself away. Dan plucked a flower from a vase and waved it out of the window. As much of a stampede as two small goats could muster ensued, before they leapt onto the window ledge as deftly as if it was their favourite way up the mountain and stuck their heads into the room with an expectant, 'Ma-a-a-a-a, ma-a-a.'

His family was speechless. Then his mum started laughing in that way of hers usually reserved for more obviously happy family occasions, whilst Benny showed them to his sleepy baby, whispering, 'See the goaty, the nice goaty's hungry isn't he?' Dan watched his dad watching his mum, seeing his relief at the laughter ringing out of her like a peal of bells.

Before they left they gave him some money so he could make his calls and buy more lip salve. It felt strange in his pocket, the currency of another world. With his supplies topped up, he watched them go, waving out of the car window.

He hurried to the payphone, remembering that he owed money to the woman in the shop, struggling to recall the most important numbers in his little black book. He tried to read the display on the phone to see how much money the woman in front had got left. She shooed him away, irritated. It said 86p. He hoped it wasn't a local call. After an eternity he heard her say, 'Yeah. Yeah, alright ... yeess! Bye, take care, bye, yeah... I love you too. Course I'm missing you ... no, I told you they gave me some antibiotics... I did, OK, alright, bye...'

He got his money ready, hopping from one foot to another. He could hardly wait to talk to a few chums. '...Can you put mum on now? ...Yeah, I know all this is very difficult for you, but how the hell d'you think I feel? ... OK. Sorry. Bye...' She fed the slot with another handful of change. Dan was incensed, he considered trying the, 'Please, it's an emergency!' ruse, but didn't think it would wash with her.

At last she completed her long drawn out valedictions. He fumbled with his change and dialled his mate Stuart from college's number. His hands were sweating. He felt nervous. It was ringing. His girlfriend Becky answered.

'Hello.'

'Hi! B! It's me Dan, I'm in hosp...'

'Hang on, I'll get Stu.' Weird, maybe she was in one of her bad moods. He watched the countdown on the dial, hearing muffled voices on the other end. It sounded like Stu saying, 'Well I don't bloody know what to say to him either...' Surely not – he wasn't one to be lost for words. Eventually he heard him pick up.

'Hiya, Stu! How's it going?' he said, trying to sound normal. An almost unrecognisable voice said, 'Oh, hello Dan, I heard what happened. Em, sorry, we've got people here, I can't really talk now... Look after yourself, bye.'

The phone went dead.

Oh well, obviously a bad time. He'd try him again later. He pressed 'follow on call' and dialled Jenny's number. He'd had a soft spot for her ever since they hooked up on the ferry to Boulogne and got pissed together on a bottle of duty free vodka, sitting out on deck, watching the White Cliffs dissolving into the haze along with their wits, fantasising about foreign tomorrows. He'd helped her wipe the vomit off her camera after her attack of what she maintained was seasickness. A dad-like voice came on the line.

'Tring 261, Allcock speaking.' Dan wanted to say that it sounded funny saying 'Tring', as if it was de rigueur to reply to the phone itself first. Instead he cleared his throat and said, 'Oh hello, Mr Allcock,' trying to dispel the image that the literal visualisation of his name conjured up, 'is Jenny there?'

'Who's speaking?'

'It's Dan, Dan Blake, from College.'

'Hold on a moment.' He heard him call out, 'Jennifer! It's someone Blake for you!' He listened to more kerfuffle at the other end. He fed some more coins into the slot and watched with dismay as his remaining change shrank in his hand.

'Hi, Dan.' There followed a more than pregnant pause. God, news travels fast! He realised that he was now the object of the gossip that he'd once enjoyed with the rest. He muttered something about how it would be nice to see her. She replied unconvincingly that it would be nice to see him too, but she had a thing about hospitals, they always made her feel a bit funny... Like boats, he thought, as another arrow pierced his heart.

Suddenly the pips went. He relayed the number to her and then hung around the phone for a while, giving her the benefit of the doubt – maybe she had to go to the loo or something – till the silent truth could no longer be ignored. Tears came to his eyes. He wished his family was still there, he felt abandoned.

After supper, he crossed the expanse of parched ground to Lime ward, hoping that the Elf had returned. She hadn't, and according to the Bitch, she wouldn't be back till the morning. Anna was curled up on a tattered sofa, cuddling a soft toy and sucking her thumb. She looked at him, withdrew it slowly from her mouth and asked if he wanted to go for a walk. He replied that he was a bit tired and escaped. She was starting to give him the serious creeps.

He went to the bus stop and waited for nothing, thinking about his parents as he watched two small blue butterflies perform a pas-de-deux. His dad had once told him, when in lyrical mode, that marriage was a dance, and watching the frivolous insects as they came close, spiralled together, then strayed, reasserting their independence before excited re-entry of each other's airspace, he thought he knew exactly what he'd meant.

Jack appeared out of nowhere, sat down next to him and lit a cigarette.

'Look at those two moths fighting,' he said.

19

Art

The next morning he was about to set off in search of her again when he was stopped by Steve, who told him not to disappear, because the Occupational Therapist would be along shortly to give him his programme for the next fortnight.

He whiled away half an hour talking to a voluntary patient called Rupert, who said he was a society photographer. That meant high society, not society per se, he explained. Dan wondered why he hadn't checked himself in to somewhere a little more salubrious than this. Still, he seemed amiable enough, Sloane or not.

He told Dan that he was suffering from SAD, which meant Seasonal Affective Disorder. He said that if it hadn't been for the fact that he'd had to do an important wedding in April, he'd be in his villa in Menorca by now. Unfortunately, it had coincided with a bleak overcast fortnight. It had put him on a right downer, before he could book a flight out to the sun that he needed in large doses to stay sane – or get to the doctor's in time. For the last God knows how long, he'd been lying on his bed with the curtains closed. Dan pointed out that England was in the middle of a heatwave, but Rupert said that when he was down he was down, like the Grand Old Duke of York, and there was nothing he could do about it until the antidepressants kicked in.

Anyway, his cousin, who, incidentally, was a culinary stylist, which he explained, is a person who takes photos of food for recipe books which make the rest of the world feel inadequate, had booked up the villa for the rest of the summer. It was obvious that Rupert felt resentful. Dan could sense that there was more than a little rivalry between these two artistes. He went on to say that if he couldn't have it all to himself (which he absolutely had to for it to do any good) till after his cousin's kids had gone back to school, then there was no point in having it at all. Dan agreed that it was rotten luck.

A thin-lipped woman came into the dayroom and sat down next to Rupert, recognising him as one of her own breed, or the nearest thing to it that circumstance could provide. She was dressed in a shapeless summer dress with a string of pearls round her neck. Her hair was tidily clipped back. She looked like a mother at the school gate. The sort that Dan would have preferred on the occasions when his mum turned up dressed in what he considered to be the most embarrassing outfit in the history of the world.

'Off somewhere nice, Elizabeth?' enquired Rupert in his dark brown voice.

'I'm just waiting to be collected for my ECT,' she mewed.

'ECT?' said Dan, horror-struck. 'Why are you having that?'

'It's for my depression.'

'But it's barbaric! You can't let them do that to you!'

'Actually, I do think it helps a bit.'

'Really? How fascinating,' said Rupert, propping his head on his chin and nodding, riveted, as if considering putting himself forward for a blast or two. Dan looked at her. She was like someone from Victorian times, who, if a doctor had proposed it, would have allowed a bird cage to enclose her head complete with imprisoned songster, this being the very latest cure for female melancholy. A man appeared, and led her away for what seemed to him to be nothing short of vivisection.

A woman in a denim dress was standing in the doorway.

'Is Daniel Blake here?' She looked around the room.

'Yeah that's me,' he said, putting up his hand.

'Hi!' she said brightly. 'Let's get you sorted out with some things to do!'

He'd been put down for Art and Dance Therapy, something called Woodland Workshop, which sounded like somewhere the Seven Dwarves would go hi-ho-ing off to work (another seven, he noted), and a session called 'Improve your Concentration'. She said that there wasn't any Horticultural Therapy at the moment because the therapist was off sick. She seemed like a nice enough person, about five years older than him and not too pushy. She opened an old leather music case into which she began to put her paperwork. As she flipped the lid back over Dan caught a glimpse of the name of his old school written underneath her name in a juvenile hand, and under that it said 'Chamberlain'.

'Is that your old schoolbag?' he said, about to be blown away by the smallness of the world.

'Yes it is, why, did you used to have one like it?'

'No, but it looks like you and I were at the same school. Weybridge College. I was Head of Chamberlain House.'

Her reaction was not as he expected. Instead of asking him if he remembered Mrs Butt, or something like that, he felt a seismic shift that sent her redrawing her mental map, trying to fit him in to somewhere where she would have never imagined that he could possibly belong. She said that it was nice to meet him, and left hurriedly. She needn't have worried – she was OK, but he didn't want to hang out with her.

His first session was to be Art Therapy with someone called Peter, at eleven thirty. He had an hour to kill before this new pursuit, so he set off for Lime again, powerless to resist its call.

As he approached, a beat-up Mini drove up and out got the Elf, saying goodbye to a woman who he assumed to be her mother. She was crying as the car drove away. He stepped in and put his arm around her. He didn't know what to say as she sobbed into his T-shirt. She told him to wait for her to dump her bag upstairs, which she did, returning with fresh make-up applied.

'Can we go for a walk?' she asked, 'I haven't got long, I've got to see the doctor.' She told him that the last time she'd been home she came back so high that they'd put her in acute, and that she was glad they hadn't put her in there this time because something amazing had happened, and she couldn't risk getting too upset.

'What's happened?' he asked, thinking that there must have been some cause for celebration on the home front. Maybe she'd been crying for joy.

'Wait till we get somewhere private, then I'll show you.' Curiouser and curiouser.

They found a quiet spot between the pharmacy, where she explained, all the drugs were kept – that's why it looked like Fort Knox – and the nurses' home. They lay down on the grass. The proximity of her was almost more than he could bear. He moved closer to her and looked at her face as she lay with her eyes closed, all traces of her earlier tears gone. If he didn't kiss those cherry-red lips soon he was going to burst. Carpe diem, he decided, as the Weybridge College motto instructed, propping himself up on his elbow.

She looked up at him with the pupils of her greenish eyes dilated with either desire or tranquillisers, and allowed him to proceed. It would have been better if his lips hadn't been so chapped.

'So what's this amazing thing then?' he said, trying to keep his cool. He didn't want to push it.

'I'll show you,' she said, smiling up at him, and started to pull up her top. Maybe there had been no need to be so gentlemanly after all. Then he remembered Anna's thighs, and felt his stomach go tight with dread. She reached behind her back to undo her bra, then took his hand and placed it on one of her breasts.

'There!' she said, still smiling. He removed his hand and looked at it. It was wet. He jumped back as if he'd been stung by the wasp that was hovering nearby, scattering dust like a low-flying helicopter.

'What the...?'

'It's milk, silly. Isn't it amazing, I'm pregnant!'

His head was reeling. It was amazing yes, but not in the way that she obviously thought it was. It sounded petty, but it had to be said, 'So, you've got a boyfriend, then. Have you told him the good news?' She laughed.

'No, you idiot, I haven't got a boyfriend, in fact I haven't even had sex... Not for ages anyway ... it's ... you know...?'

'Know what?' He really did not want this girl to start messing him about.

'Immaculate conception!' she said, gazing ecstatically at the sky. He waited for her to say she was joking. Suddenly she sprang up and said it was time for her to go and see the Doc, presumably for her first antenatal check-up.

Feeling as sceptical as Joseph and with a leaden heart, he set off for Art Therapy. As he walked past the ECT suite, the door opened and Elizabeth was wheeled out in a chair that she hadn't needed earlier.

'Hi there, Elizabeth! Are you OK?' Her dazed face looked at him blankly as if she had never seen him before in her life, confirming his ghastly suspicions. He felt glad that no one had suggested this treatment when he was depressed. In the state that he'd been in he probably would have gone for it as well. If someone had told him that sitting on a pile of hot coals would improve his mood, he'd have jumped at that too. He wondered whether he should suggest to the doctors that they should give her a couple of generous lines of speed, since he truly believed that's what had saved his life.

He paused outside the door of the Art Therapy room. He wasn't sure what to expect. He knocked, went inside and was hit by the chalky sweet smell of powder paint. He looked around at an art room, the likes of which could be found in countless schools throughout the land. A man, a mixture between a hippie and a gypsy, got up from a desk and came over to him, holding a register.

'Hello there! You must be one of our new recruits. What's your name?'

Dan told him and he ticked his list. He introduced himself as Pete, and indicated that he should sit down at one of the little square tables that were arranged around a central space. In the middle there was another table. Upon it was a standard issue still-life, arranged on a bit of hard-to-draw drapery.

'Do you mind just sitting for a bit while we wait for the others?' Dan said that he didn't.

The room was an exhilarating muddle of colour. Big tins of powder paint were stacked precariously on top of one another with traces of their jewel-dust contents caught in the rims around their lids. Teetering columns of brightly stained plastic cups rose from a forest of paintbrushes in glass jars. Oblong palettes, the type that could take four lovely new cakes of bound pigment, were piled up, fitting together like squashed giant Lego. There were rolls of paper, piles of paper, a chest full of different coloured paper, boxes of watercolours, sets of chalks, and all the stationery of an office kleptomaniac's wildest fantasy. Wonky easels were tangled up together in one corner, and next to the obligatory filthy sink there were metal bins with

'CLAY' written on them in drippy white paint. It was exciting, the whole place overflowing with the wherewithal for great works yet undone. The rolls of blank paper as terrifying as the vast vacuous universe before God got it together, knowing that he could be on the verge of an Almighty cock-up.

Posters lined the walls, punctuated by examples of patients' work. His eyes flitted over the printed images, some of which he recognised, or thought he did, until they alighted on a print of landscape that even someone who knew less about art than him would know was by Van Gogh. It drew him out of his chair till he was standing before it. Underneath the image was written, Vincent Van Gogh: A cornfield with cypresses. 1889. London, National Gallery.

1889! A hundred years ago, it didn't seem possible. He stood entranced before this image feeling his solitary vision of the world become something shared. For some reason this distillation of an afternoon plucked at his heartstrings, sounding a chord that brought tears to his eyes, something which seemed to be becoming an embarrassingly regular thing.

The first thing that rang true was the greeny colour that the artist had used as a background for the living clouds, swooping, swirling mythical beasts whipped up by the wind, inspiring the trees to dance a saraband as they rippled with luminescent life. Behind them were purple hills with lilac highlights that looked as if they were yet to settle – a fluid mass of unformed planet, being forced skywards by a subterranean Hercules. In the foreground was a sea of dazzling corn, and as he looked, he could have sworn that he heard it swishing in the ethereal tide.

He hoped Jack was in this group, because the sky did look whole, as if a plane could, after all, do it some serious damage. He suddenly remembered another picture by this man – a self-portrait, just after he'd had a go at his ear. Hadn't that face been green? Far out! This really was freaky. Everybody knew that Van Gogh had 'suffered from bouts of insanity', to put it politely. He'd heard that his paintings went for silly money these days, and hoped that the man was somehow aware of this, wherever he was, and enjoying a protracted last laugh.

He went back to his seat. The therapist called him over to where a quiet woman was painting a picture.

'Dan, this is Suzanne.'

The woman looked up and nodded, before attacking her creation with a vengeance.

'Can I have a look?' he said in a reverential whisper. The woman nodded again. He peered round at her piece of paper taped to a drawing board on an easel. He was looking at the antithesis of where he had just been. A dark, grey, empty landscape, where no living thing could survive, under a punishing sky to which she was adding layer upon layer of blackness.

It was nightmarish. Post-nuclear, contaminated, airless, terrifying. Hellish. Not a smouldering hell, full of the shrieks of penitence, but a dead place, a silent void, the sort of place you'd kill yourself to get out of. This time his heartstrings twanged with a discordant yelp of recognition, triggering the tear ducts again.

Pete led him away, apologising for upsetting him. Dan was now back in the full beam of the Van Gogh and was perfectly OK.

'Is that how you're seeing things at the moment?' said Pete.

'No – that is though,' he said, pointing to what was now his favourite painting.

'Oh right, that's interesting, I'll have a chat with you about that later.'

He felt good. Here was a man who was not going to ask him to take seven (seven!) away from a hundred backwards, at least he hoped not.

The door burst open and in walked Tim, followed by five or six people that he didn't know, and one who he recognised as the germ-free adolescent from OCD. They chose their places and sat down, Tim, with a fist full of felt-tips, next to Dan. Pete was in the middle of the room putting the still life into a cardboard box. An arty-looking bloke who looked older than Pete, in a black turtleneck, sitting with his arms folded and a supercilious expression expertly painted on his face said, 'Très surreal, I'm sure!' to which Pete replied, 'Good one Mike!'

A woman in excruciatingly tight jeans walked in.

'Hi there, Michel,' she purred, squeezing her way up to the free seat next to his.

'His name's Mike,' said Tim.

'Well he told me it was Michel, and,' she looked at him alluringly, 'I think it suits him. He's going to paint me, you know.'

'I bet he is!' said Tim. Everybody laughed. Pete moved the cardboard box aside and sat on the table.

'Thanks for coming everyone. I thought that today we could do portraits. For the first half, do one of the person on your right, and for the second half I'd like you to do a self-portrait. No mirrors – I want you to do it from memory, OK? Use whatever you want. If you really want to do something else, or if you've got something to finish off from last week, that's OK as well.'

'Cool,' said Tim, 'what about some life drawing?'

'I don't mind modelling,' said the Venus in blue jeans.

'Thank you Pamela, but I think we'll stick to portraits for now,' said Pete.

'O-oh,' moaned the lads.

A latecomer arrived, a rotund Asian man of about forty-five with a shiny bald head.

'Hi there, Rajiv!' said Pete, 'It's portraits today, your favourite.' Rajiv chuckled happily, sitting down on the other side of Dan. Paper was passed around and everyone sorted themselves out with their preferred media, except for Tim and Rajiv, who was clutching a rather fine Parker pen, which Tim said, was all he ever used.

Dan thought it best to stick to pencil, and hunted around for a rubber. He looked at the man to his right. This was going to be difficult. Rajiv was never going to sit still enough for him to even begin. The man's shoulders were going up and down as he chortled with mirth, executing a bold portrait of the obsessive-compulsive, which although it could never be described as a likeness, did manage to capture some elusive yet essential quality of the spotless person by his side. Tim was expertly transforming Dan into a slick cartoon character. He leant over and whispered that about twenty years ago Rajiv had killed his wife. Dan didn't feel quite as shocked by this piece of news as he would have been a week ago and wondered whether it was this that was still making the man laugh, even after all these years.

He set to work, and despite an initial reticence, soon found that the possibility of doing something that wasn't entirely without merit lay within his grasp. He quickly abandoned the pencil, substituting it for some chalks, and went wild. A silence descended on the room while all were lost in their work, broken only by outbursts from Rajiv. He reminded Dan of a really annoying souvenir that his brother had brought back from one of his jaunts in the Far East, a plastic statuette called a laughing Buddha. It had an inexhaustible capacity for electronic laughter, activated by practically any extraneous noise, which soon ceased to be funny, necessitating its consignment to a cupboard. Even then it could still be heard, cracking up as somewhere in the house a pin dropped.

All too soon, it was half time. Mike hadn't finished his portrait of Pamela. Even though she was quite close, he was holding out his stick of charcoal and moving it professionally this way and that, his eyes scrunched up as if he were staring at the sun. A few people got up and made themselves a hot drink from the kettle in the corner. The obsessive-compulsive was at the sink, scrubbing at his hands with a nailbrush.

Dan wished he could stay there all day. Pete came over and asked him how he was getting on, to which he replied that he was really enjoying himself.

'So you like Van Gogh?' said Pete, pulling a book out off the shelf above his desk. 'You can have a look at this. It's got a lot of his work in it.'

Dan flicked through it, feasting on the images. He stopped at one that showed the sun spreading thick buttery-yellow rays onto a toasted landscape.

'That's exactly what it's like!' he said, awe-struck again.

'Is that how the sun looks to you?' said Pete, with no hint of anything other than interest.

'Yeah – it's amazing ... I didn't think anyone else could see it...'

'Does that make you feel better?'

'Well, I feel pretty good at the moment anyway, but yeah, I do think it makes me feel even better.'

The second half of the session flew past. Dan produced a jolly image of himself in a bright landscape. It was like a child's painting really, with no method whatsoever in his madness, but he was pleased with it anyway.

On his way back to the ward, feeling worn out from his exertions, he ran into Jack at the bus stop.

'I thought you might be at Art Therapy, there was something I wanted to show you,' he said.

'They've banned me from all so-called therapy at the moment, my son. Except for drug therapy, surprise, surprise.'

'What for?' It seemed odd to take away therapy. Did they want you to get better or not?

'I had a run-in with the goody-goody gardener, that's

all.' Then, changing the subject, he said, 'I saw you sneaking off down the field with what's-'er-name earlier, you little rascal.'

Dan hoped he hadn't told Alec, which must have been understood because Jack gave him a wink and said, 'Don't worry, mum's the word.'

'Funny you should say that,' said Dan, 'because she's pregnant.'

'Crikey mate! You don't waste any time do you?'

'Very funny, it's nothing to do with me.'

'Well how d'ya know she is then?'

'I know she is ... cos she's got ... you know...' Dan made outpouring gestures in front of his chest.

'What d'you mean,' said Jack, copying his gesture, 'big tits?' They started to walk back towards Ash.

'No, I mean she's got, you know, milk.'

'That doesn't mean anything, you want to talk to Joanne about that,' he said, enigmatically. As soon as they were in the ward Jack hurried over to her. She was sliding up and down the corridor in her socks to the accompaniment of the HDM in full swing.

'Hey Joanne! C'mere a minute.'

She skated over to them, out of breath. Jack whispered something in her ear, using what he had obviously thought was quite a descriptive gesture after all, to illustrate the Elf's condition.

Joanne was saying, 'Yeah, I did, yeah, could be, most probably...' Then she turned to Dan and said, 'Do you know what medication she's on?' He said that he didn't have a clue. Come to think of it he wasn't really sure what medication he was on, he thought he'd heard someone mention lithium, which you got in little batteries...

'What's that got to do with it?' he asked, confused.

'Well, guess what? Lactation is a side effect of Haloperidol. It happened to me when I first got here. I'll never forget my sister's face when I showed her, her eyes nearly popped out of her head! Imagine giving that to a girl who's off her head anyway! I was really freaked out, I can tell you, I'd only just had an abortion,' she said, unabashed, 'So you can imagine what I thought! I hit the bloody roof when I found out, didn't I Jack?'

'You certainly did my girl! Proud of you I was!' he said. Then, as though he hadn't considered it before, he added, 'Makes you wonder what it's doing to the blokes.'

Christ, yeah, thought Dan, hoping that he wasn't on it. He made a mental note to find out more about his medication as soon as possible. Joanne said she was going to go and talk to Kate and Jack said he was going to give that sour-faced bitch in Lime ward a piece of his mind, even if she was only a nurse. Dan tagged along, hoping that he hadn't done the wrong thing.

They marched into Lime on their mission. The Elf was talking to Anna. Joanne joined them. Jack and Dan hung back whilst the girls formed a tight huddle. After a bit, she came back with her report. They'd done a pregnancy test, which came up negative, then told her that yes, it could well be a side effect. Dan's heart flipped with relief. He could now dismiss the vision of leading her, heavy with child, down the local high street, on a goat.

Jack was livid. He stormed into the office and slammed his fist down on the desk in front of the rigid-haired Bitch, who stood up and eyeballed him challengingly.

'Do you lot think it's funny to make young girls think they're pregnant, or what? Didn't anyone stop to think about it before ladling the stuff out?'

'I'd like you and your friends to leave this ward now. This is absolutely none of your business. Do you want me to call security?' The Bitch was swelling up like a hot air balloon.

'Yeah, go on love, then they can cart you away and give you some, and we'll see how you like it!'

Jack looked at his audience, which was, for once, appreciative. He spun round and stormed out of the ward, Joanne by his side. The Elf slipped her arm through Dan's and they followed them back to Ash. Dan decided against asking her how she felt.

They made their victorious re-entry just in time for lunch. Gerry was bossing Mr Atkinson about again, telling him to put on his socks and shoes and that it was stupid to wander about in bare feet.

'Look you! Who d'you think you are, talking to 'im like that? Leave 'im alone! I'm going to report you. Just you wait!' Jack was on a roll.

Alec was at the end of the corridor, his jealous laserbeam stare burning into Dan. As they approached, all following their leader, he started to chant Number 1 in the hospital hit parade, '*THE LOON-A-TICS ARE TAKING OVER THE ASY-LUM...*'

Malcolm came over to see what was going on.

'What's all this then, dissension in the ranks?' Hunger, however, dampened the revolutionary spirit. The Elf headed back to the main dining room, and the rest of them got in the queue for shepherd's pie.

20

Duncan and Jake

After lunch, Dan escaped from Alec and Jack and set off once again across what was becoming the well-worn path to Lime. Still within earshot of Ash, he heard his name being called. He looked round to see Colin leaning out of the office window.

'Dan, I've got a friend of yours on the line wanting to know if you'd like a visit... His name's Duncan ... and he says Jake wants to come as well... Shall I say yea or nay?'

Duncan and Jake? Who told them? He hadn't heard from them for ages. Funny, he was only thinking about Jake earlier.

'Yeah, tell them to come, and to bring Cerbie!' Colin's head disappeared then reappeared.

'Sorry, no dogs allowed,' said Colin, shrugging his shoulders as if he didn't know why not either.

'They say they'll be along soon.'

Dan didn't know what to do. He didn't want to miss them, but he had no intention of staying in the ward all afternoon. Not now that the sun wasn't so strong, and especially not now that the Elf wasn't off limits after all. He decided that he would just know when they were around. If Duncan was still driving that heap then he'd probably hear them coming.

He could see it now. The yellow Opal Manta that Duncan called 'The Fruit', and his insistence that it was a 'bloody good motor', despite its best efforts to prove otherwise. On the day that they'd turned up at his parents' house to take him to Cornwall, it had refused to restart, making a mockery of the farewells that had just been made. Dan's dad had come to their rescue, shaking his head, despairing of such a useless bunch, armed with his tools and an encyclopaedic knowledge of engines, which the new drivers couldn't be arsed with.

He hadn't really known Jake, but Duncan was the younger brother of a mate of his brother, so now and then circumstance had thrust them together, and on these occasions they'd always had a laugh. It had been Dan's brother's mate that had suggested to Duncan that he should take him along, and Duncan had agreed, which was kind, because taking someone on holiday who had recently tried to top himself wouldn't appeal to most.

Maybe it was because they were both studying classics, of all things, so they had an interest in the practically dead. Or perhaps because Duncan was an aspirant Goth, the type that paints its bedroom black, hence the bleak midwinter break. It could have been that having a clinical depressive in tow was his idea of good company, not a charitable act at all.

Dan's parents had been hesitant. His brother had said that it might do him good. Dan kept saying that he was feeling better, and everyone wanted to believe that it was true. Inside, he felt exactly the same, if possible maybe even worse, since his sense of complete failure had been compounded by his inability to do away with himself, which, he was still convinced, despite all the words to the contrary, would be the best thing for all concerned.

Cornwall seemed to offer the perfect solution. Where there was the sea, there was the opportunity for a staged accident. He could fall off a cliff, or drown, accidentally on purpose, sparing his parents the shame of his suicide.

'What a tragedy,' they'd say, 'Just when he was starting to get better too... What sort of person would leave a banana skin on a cliff edge?'

He saw himself, stamping on it, making sure the mark of his trainer was clearly visible, careful not to leave fingerprints, positioning it carefully to indicate his fatal trajectory. But what to do with the banana? Chuck it into the sea of course, he sure as hell wouldn't be feeling hungry. And when it had all gone down in history, when his parents were dead and buried, his great-nephews and nieces would laugh about it. 'Oh yeah,' they'd joke, 'Great-Uncle Dan, you know, the one who went bananas...' If only it could be that funny.

When The Fruit did eventually get going, he looked back at them as they waved optimistically, for what he hoped would be the last time. It wasn't that he didn't want to see them again, more a case of hoping that they wouldn't have to see him again.

He sank back into the furry seat cover, deciding that it wasn't anything to do with them anyway. He knew that was ridiculous, but he just couldn't fit them into the equation. It was a relief to get away. He was sick of the watchful eyes, the exchanged glances as his face remained set in stone, while everyone else expressed their humanity one way or the other, as the television broadcast news of fresh disasters. He had no feeling other than a longing for release. It was merely a question of his body catching up with his already dear departed soul.

He was sharing the back seat with Jake's dog, a huge Alsatian by the name of Cerberus. Animals usually liked him, but this one was the exception. He tried to pat him when he got in, but the dog flattened his ears against his head and curled his upper lip, revealing his wolf-like fangs and giving a low throaty growl. He snatched his hand back.

A forbidding ridge had appeared down the length of his back, bristling with animosity.

'Pack it in, Cerb!' said Jake, reaching behind him to smack his four-legged friend. 'Sorry mate, he's not usually like that. He'll get used to you in a minute.'

The growling stopped, but the hound sustained the ridge-backed, teeth bared, totally wired pose for the rest of the nightmare journey. Dan squeezed himself against the opposite door, trying to get as far away from those teeth as he could.

'Great name isn't it?' said Jake. 'It's the name of the three-headed dog that guards the doors of Hades, you know, Hell.'

Dan agreed that it was, then, thinking about it, wondered why he wasn't greeting him like the hopeless sinner he was. Maybe suicides weren't good enough for hell.

'I thought that was Janus,' said Duncan.

'Nah mate, he guards the doors to somewhere else, schools maybe ... or backsides.' They roared with laughter.

'Lighten up back there!' said Duncan, eyeing their pale passenger in his mirror.

'Yeah, don't worry. He won't bite. He'll chill when you do.'

Dan recognised this as a Catch 22 situation. He knew that the dog, with his intuitive powers, sensed that despite being disguised as a human being, the creature next to him was something very evil indeed.

'Shame you haven't got a cake mate!' said Jake.

'What are you on about?' Duncan was one of those drivers that turn to face the person they're addressing in a very worrying way.

'Cos Cerberus can be appeased by a cake, that's why.'

'Typical bloody dog! But surely that would be three cakes?'

About three miles into the journey Jake told Duncan to pull over because he needed, as he called it, some refreshment. Duncan swerved into the next lay-by without giving any warning, causing the driver behind them to brake suddenly and toot his horn angrily.

'Wanker!' he jeered, as Jake removed the sun visor from its plastic hooks, spitting on the little mirror and giving it a polish with his sleeve, before placing it on the open door of the glove compartment.

Dan watched from the back seat. He wondered if there was anybody left on this earth that kept a pair of gloves in their glove compartment. This innocuous little in-car cupboard with its absurd name seemed to epitomise the claustrophobic, suburban orderliness that could cheerfully suffocate any hopeful aberration. Whereas people may have once just stuffed their gloves into their pockets, or even done without, here was a command that they be folded up and inserted neatly into their very own place. Why did anyone need driving gloves anyway? It wasn't exactly a dirty business. He supposed it harked back to the golden olden days when the driver 'really knew he was driving', pitting man and machine against the elements as his good lady wife hung on to her headscarf. So it was nostalgia that kept this name a feature of the modern motor. What a pathetic race, he thought, full of rosy rear-view fantasy. Unlike him, who when looking back at his short life saw nothing but a catalogue of disasters and culpability. Every single thing that he had ever done had been a mistake. If only he'd been a good boy and put his gloves away tidily, perhaps everything would have been alright.

'This'll help the journey go a bit quicker!' said Jake, as he arranged three lines of white powder artfully on the mirror with a razor blade. He took a tenner out of his wallet, rolled it up and bent his head ceremoniously, hoovering up his line before passing it all across to Duncan, who did the same. He then handed it over to Dan.

'A bit of whizz'll perk you up mate!'

He took it, thinking that although it would be wasted on

him, it would require fewer words to comply than refuse. As the vile toxic sludge crept down the back of his throat, he decided that hastening proceedings wasn't such a bad idea after all. He closed his eyes and pretended to be asleep, not a state usually associated with amphetamines.

A while later, Jake looked round with pinprick pupils.

'Are you getting a buzz off that back there? Oi Cerb, lie down!' He tapped the dog on the snout to no avail. Dan said that he was, but in truth he was feeling no effect of the drug whatsoever. It was like giving half a Junior Aspirin to someone who'd just had an unanaesthetised lobotomy.

With their body clocks adjusted, Duncan and Jake talked gibberish to each other for miles, arguing about what exactly was wrong with the radio. After an hour or so they stopped at a service station for more fags and petrol, letting Cerbie, which almost made him sound cute, out for a sniff about and the rest. Dan almost enjoyed those ten minutes without hot dog breath reminding him of the imminent ripping out of his throat – which, despite solving the problem, would have been too horrible a way to go, even for him.

Another line of speed and they were off again, this time with Jake at the wheel, an experience which under normal circumstances would have been hair-raising, since he'd only passed his test that week. By the raised hair on the indefatigable dog's back, Dan could see that the only terror around was being instilled by him. Anyway, there was absolutely no chance of them crashing, even if Jake were to totally surrender the small amount of control that he did hold over the vehicle, because according to the apparent workings of fate, his death wish would be studiously ignored.

Several hours and countless near misses later, Duncan announced that they were nearly at Land's End. Dan wiped the steam off the window and looked out. It sounded like a fitting place to be. All he could see was darkness and raindrops making their quivering sidelong way across the glass like the tears of an inconsolable God. The only thing he could remember about the journey apart from the dog's silent accusation was a fleeting glimpse of Stonehenge, which he'd visited in another life with Fran, certain that just like the wondrous ancient monument to who knows what, their love would stand the test of time. He'd turned away from it, nauseous with disgust, as if it had cheated him with its insinuations of eternity.

If he'd been expecting some dark romantic dwelling to act as terminus to his botched life, he was to be disappointed. Despite the fact that Duncan had spent every summer of his childhood that he could remember there, they experienced considerable difficulty in finding the place. He said that it was because his dad had always driven there in the past, and that he'd never really known where he was. More through luck than judgement, they finally pulled up outside a bungalow that looked as if it had been transplanted to Cornwall from the outskirts of Weybridge. Cursing, Duncan tipped out the entire contents of his holdall before finding the keys in his trench coat pocket, just as Jake was about to break in.

It was freezing. It was worse inside than out. Jake said it was colder than Triton, which he knowledgeably informed them was the coldest moon in the universe. Duncan replied sarcastically that it was a shame that they'd forgotten to bring along the Trivial Pursuit. Dan shivered while Duncan went in search of the central heating, reading from the list of instructions that his mum had written out for him. Necessity had forced him to resort to this embarrassing note, and as he went from light switch to light switch, revealing the bland horror of the holiday home in all its glove compartmental mediocrity, his credibility as Weybridge's answer to Ian McCulloch waned irrevocably.

After Duncan and Jake had squabbled over who was

more likely to require the room with the double bed, they came to a compromise. It being the property of Duncan's family, it was deemed that officially, he should have it, but in the unlikely event of Jake pulling and him not, he could have it for that occasion. Dan was offered the back room, about the size and temperature of a deep-freeze, which suited him fine.

He lay down on the bed and curled up, hoping that he wasn't expected to be sociable. His brother had made it clear to them that he was 'convalescing'. He hoped that would be sufficiently off-putting to the two lads, for whom practically any reference to a physical reality that didn't pertain to women lay somewhere on the border-line between an embarrassment and out-and-out taboo.

He wasn't going to get away with it that easily however. Jake, his runny nose rosy from much post-snort rubbing, giving him the quite justifiable, if erroneous, appearance of having a bad cold, barged in with his gear and a dress-ing table mirror. Dan sat up as he got a few more lines drawn up and partook in what he saw as a way to show some sort of willing.

'Just help yourself to it mate, there's plenty of.' Duncan joined them, then said that they should go to the pub, which was just down the road.

It's usually the case that distances that a youth perceives as long, turn out in adulthood to be short. In this case the opposite applied. As they braved an unabated lashing from the liquid icicles, Duncan said that they must have moved the fucking place down closer to the seafront. When inside, one of the few locals said that it was a funny time of year for a beach holiday. Duncan said defensively that he felt quite inspired. The self-appointed pub wit, still laughing at his initial jibe said, 'Inspired to do what? Kill yourself?' Dan's half-dead self twitched involuntarily. Did they know?

They began a marathon sesh with brandy, to warm

them up, then moved on to just about anything they could think of. Here was one area where Dan could prove his worth. He drank them under the table, pouring drink after drink down his throat like buckets of water onto a forest fire. The alcohol too went unnoticed by his malfunctioning system. It didn't surprise him in the least. He had become subhuman, all sensation had been dispensed with, except for pain, and that was soon to follow, if things went according to plan. However, choking to death on his own vomit in Duncan's uncle's holiday home was, if slightly less appalling than the idea of being dispatched by Cerberus, still not what he had in mind. He thought better of one last drink, just in case it was the one to tip the balance.

On their way home, Dan supporting the two toxic wasters round their middles, the rain stopped, and an unearthly stillness descended. As they stumbled towards the bungalow with the name 'Seaview' painted on a varnished slice of wood by a liar, the crystal silence was shattered by Cerberus, howling like his mythical namesake. Duncan opened the door and the dog bounded out, wagging his tail and rubbing against Jake, until Dan crossed the threshold, at which point he began snarling again.

'Bloody hell mate, he's really not into you at all is he?'

They spent the next two days doing a lot of speed, avoiding the worst of the weather and playing cards. At least Duncan and Jake played, while Dan stayed in his room, picking over the bones of his life like a starving vulture, desperate to find one morsel of flesh that would string out its existence for another day.

21

Day one

When recalling what happened next, he found it impossible not to wax Biblical again. ...And on the third day he rose again from the dead. Resurrection. It didn't happen with a bolt from the blue, rather a tiny bubble that formed half-heartedly in the fathomless, putrid depths of his contemptible self.

He'd been taking Jake at his word, shoving white powder up his nose like there was (he should be so lucky) no tomorrow. It wasn't that he wanted it, or that it was in any way pleasant, it was just there, and it was bad for him – like fags, at the tip of the suicide iceberg. Jake and Duncan had gone to the pub, leaving him and Cerberus to their own devices. The dog was still giving him the widest berth possible, lying under the tiny kitchen table as if it could protect him from the dark forces lurking in the back bedroom.

He was lying on the bed, staring at the arctic landscape of the Artex ceiling, endlessly plotting his own demise, when he felt the minuscule eruption. He clutched his stomach, not daring to breathe. Then nothing. Maybe he'd imagined it, like a straw-clutching relative insisting that they'd seen a blip on a flatline. But hang on, wait, there it was again, no, it wasn't gas. It was liquid. It was water, water rising in a desert, a tiny droplet. Oh please God, please... He didn't dare to move his hands, as if protecting a spark. That's what it was, a spark. Oh please God, let it take! Whatever the fuck it was, air, water, fire, he willed it to stay. It was the closest thing to life he'd felt for months. Then it went as quickly as it had come, as if it wasn't worth the effort after all.

Cruel torture! He broke into a cold sweat. Enough! This was it, Daniel Charles Blake, your time is up. He'd do it now. There was no point in putting it off any longer. While they were at the pub. They wouldn't even notice he was missing until the next morning. He was going to go down to the sea and let it do its worst. It was still stormy. He wouldn't stand a chance. All he had to do was to wade out and let it swallow him up. Couldn't be easier.

He sat up, sick with the same feeling that he'd felt as he'd swallowed pill after pill, grieving for himself like the sole mourner at his own funeral. Just as he was about to stand up, there it was again, that distant bell chiming life across the wasteland. He lowered himself gently back into a horizontal position, sweat running off him like a melting snowman. His breathing was fast and shallow. He tried to calm it down – he couldn't risk anything disturbing the exquisitely fragile thing.

Several hours passed on this life or death rollercoaster. He urged the embryonic life form to tread carefully. He kept repeating his dad's advice to his sick child, 'Little steps, little steps.' He lost contact with it often, sending his heart into a frenzy of panic, but it kept coming back, picking itself up time after time to make the long journey home.

He was thirsty. Quick, he had to drink, had to give the little thing what it wanted before it perished. But that meant having to move from this, his lifebed. He was petrified. What if it went away again? And this time never came back? He reassured himself with the thought of the sea, and suicide. Still there, singing its siren song.

With the stealth of a cat burglar, he got up, went to the door and turned the handle. The door opened. He shrieked at the sight of a huge shadowy beast, standing square before him.

'Jesus Cerberus! You nearly frightened the life out of me!' He groped around the darkness inside. It was OK. It was still alive. Cerberus cocked his head on one side, pricked up his ears and sat down, sweeping the floor with his mighty wagging tail.

Dan's head was spinning with the implications of this sudden change of canine heart. Did this mean that it was for real? That this change in his body chemistry was perceptible to the dog? Was it coincidental? Had he just decided that the sick human wasn't dangerous, just pitiful?

He knelt down before what no longer looked like the jaws of death and put out his hand. A wet nose pushed forward, then the dog began to lick it, with a slow rasping caress. The thirsty thing clambered up into his heart and did a jig. He put his arms around the hound and sank his face into his voluptuous mane. The doggy smell assailed his reawakening sense as if it was his mother's perfume. By the time he finally pulled away, the dog's neck was wet with his tears. Cerberus proceeded to lick his face, which, even at this most unusual moment, was going a bit too far. But what was this? He felt the dormant muscles of his face crank his mouth upward into ... what was that thing again? Ah yes, a smile! He was amazed that his face didn't crack and fall to the floor in pieces.

He stood up. It was OK. It was cool. It was still there. The bathroom door was open. He filled up the tooth mug and drank the icy water. He could feel it as it wended its way downward, fizzing like caustic soda into a blocked drain. He refilled the mug again and again, while the dog waited patiently at the door, still beating time with his tail. Deciding that he could take this further, he shed his clothes, suddenly oblivious to the chill. He stood under the shower, gulping in what he could, while the rest cascaded over his body till he tingled, thrilling, euphoric, having, he was now pretty sure, returned from what had not, after all, been the point of no return.

He stepped out of the shower feeling as if he'd had a total body transplant. The mirror said otherwise. Despite a flickering light in his eyes, he looked sallow and depleted, spindly, with the pallor of an etiolated plant. Still, he was, to himself, for a change, a welcome sight. He resolved to burn, or at least chuck out, that stinking heap of clothing on the floor, now an outgrown carapace.

Still cautious, still half-unbelieving, he went back to his room and rummaged in his bag, pulling out a tracksuit that his mum had washed and folded, and pulled it on. It brushed against his clean skin like silk. It felt nice. He wanted to wrench open the painted shut window and shout it out to the obscured heavens. How could he ever express how fantastically nice it felt that something felt nice? Dan the astronaut, home at last after a prolonged mission to the dark side of the moon, trying to explain that to him, the word 'mundane' now spelt exotic, rare delight. The dog had got hold of one of his socks, and was inviting him to join in a game of tug-of-war, as if it was his job to initiate him back into the realms of pleasure. As they played, the front door opened and Duncan and Jake, more than a little worse for wear stumbled in.

'We've brought you some chips,' said Duncan, proudly letting off a loud beer 'n' vinegar belch.

'Look's like the door of Hell's open to you at last, mate!' said Jake, looking at his dog, who was rolling around like a daft puppy, sock in mouth. Dan took the cold, soggy chips from Duncan before he ate them all. The thing that had now overtaken him needed nourishment.

'Blimey, you were hungry, must be the sea air,' said

Duncan, collapsing onto the sofa.

'Yeah, must be,' said Dan, who decided not to reveal his secret, like a scientist who'd just discovered microbial life in a fragment of a Martian meteorite and didn't trust himself not to break the slide.

'Anyone for a night-cap?' said Jake, untwisting the bag of speed.

'Christ! Can't you leave that stuff alone for a minute? You're unreal! When do you sleep?' said Duncan, yawning. Jake looked at Dan inquiringly.

'I think I'll give it a miss too, thanks.' As if he'd give drugs to his newborn baby!

'Lightweights!' said Jake, who said that in that case he'd do without as well. Before too long they went to their rooms, and their snoring commenced battle.

Dan sat in the darkness, listening to the wind sweeping away the silver gilt-edged clouds. He lay down on the sofa with his legs dangling over the end, positioned so as to watch the sky, the moon beaming brighter as the cover dispersed. He thought he could hear the hoot of an owl, then decided it was more likely to be a gull, an airborne town crier bearing news of the miracle that had come to pass on their doorstep.

Cerberus joined him on the sofa, threatening to squash him flat. They wriggled about till they were comfortable. The dog was the first to fall asleep. Dan looked at him and stroked his head. Jake had got it the wrong way round, it wasn't that the gates of hell were finally open – it was that Cerbie hadn't been going to let him through. And he hadn't even had to give him a cake.

They woke up together. He could hardly bear to venture further into consciousness for fear of finding the feeling gone. He went into the kitchen for a drink. The clock on the wall said half past four. He drank some milk from the carton, and poured some into a bowl for the dog. He lapped it up noisily, then trotted into the hall, coming back with his lead in his mouth, casting his eyes in a front-doorly direction. Dan didn't need to be asked twice, so after brushing his teeth vigorously, a task that suddenly seemed worthwhile, he donned several layers, grabbed his fags and stepped out into his New World.

He set off slowly at first, savouring the smell of the night, pinching himself. He remembered his brother telling him about when he got his glasses and saw the stars for the first time, and knew just how he felt. Cerberus trotted along until his eagerness got the better of him and he broke into a rolling canter. He looked back at the dazed human behind him, spurring him on.

After dragging himself around for what seemed like an eternity, the idea of running was strange. But he tried it, feeling the blood pumping oxygen around his limbs, bringing them back to life. To feel his physicality as a pleasure rather than a curse was indescribably wonderful, and he tore down to the water's edge like the Flying Scotsman, with steam clouds puffing out of his mouth.

He would never forget that walk, that dawn, for as long as he lived. He sat down on a piece of black rock jutting out of the sand like a new tooth, tears mingling on his lips with the sea-spray. Cerbie dug an impressive hole as the tide clawed back the land, the first glimmer of a new day drawing a faint line on the horizon. At first it came and went, just like his life force on the previous night, till it couldn't be held back, spreading a pale glow from the unimaginably distant fire of the rising sun. He wondered if the sun itself would appear, but then remembered that it rose in the East. He didn't care. This was the most beautiful dawn in the history of time. He was born again. It was Day One.

He reckoned it must be about six or seven by now, maybe later. In the half-light he went over to the call box, found some change in his pocket and called home. His mum answered the phone, her sleepy voice becoming anxious.

'Mum, mum! I'm better! I can't believe it, I'm better!' He was running out of money. 'I'll see you soon, isn't it great?! I'M BETTER!'

He walked on and on down the front, devouring everything he saw with his descaled eyes. He was joined on the beach by the odd early bird, who despite calling their dogs to heel at the sight of Cerberus, greeted him as if he were anybody, a normal person. A normal person! Oh to be a normal person, he thought, as he returned their good-mornings, as if, like them, (although it was just a guess) he had just woken from a blameless night of slumber.

He looked around in vain for a café that wasn't boarded up, craving sweet tea and hot-buttered toast. The only thing he could find open was a small Spar shop. He went in, leaving the dog to steam up the glass door and looked around, his mouth watering at the sight of Battenburg cakes and French Fancies. No, he was going to be sensible with his crumpled tenner. He'd surprise his long-suffering friends with a cooked breakfast. God! He was going to make something, to do something! He still couldn't get his head round it.

Just like an ordinary, everyday shopper, he got what he needed and turned to leave, coming face to face with the newspaper stand, groaning under the weight of grim headlines. His stomach turned over at the glimpse of another dimension to this new reality, and he dropped the eggs as if he'd been hit by an aftershock. His instinct was to run for shelter back into the dark, familiar place, Christ, he wasn't ready ... maybe he never would be...   He started shaking.

The woman behind the counter rushed to his aid.

'Are you alright there ducky? You look like you've seen a ghost!'

She called to a spotty youth to get something to clear up the mess. Three of the six eggs were broken. She told him not to worry, giving him another box and waving away his offer of payment.

Still trembling, he stepped back out into the morning, trying to breathe deeply, remembering someone telling him that you couldn't panic and breathe deeply at the same time. There was a fight going on his head between yesterday and today. Thankfully, today had the upper hand. Its beginner's luck sent yesterday packing with a direct hit and he stuffed the thought of suicide back into its rightful place. In the cupboard that you never bother to look in. That one day you'll clear out, because if you haven't used any of the junk in it for years then you're never going to, but then, better not, you never know, one day, perhaps.

He set off for the bungalow, with Cerbie sniffing at the bag swinging by his side. By the time breakfast was on the table the rain had set in again. The greasy smell of the fry-up coaxed Duncan and Jake from their pits, and they emerged from their rooms hung-over and haggard. Duncan said he wanted to go home. There were no women here and the weather was crap. He said that he'd have been less bored at home reading the Iliad, and that was really saying something. Jake agreed.

On the road home, Dan leant his head right back till he could see the sky out of the back window, hoping to God that the demon drivers wouldn't crash the car today – that really would be too cruel. Cerberus commandeered seven-eighths of the seat, lying on his back with his four legs in the air in a balletic pose, his head on Dan's lap, jowls flopped into a lazy grin.

On the home stretch Duncan said, 'Sorry about the shit holiday, mate!'

Exchanging glances with the dog, Dan said that he'd enjoyed himself, thinking that that was the understatement of the millennium.

This walk down memory lane had led him to not to Lime, but to the bus stop, where his reverie was broken by a female voice from somewhere nearby.

'Boo!' The Elf popped out from behind a bush.

'I've been watching you. Talk about deep in thought! You've been somewhere else, was it nice?' He looked at her and smiled. Yeah, he thought, it was nice, but this was much, much nicer.

He thought it better not to mention the milk thing. She might be a bit embarrassed. Like he was when Joan started crying because her legs had never been so painful, just after he'd told Jack that he was sure he'd healed her. They sat in companionable silence as if they'd known each other all their lives. He took out his fags and offered her one of the remaining two.

'That reminds me,' she said, 'I've got something for you.' She delved into her basket case and fished out a packet of Rizlas. She took one of his cigarettes, and made it into two roll-ups.

'There you are, that'll make them last twice as long. If you halve things then you can have double,' she said, lighting them both and giving one to him.

As their fagettes burnt up like shooting stars, they heard a car bouncing over a sleeping policeman at high speed. It was The Fruit. They were here!

Dan ran after it, jumping and waving. Despite the veto, he could see Cerbie's head bobbing about on the back window ledge like a ginormous nodding dog. The Elf followed some way behind. The car screeched to a halt and Duncan and Jake sprang out. Cerberus bounded over to his old pal, nearly knocking him over.

'It's great to see you guys! Thanks for coming.'

The summer didn't suit them, they looked decidedly unnatural, even embarrassed in their light clothing, like shaved cats.

'Cor, is she part of the treatment? You lucky beggar!'

said Duncan, as he watched the Elf approach, then added, 'We haven't got long, sorry mate. We're on our way to Brighton.'

The Elf said she'd leave them to it and walked off in the direction of Lime. Duncan could scarcely hide his disappointment. Dan got the feeling that a romance with a psychiatric patient would be right up his street. They wandered about the grounds, out of sight of the office, Cerbie sniffing at the ground happily as if it was just any old park. They made a sort of awkward small talk and chain-smoked. Once again, Dan found that he had to put them at their ease by being ultra-normal. He wondered what they'd expected.

Jake seemed to be really stressed out, as if he couldn't wait to get away. They walked back to the car. Dan was saying goodbye to Cerbie when he saw Duncan nodding at Jake as if to say, 'Get on with it then!' Jake coughed, ran his fingers through his hair, looking this way and that. He approached Dan and stood before him, coughing again. Dan could see two of himself looking very funny in either lens of his mirror sunglasses.

'Listen Dan, I wanted to tell you, I mean I wanted to come and see you anyway, but I just wanted to say that, you know, I've been feeling really bad about what happened, the whizz and all that. I shouldn't have given you any. I know that now. I'm really sorry mate. I feel as if... This is all my fault!'

Dan assured him that it wasn't, and they sped off to Brighton, tooting and waving. He hadn't told him that in fact he considered him to be his saviour, thinking that it could have been an even greater burden.

22

Dance

At eleven thirty the next morning he found himself in the short queue outside Dance Therapy. If it hadn't have been for the fact that Joanne had told him it was really good, he would have skived off. It sounded a bit too much like 'Music and Movement' that he could still remember from junior school.

Even though he always felt as foreign as a deep-sea diver in the murky underworld, he liked going clubbing with Mat, who could dance just by blinking. He could see that many people derived a great deal of pleasure from flinging themselves about, but he was of the opinion that it was better to leave it to those who knew what they were doing – like Joanne, who just had it, whatever it was. He watched her as she shimmied up and down the corridor impatiently, as if her first steps had been a dance. Admittedly, in the days leading up to his admission this reticence had, like all other inhibitions, gone out the window, but had been the first to return, cap in hand.

Before too long a small but perfect specimen of manhood minced down the corridor with impressive bulges in all the right places. He said a breezy good morning to his class as if it was the Ballet Rambert and unlocked the door of a high ceilinged room with large windows and a shiny wooden floor. There was a stereo in one corner and several large beanbags arranged casually about the place.

Apart from himself and the HDM, the rest of the group was, worryingly, female. Dan was relieved when the door opened and someone whom he'd never seen, a Chinese-looking bloke, came in. The rest of the class consisted of Joanne, Pamela from art therapy, in a slinky red dress, and about four other women of varying age, shape, size and colour. The man, who had removed his tight tracksuit bottoms to reveal a pair of even tighter tights, introduced himself as Simon, and told them all to take off their shoes and 'limber up'.

He remembered scenes from the Kids from Fame, in which scores of beautiful people in leotards would flex their perfectly honed limbs and arch their supple backs. Still, he was glad to be rid of his hot, lumpen trainers that would have managed to inhibit a clog dance. Not that he was going to do any sort of dance, he'd already made up his mind to say that he didn't feel well and that he'd prefer to just watch.

Whist the others were striking poses that looked like stills from a beginners' aerobic class, (apart from the chinesey guy and Joanne, who were advanced), straining over their expansive spare tyres to their distant toes, he approached the man who was sorting out some music. He made his excuse, which was drowned out by a sudden loud buzzing interference from the radio. He slammed his hands over his ears, wincing as the distorted noise bore into his brain. Radio signals that were not tuned in properly were his head's pet hate.

'Sorry, wrong button!' said Simon, turning round and asking him to repeat his request. This Dan did, to no avail, being told that it really would be better if he joined in with the rest. Clapping his hands, the dance therapist turned to the group and said that today they were going to work with some African rhythms.

'Wicked man, nuff respect!' said the HDM.

'To begin with, you can do whatever you like, but in a circle around me. If one of you feels you have more to offer, then come into the centre, and I'll join the wheel, and so on. OK?' He pushed the button on the tape deck. The music started and the wheel was cranked into action. As if it could have possibly mattered he rushed back to the buttons and said, 'Whoops sorry. Wrong side!' He switched it off and turned the tape over. Dan thought he was having a déjà-vu, or rather entendu, as the group was set into motion again by what sounded like exactly the same thing. 'Simple Simon Says...' popped into his head.

'This side is better quality,' said the man as the music promptly receded into nothingness. 'I do apologise,' he said, going back again to fast forward it and try again.

After their two frustrating false starts, at last the dancing began. Apart from the advanced class, the rest of them would have been better off joining hands and doing something they felt safer with, like the Hokey-Cokey. Joanne was the first to become the axle, really going for it, the Woodland Park disco-dancing champion. She could have happily held centre stage for the entire session, but Pamela elbowed her out of the way, doing her version of the Dance of the Seven Veils (that's Seven Veils, not Six Veils), whilst making as much eye-contact with Simon as her contortions would allow. That she was barking up the wrong tree was obvious even to the most innocent amongst the rest.

Dan did his best to go with the flow. He bent his knees in what he guessed might be the appropriate places. He was trying to smother the serious fit of mirth that was threatening, as he saw the HDM tugging at the Oriental's sleeve, forcing him to watch his attempts at Kung-Fu fighting to the music of the African bush, as the guy, who was called Tom looked at him in astonished incomprehension. Not a moment too soon the music came to an end.

'....And rest,' said Simon, exhaling from his perfectly pursed lips with his eyes closed, reminding Dan of a butter-wouldn't-melt-in-the-mouth choirboy. Some of the group collapsed exhausted onto the beanbags. Others pranced about, champing at the bit like racehorses.

He told Simon that his headache really was quite bad and that he wanted to go and lie down. Simon said it was a shame because it looked like he was enjoying himself. Dan wondered how on earth he'd given that impression, feeling quite sorry for the deluded bloke. He waved at Joanne, and left. He was dying for a cigarette.

Back in the corridor, he looked around hopefully for a smoker. There was no one about. He pushed through two more weird transparent yellow rubber flaps and found himself at the back of the building, by the staff canteen. He headed for it, sure that he could get a fag in there from someone. Just then he saw Jack, walking purposefully in the direction of the gates. He called out, making Jack signal wildly not to draw attention to him, then gesture that he should come over.

'Wotcha my boy! I'm just going for a bit of my favourite therapy. C'mon, I'll buy you a drink.'

'What, you mean out there?' said Dan, pointing through the gates to the outside world.

'Yeah, can't see anything stopping us can you?'

Apart from the Mental Health Act, thought Dan, feeling ambivalent about the plan. It wasn't that he was averse to a bit of law breaking, rather that he didn't really want to find out where he was. Life was easier on the inside, for the time being.

Jack led the way.

'And for God's sake, try and look normal.'

'What do you mean?' He felt insulted.

'You're doing the Largactil shuffle mate! Try and let

182

your arms relax, you look like a bleedin' puppet – else they might not serve us.'

Dan tried to do as he said. It was hard work, the moment his concentration lapsed, he could feel his arms rising up and his walk becoming stiff. He might as well have had 'Beware! Escaped Lunatic' emblazoned on his T-shirt.

They sauntered casually through what Jack called 'Checkpoint Charlie', past a security guard who looked like he might rush out with a machine gun and demand to see their papers. Soon they were walking down a street of 1950's semis. Dan bet you couldn't give these houses away. Being next door to Woodland Park would hardly rank as an estate agent's selling point.

At the end of the road there was a busier thoroughfare, with buses, cars, people with shopping bags, children, and cafes. He was amazed at how alien this world was, even after a short time away from it. It was scary, bright and noisy, too busy. He wondered if Sparrowman ever ventured into this place. He doubted it. If he couldn't handle it after however many days it had been, there was no way that the old man could. So much would have changed. It would be like coming back from the dead.

'Quick, in 'ere!' said Jack, pulling Dan into a shop selling crystals, joss sticks and the like. The New Ager behind the counter asked them if they needed any help. Jack said that they were just browsing. Dan looked around with eyes on stalks as if he were in Aladdin's cave. The whole place was sparkling with coloured light, dappling Jack's face, as the pendulous magic stones swung from the ceiling.

'That Australian just walked past, you know what's-his-face from acute ... Dave, that's it,' whispered Jack. 'He didn't see us though. C'mon, let's go!'

Dan didn't want to go to the pub. He wanted to stay in this crazy temple of a place with the mellow bearded dude. The smell of incense intensified as the man lit a small purple cone on a brass tray. The shop seemed to be out of place, as if it had just fallen off a magic carpet en route to Kathmandu. If he stayed long enough he was pretty sure that the guy would skin up. He envied him – his seemed to be the perfect job. Jack bought a packet of incense sticks so they wouldn't look mad, and gave them to him in a fatherly way when they got outside.

At the end of the road stood an old Victorian pub, commandeering the entire corner. They went into what was called the 'Saloon Bar', as if it was the watering hole of cowboys. Slim pillars with ornate capitals stretched from floor to ceiling, surrounded by chairs and tables on a threadbare carpet. Round the edges, under decorous frosted glass were cushioned seats covered in old red velvet, speckled with cigarette burns. The place smelt of beer, fags and disinfectant. There was a sign over an open doorway that said 'Through to Lounge', which sounded to Dan like an invitation for a nice lie down. He felt done in. The day was close and sticky and the journey to the pub had been made even more tiring by trying to remember to disguise the unsavoury fact that he was a nutter.

'So, what can I get you?' said Jack, rubbing his hands in happy anticipation.

Dan had to think about it. Really, he was craving a Coke, but thought that would be too disappointing for Jack, so he asked for a pint of lager. Jack came back with two pints and a large scotch. He asked Jack if he'd lend him the money for a packet of fags. Jack obliged, blissfully generous before his beloved drink.

They smoked and drank in silence, the blue smoke swirling into a greenish haze against the sweaty yellow ceiling. Dan was only a short way into his unpleasant drink, feeling like a child unable to understand how adults could enjoy such a foul taste, when Jack was ready for more. He went back to the surly barman, who was polishing glasses with slow deliberation. His tongue was making an accusatory bulge in his cheek, as if he knew exactly who they were and was weighing up whether to call the authorities, or make the most of the scant pre-lunch trade that was inevitably made up of weirdos, drunks and bums. Dan remembered an old dole-queue joke.

'Hey Jack, what's green and gets you pissed?'

'Eh, dunno ... mouthwash?' replied Jack, downing his whisky.

'A giro!' said Dan, finding it even funnier that he used to.

'We better get back, it's almost lunchtime. We'll be missed,' said Jack. He seemed remarkably sober. Dan, on the other hand, was floating hopelessly adrift on a medicated sea of beer, swaying with its motion, oblivious to the time of day, or anything. He went to the Gents and managed to complete the highly complex operation, giggling to himself.

They walked back to the hospital past the un-des reses. Dan felt as if he was wearing moon boots. His head was spinning, 'Jesush Jack,' he slurred, 'that must have been bloody shtrong lager, I'm absholutely off my head.'

Jack agreed that he was, and that it was 'bleedin' obvious.' Action had to be taken. A sugary snack before they got back to Ash, that might help. He told Dan to wait, whilst he rushed into the staff canteen and bought him a giant chocolate chip cookie. Dan wolfed it down, glad that Jack declined his offer of half, saying that it was all for him.

'Feeling better now?' Jack asked, anxiously. Dan replied that he'd felt better, but before he could finish the sentence, he put his hand to his mouth and accelerated towards the herbaceous border, where he was violently sick. Jack gave him a tissue to wipe his mouth and one of his Extra Strong Mints, which burnt his sore mouth like brimstone, but left a better taste.

Feeling marginally more normal, but with no recollection of the rest of the journey, he found himself back in Ash where lunch was being served. He felt his stomach lurch at the thought of food, so he waved his face about a bit and went to collapse on his bed, with a terrible case of the whirling pits. He was called for his medication, which he moved around his mouth as it was checked, before rushing back to his room and spitting it out the window before he was poisoned.

He slept until teatime and awoke feeling strangely OK. He topped himself up with tea and biscuits, washed his face and brushed his teeth, reminding himself that he must research his medication. He excused himself from the difficult sounding task, thinking that perhaps it was better to leave it for now, it might bring on another attack of vomiting. He went into the dayroom and sat down wondering what to do next. Colin came in and asked if he was OK – he'd noticed his lack of appetite at lunchtime. Dan looked over at Jack who was snoozing in an armchair and said that he was fine. He'd just been a bit tired after Dance Therapy, that was all.

The goats were standing with their heads inside the room, droopy eyed and lethargic in the quiet afternoon heat. Alec was sitting with his mum. She seemed to have warmed to Dan, which Alec did not like one bit. To make matters worse, in walked IRA and the Elf, who sat down next to Dan. The Elf said that she wanted to go for a walk and did they want to come?

IRA said he wanted to watch the cartoons, so with Alec's eyes accompanying them out the door, Dan and the Elf walked up the corridor.

'Alright Nelson?' she said to Mr Atkinson, who was sitting in his usual place, rocking to the music on his very own Walkman. He raised his hand, smiling at them as they passed.

'His name's Eustace,' said Dan, proud of his inside

knowledge.

'Yeah, and my name's Kate,' she said, taking his hand as they left the ward.

She led him into the walled garden and they sat down in a shady corner. She took two toffee lollies out of her little straw suitcase and handed him one. They lay back on the warm, scented grass with the sticks protruding out of their mouths as they rattled the candy against their teeth. Dan crunched his up, thinking that there were better things that he could be doing with his mouth, but the Elf sucked hers tantalisingly slowly, taking it out of her mouth now and then to inspect it as it shrank away. He asked her why IRA was here, expecting his release from prison to have been after serving time for a despicable crime, having been caught with traces of Semtex under his fingernails.

'He's a joy-rider, he got locked up after getting caught a few times, then he got depressed in prison so he came here. He's really sweet. He gave me this.' She showed him a tiny flower carved in wood that she'd wrapped in tissue and put in an empty matchbox.

'He's really into you isn't he?' said Dan, thankful that his crime hadn't been a) a pub bombing or b) GBH inspired by sexual jealousy.

'Don't be silly! He's got a girlfriend. Didn't you see her last time she visited him? You should see the present he's making her – are you down for Woodland Workshop?' He said that he was.

'You'll see it then, I won't say anything else so it'll be a surprise.' He was less excited by the promise of IRA's creation, than by the possibility that the girl by his side might only have eyes for him.

As he looked at her profile, pale and fine-boned, he realised that he knew nothing about her at all. Come to think of it, she knew nothing whatsoever about him either. Although this lack of exchanged information seemed to be unconscious, it may have been a deliberate kind of un-consciousness. Like a holiday romance, where two other-wise disconnected lives are thrown together in what they are sure is a fated temporary togetherness. To speak of other lives would be to betray the reality, the hoped for longevity, of this dalliance at some orbital crossroad. He remembered Jack telling him that this was the best holi-day he'd ever have and as he lost himself in a kiss, he was starting to believe it.

She told him that she had written a poem. It was called Bye-bye Peridol, (as oppose to Haloperidol, her phantom impregnator), even though they'd put her onto Largactil now, which she said was just as bad, only in a less obvious way.

She told him that if you spat out the Largactil and just swallowed the Kemedrin, the side effect pill, it was much nicer. He said he'd try that next time, he was pretty sure one of his pills was called Largactil. He told her that he loved poetry and that he'd love to hear hers. She took out a notebook, which she said was full of it. He asked if he could have a look, but she said no, she was shy, and any-way, most of it was private.

She coughed, then blushed, telling him that it was only a ditty, not a proper poem, then began to read:

Bye-bye Peridol
Dear Doctors and nurses, please hear my plea,
You've messed me right up with your chemistree
Give me back control of my own bodee...

Then she stopped and said it was rubbish. He said he thought it was really good, and that it was amazing that she could get anything together at all while she was on medication, because all he could do was think and doo-dle, which was annoying, because there were loads of things that he wanted to say.

Time thwarted their delight by passing impolitely quickly, and their stomachs told them that it was approaching suppertime. He said that he'd like to see her later, but she said it wasn't a good idea, because her mum was coming to see her. In an agony of unspent passion, they tore themselves away from the important business of their summer love, as if one or other's parents had decreed that today they were going to visit Knossos, and no, they couldn't stay at the hotel on their own. She said she'd see him tomorrow and he gave her another kiss, relying on it.

23

Marianne

That evening he had a game of pool with Tim, who said that he was going home soon. He said he needed to get his head together if he was going to go back to college in the autumn. The autumn, college, both these things seemed as remote as retirement to Dan. His college had granted him a year off, keeping his place open, having been informed of his 'breakdown' by his family. He didn't want to go back. In fact, the very thought of it filled him with dread. What good was a bad degree in French going to do him anyway? Tim, on the other hand, said that he couldn't wait to get back because his college was brilliant.

After a couple of games, Benny and a lanky bloke called George came in, demanding their turn. They said that something was happening in the main building – there was an ambulance and a police car over by Oak. Dan and Tim set off to find out what was going on. As they approached the side of the building that housed Oak, Dan felt a sense of foreboding – for once, the noise of the television wasn't blaring out of the ward window.

A policeman told them to stay back. The back doors of the ambulance were open and a paramedic was busy inside. After about five minutes there was quite a crowd gathered. No one seemed to know what had happened. Suddenly, a stretcher appeared with a body shaped lump under a white sheet. Dan saw part of a foot protruding from it, with traces of red nail varnish still clinging to a toenail.

'Fuck me, it's a stiff!' said Tim. Dan thought he was going to pass out. Whoever it was, was loaded into the ambulance which, after some scurrying about of doctors and nurses, drove off, with no sirens wailing and in no great hurry.

He'd always thought that when the sirens were silent, it meant that everything was OK, the ambulance was empty. Now he realised that it was when they were screaming for people to get out of the way that there was hope. He wanted someone to come out and say that the dead body had belonged to so-and-so, who'd died with a smile on their face at the age of ninety-seven.

Suddenly Krish and Spide appeared.

'What happened?' asked Tim. Dan wasn't sure if he wanted to know.

'A woman called Marianne topped herself. She'd only been here a few days. Yeah, managed to sneak some pills in and saved up the ones she got given... Dead a few hours before anyone noticed,' said Krish, pulling his chewing gum out and winding it round his index finger.

Dan thought he was going to puke again. He told Tim he'd see him later and nodded at Krish and Spide. He saw Pamela sitting on a bench with her arms around herself, wailing. He stumbled across the grass, desperate to get away from the crowd that had gathered and its hushed murmurings. The news seemed to have spread pretty fast and people were making their way towards Oak like rubbernecks at a car crash. He could see Jack and Alec in the distance, heading for the bus stop. He couldn't face them either, so he dived into a side door of the old building and found himself in the corridor that led to the church.

The church! That was the place to be, surely. He ran the last ten yards or so, but the door was locked and the rose window's light was cold and dim. Just when he needed him most, God was out. He turned back. Call home – that's what he'd do. He ran to the phone. Typical, a piece of paper was taped to it that said, 'Out of Order'. He picked up the handset and it buzzed with life. Yes! He dialled his parents' number with trembling fingers. There was no reply. He tried Mat's number. A female voice answered. When he tried to push the money in, he found that he couldn't. The slot was blocked with what looked like a half sucked boiled sweet. He dropped the receiver and stepped back, bashing into someone who was walking past.

There was a crash as a box fell to the floor. It was the man from the Games Room. Dan muttered his apologies, bending down to pick up cassette boxes that had scattered across the corridor. They slipped through his fingers and came to pieces. There was a crunch as he trod on one. The man told him not to worry and asked if he was OK. Dan blurted out what he had just witnessed and the man nodded, saying that he'd just heard about it himself. Leading Dan back into the deserted Games Room and into his office, he put down the box and offered him a seat. He cleared some papers off his desk, shut the door and sat down opposite him, taking his hands in his.

This time he really couldn't help it. Tears rolled down his cheeks as he gripped the man's hands. Eventually the flow lessened, leaving him gasping, his chest lurching spasmodically. He said sorry. The man said there was no need to be sorry, and that everyone was very upset. Dan said that he didn't understand – he wasn't really crying for the poor woman, he was crying for himself, which stupid, because he was fine really, he was happy. The man looked at him and said that he didn't look very happy and would he like to talk about it? Dan looked around at the dusty little office, full of LPs, all labelled neatly. It reminded him of Mat's place. He said that he wouldn't mind – if he was sure he wasn't too busy. The man said that he wasn't, and to call him Bill. He made him a cup of tea, putting an ashtray in front of him in case he wanted to smoke.

He began to pour out his tale. The words came tumbling out, tripping each other up in their hurry. The details, he knew, were irrelevant now, but still, he told him how Fran had left, then come back, then left again, then reappeared, trying to be kind, but making matters worse, giving him hope, then saying that of course, she was still seeing Him. But it wasn't just that. He was frightened. He didn't really know what of, just everything. He didn't know what he wanted to do, what he wanted to be, and even if he did, he was pretty sure that he wouldn't be able to get it together. It all seemed so difficult, so pointless.

His desperate rebounding, the drunkeness, all the things he regretted. God, it made him cringe, thinking about it. Trying to get it together, to be positive about France, but when he got there, feeling totally lost and alone. He got ill, just a bug, but he couldn't shake it off. The people he was sharing the stark, ugly flat with got bored with him, so he lay on his half-collapsed camp bed, fretting, feverish. Anxiety set in, covering him like a pall. Anxiety wasn't a strong enough word for it. Terror more like.

He found it impossible to put it into words – it was as if he had a time bomb ticking inside of him. More and more it ate into his brain, panic, dread... He was desperate. Company didn't help, just intensified his feeling of isolation, of difference. Of failure. Why wasn't he coping? Other people were. They were making friends, speaking French, sending postcards home, casting aside heartache and homesickness, starting new romances. He was outside in the freezing cold, a beggar looking through the window of a happy home on Christmas morning.

And it got worse. From where he was, the beggarman

started to look like a winner. Now he was trapped behind glass, like some sort of demented mime artist. He had to get away. He wanted England. He told everyone that the doctor said he should go home, that his bug was bad. People seemed to buy it. They were probably glad to get rid of him. He was cramping their style. On the train back to Boulogne he tried to be normal, to read and look out of the window, but his mind was racing, frantic, searching for somewhere to hide. It led him into what he thought was a ditch, where he could lie low until it passed, but found himself falling into a bottomless pit. He managed to reach out and grab the edge, and that's where he was when he got to Dover. Clinging on for dear life.

Home was no solution. His parents were dismayed, disappointed, exasperated. He said he couldn't face the flat. Anyway, he couldn't go there because he'd sublet it to his mate John. He told them he wanted to stay for a bit, just till he got his head together. They said he could, but that he'd have to get a job and pay his way.

He tried to explain to Bill, that although it might sound perfectly feasible now, at that point, well, they might as well have told him that he'd have to go and climb Mount Everest in bare feet. Which, come to think of it wasn't unlike how it felt just getting through a day.

The unbearable days, the horrific nights, the endless weeks that turned into months. Pleasure became a memory, food turned to sawdust. The scampering upstairs to hide when the doorbell went, the agoraphobia, the claustrophobia, the terrible tension. Every fibre strung out like perishing rubber bands at breaking point. Then disintegration. A falling to ruin. No, a demolition. Slow and violent. God, his hair even started to fall out! The self-disgust that matured into loathing. The horrible taste of himself. At first sleep had offered some fleeting release, till the nightmares began. Night after night, strapped into a chair and wheeled into an arena. The audience everyone that had ever featured in his life. Braying and pointing, laughing, their voices a piercing chant, wrenching him out of sleep and reducing him to knocking on his parents' door once more a child with the heebie-jeebies.

It was unreal. He remembered looking at his hands, amazed that they'd once been useful. Staring out of the kitchen window for what seemed like hours, the task of making tea reducing him to tears. Until one day the tears just stopped. His humanity packed and left. The aged family cat staggered off to die and instead of grief, he felt envy.

He paused to light a fag, thinking of what Anna had said about how cutting herself was better than feeling nothing. Yeah, maybe she had a point.

'Go on,' said Bill.

Dan told him how suicide appeared on the horizon like an oasis. It was logical. He needed to be put out of his misery. No one had told him that he could recover. No, that wasn't true, everyone did keep saying that it would pass – but what the hell did they know? They were getting sick of him. They'd be glad to get rid of him too – he could see it in their eyes, their faces set, their compassion supersaturated. He didn't blame them. God, what a relief – there was a way out! He was aching from the strain of hanging on. Down to his last few breaking fingernails. He was exhausted. He'd tried his best, done his bit. No one could expect him to bear it any longer. He kept thinking of that song in the 'Messiah' that they'd done at school that went, *'Death, death, Where is thy sting?'*

He felt angry, thinking about it, that no one had taken him seriously. He'd begged for help, or felt as if he had. He'd even asked if he could see a psychiatrist – he knew he was crazy. He'd been to see a counsellor who suggested that he tidy himself up a bit and do some sport. He remembered it as the only time that he had laughed in months. The doctor gave him antidepressants, but they gave him a seriously bad trip. His bed turned into a slab of stone and his bedroom was a slimy dungeon. He couldn't get up, but knew he was a beast, half man, half woman. All he could do was raise his hands as far as he could to see them begin to sprout hair like a werewolf...

He paused to look at Bill expecting to see him recoiling with horror – which he wasn't. When his parents had been at work, he'd spent hours on the phone to the Samaritans, who were kind, but only helped pass the time as he plucked up the courage to do the inevitable. Maybe he just couldn't face being a man. Maybe he was just too soft. He was impotent – totally. Mentally, physically, emotionally, the lot. How could he ever be a man? He couldn't even get out of bed.

If only someone had said that they knew how he felt. But how could they? If you're not suicidal the possibility of feeling suicidal is unthinkable, unknowable. To be alive is to wish to stay alive, the impulse, stronger than any other is for survival. You might send a million people into the gas chamber because you feared for it. You might even resort to cannibalism.

He said he didn't think that it was the coward's way out and that he bet people were already saying that the woman had been selfish and weak and an egomaniac, but that actually he thought she was brave. The point was that you didn't have an ego. That was what made you want to die, because you're nothing without an ego. That doesn't mean you have to have a huge one. He looked at Bill, who nodded understandingly.

But how to finally let go? That was the sting. He knew it was never going to be easy. He knew that there was going to be that moment before oblivion, when the 0.0001% of himself that wanted another go would beg him to reconsider. But it would be too late, he'd be unable to respond, to undo the undoable. Everything that crossed his field of vision became a murder weapon. His mum's macramé plantpot holder was a noose, the kitchen knives were daggers, the car a generator of carbon monoxide, his dad's razor... The medicine cabinet.

It was terrifying, like standing before a death squad. He could remember the taste of fear in his mouth, raw and black. Waiting for execution. Except that you couldn't just stand there and wait for it, because you were the executioner. You could say that it was different, because people waiting for execution generally want to live, whereas the suicide doesn't, but that's not true. He wanted to live – but this wasn't living, this was a living death. Anyone feeling like that would come to the same conclusion. As he said, it was logical.

He said he'd felt brave as he'd taken all the pills he could find – painkillers, most of them, which seemed to be the obvious choice, washing them down with brandy, writing his apologetic note to the world. Bizarrely, it seemed like the only positive action he'd taken in months. Hearing his parents' snores as his limbs went numb and his heart took on an unusual rhythm, which was the last thing he remembered.

He paused at this point and Bill put his arm round him, saying nothing. Dan told him about waking up in hospital, in a side room. Being told by a doctor that there was no way of knowing how much damage he'd done to his liver and kidneys, 'We'll just have to wait and see.' He'd asked if he was dying, the doctor said the same thing again, that 'We'll just have to wait and see.' A nurse came in and put some bread and jam on his locker. She said he had to eat it, and, 'What did you do that for, how could you be so selfish? What about your poor mother?' She didn't understand that at that point it seemed selfish to carry on living, since he was only a burden. His mum and dad at his beside, looking so pale, his brother flying back from his travels to be with the family.

Where every other patient was a hero, he was a villain. Like a woman who'd had an abortion in a ward full of others having fertility treatment. A man with no legs wheeled himself over and when he'd told him what he'd done he'd spun away saying, 'Feeling sorry for yourself were you?' That was the point – the man with no legs was a hero, but depression takes away the capacity for heroism, you did feel sorry for yourself. Really sorry. People kept telling him that he was lucky to be alive, but he didn't agree. Looking back, he now knew how lucky he was and that when he saw that foot sticking out from under that sheet, he'd seen himself lying there. He did think about the overdose a lot, but that was because he could, unlike that woman. He told Bill that at least she had got what she wanted, even though it wasn't really what she wanted. It was the illness telling her it was, probably. He asked him if he thought people could kill themselves when they weren't mad. Bill said that he didn't know.

He finished his story, saying how amazing it had been to come back to life (sparing him the details of Cornwall and the speed), and how afterwards he'd levelled out and gone back to his flat. Now he was here, and he still wasn't sure why because, as he'd said, he was really happy.

He disconnected himself from the man's embrace and wiped his nose. Bill handed him a tissue and said, 'Blow!' He said that it was wonderful that he had lived to tell his tale and said that if he ever wanted to talk about it further, or anything else for that matter, he was more than welcome. As Dan was leaving, after saying thank you about a hundred times, Bill said that he looked forward to another tune on the piano.

He went back outside through the side door with his eyes puffy and swollen. It was raining softly, just enough to cool his face. There was a crowd of sombre people gathered at the bus stop. The Elf was there, her mum hadn't turned up, and she rushed over to him and hugged him, saying she'd been looking everywhere for him and wasn't it dreadful about poor Marianne. Dan held her, thanking her inwardly for bringing him back into the present tense, and he said that yeah, it was really, really dreadful, and he meant it, for her, Marianne Whoever-she-was, not for him, he was lucky, he was OK. It was history.

24

Her uncle

The next day all therapy was cancelled due to the impromptu memorial service for Marianne. Most of Oak turned up and quite a lot more besides. Dan couldn't really face it but the Elf said she wanted to go, so he went with her. Quite a few people in the church were sobbing. He suspected that like his splurge yesterday, they were most likely weeping for themselves. He didn't want to think about it anymore. He'd had a weird night full of strange and vivid dreams and all he wanted to do was listen to music, be with the Elf and get happy. The atmosphere was strange, still hushed and subdued, despite the staffs' best efforts to get everything back to normal. The 'regrettable incident' had called for meetings and recriminations. No one would have wanted to be the person on duty in Oak yesterday. The gossip was that Marianne had tried it before, and was supposed to have been being 'specialled', which meant being followed around at all times by a nurse, so how could it have happened?

He'd managed to get hold of his parents last night before he'd gone to bed – Steve had let him use the office phone, and they'd said that they'd be along the next afternoon. After lunch in the unusually quiet dining room, he mooched around, waiting for them, eking out his remaining fags with the help of the Rizlas that the Elf had given him. For the second time he felt his family approach, just as Steve had told him to go and play pool or something. When he told him that they were here, Steve said again, 'You're imagining it,' just as the door at the end of the corridor opened and they walked in. Dan smiled smugly at Steve, who said it was just a coincidence.

They were with Uncle Paul and Auntie Pat, back from their cruise and as brown as berries, who nearly suffocated him with hugs reeking of duty free scent. They handed him a bag containing a carton of two hundred cigarettes, and an enormous Toblerone. Dan couldn't wait, so he opened it, and then felt that he had to offer it around. Thankfully, there was hardly anyone about. Just as Grace was about to put a bit in her mouth, her eyes wide with anticipation, Steve rushed over and took it away from her, telling Dan for the umpteenth time that she was a diabetic.

Auntie Pat looked really upset as she showed him some of their holiday snaps. There were a lot of Uncle Paul in loud shirts and sunglasses holding the ship's railings, against the azure background of the sea. She gave him the guided tour, saying that that was there, and that was there or was it there? The pictures held no clue. He asked her why there were hardly any of her, and she replied that she'd ripped up all the ones that had made her look fat, and that only left three out of about a hundred. Uncle Paul said she'd looked gorgeous in all of them. She told Dan not to listen to him – he was lying just to make her feel better.

By and by the subject of 'the poor woman' came up and he felt his parents scanning his face, assessing his reaction. They told him that their old friends Angela and Ron had invited them up to the Lake District for a long weekend, but if he didn't want them to go, they'd cancel it. He assured them that he was fine and said that they could probably do with a break. They said they'd be back on Tuesday, and they'd come and see him straight away.

They asked him to show Auntie Pat the goats and when she saw them she became almost hysterical with laughter, which set everyone off. When the visit had run its course, Uncle Paul thrust twenty quid into Dan's hand and told him that there would always be a job for him in the garage if he wanted it. As he walked them up the corridor his Auntie Pat said, 'I'll be in here next,' with tears in her eyes.

Armed with a chunk of Toblerone and a new packet of fags, the rest hidden in his bed for safety, he went to find the Elf. He opened the door of Lime ward and looked around, hoping that the Bitch wasn't on duty. She wasn't. Anna saw him and came over.

'Why do you keep pestering Kate? She's getting sick of it you know.' Before he had time to react to this unwelcome piece of information, the Elf had appeared out of nowhere and was by his side. Anna tutted, turned on her heel and flounced off.

'She's just jealous. She really likes you, you know.'

'Oh,' he said, wishing that she didn't. They walked out into the late afternoon. Last night it had rained, he'd heard it, woken by his harum-scarum dream about hospital beds and ambulances full of Alsatians. It had left what had become their favourite place, the walled garden, lush and aromatic. They sat like two overgrown children eating chunks of the overgrown chocolate bar. She asked him what he wanted to be.

'When I grow up, you mean?' The future, however much he tried to ignore it, kept knocking at the door of this bizarre house of his second childhood. 'I really don't know,' he said, looking away.

'Don't worry. It'll sort itself out. You've got all the time in the world. We both have.' She rolled over onto her back and looked at the sky. 'Anyway, the future's only the day after tomorrow, its not some foreign country that you're suddenly going to be dumped in.' He wished he could be so sure.

'Doesn't the sun hurt your skin?' he asked.

'No, why should it?'

'It's a side effect. I'm OK now, as long as I stay in the shade.' She laughed, reaching for the basket case, out of which she took a battered cigarette box. She shook it and it rattled. Dan took it and looked inside. It was half full of white pills, some with their sugar coating half gone. He was horrified. It was a suicide kit.

'What the hell are you keeping all these for? I'm going to get rid of them right now.' He stood up. She looked upset.

'I wasn't keeping them for any bad reason. I just didn't know what else to do with them. Honest. It's just that, well you know, after the ... thing,' she said, pointing to her bosom and blushing.

He said he was going to bury them. They went over to a dark corner and he got down on his hands and knees and dug a hole with the help of a stick. The earth was hard as rock under the top, rain-softened layer. He laid the box in the earth and the Elf put a daisy on top of it as if it was a dead bird. They filled it in and Dan stamped the earth down, then scattered some sticks and stones over the top of it till it was disguised.

He asked her if she'd ever tried to kill herself and she said she hadn't, even though there had been times when she'd thought about it.

'Well don't,' he said authoritatively, gripping her shoulders and looking into her eyes. 'Don't even think about it – ever. Promise me.'

'I promise,' she said solemnly.

'Good,' he said like a parent, pulling her into his arms.

They went back over to their chosen spot. Suddenly he wanted to know more about her. That she existed solely in this place was no longer enough.

She told him that she was twenty-one and had almost finished training to be, would you believe it, she said bitterly, a nurse. She said she didn't want to go back to that though. She said she wanted to study and travel and leave the past behind her. She seemed happy to talk about future possibilities, but what he really wanted to know was why she was here. She said that her uncle had died, not a proper uncle, but her dad's best mate. He said that he was sorry to hear that and were they very close? She laughed. You could say that.

Her parents, who had split up now, had been living abroad. Her dad was in the army, so she'd been sent to boarding school when she was ten. This uncle and his wife had been made her legal guardians by her parents, and she would go and stay with them regularly, once, maybe twice a month. On the way back to school, it was always her uncle that took her back. He'd take her to the Little Chef for cherry pie and ice cream, then he'd drive up a lane, always the same place, and tell her that he had to check and see if she was 'ready'. She didn't know what he meant. He'd put her chair back and put his hand up her skirt...

Oh no, fucking bastard, thought Dan, just as well that he's already dead...

She told her tale in a very deadpan manner. How he always gave her money and said it was a secret, and that everyone had secrets and that he loved her very much and that she was a good girl. She was so stupid that it wasn't until she had sex education at school that she knew what it was all about. After a couple of years he decided that she was 'ready' and started to screw her at every opportunity.

'Rape you, you mean,' said Dan. She said it wasn't that simple because by then she thought she loved him, and that meant that it was her fault, partly. Dan said that there was no way that any of it was her fault. Her uncle had told her that it wasn't sex, because if it was she would've got pregnant, and she'd believed him. She didn't tell anyone until the day before she left school. Her friend said that she had to tell her mum and that her uncle should be locked up to stop him stealing anyone else's childhood. So she did, and it was awful. She'd tried to take it back, saying that it wasn't proper sex or else she would have got pregnant but her mum told her not to be such an idiot – he'd had a bloody vasectomy. Her parents got a divorce, and she thought it was all her fault for telling them what her uncle had done. She'd tried to forget him by going out with a string of weirdos and losers because she felt like a weirdo and a loser.

Anyway, last year he died on the golf course, just like that – a brain haemorrhage apparently. No action against him had ever been taken. When her parents confronted him he'd denied it, and that was the story that they preferred. When she heard about his death she went loopy, she couldn't tell if it was happiness or sadness. It was both. She said she didn't want to talk about it any more and made him promise not to tell anyone.

Dan didn't want to leave her when the time came for her to join her ward in the main dining room, but she laughed, saying that honestly she was fine, that she'd cried all the tears she was ever going to cry for that man. She said she wanted to leave it there, in the ground with the box of pills. They went over and looked at the little grave. She laid another daisy on the spot whilst Dan swallowed the urge to spit on it. He walked her back to Lime and kissed her extra gently.

That night he lay in his bed hot with rage, wondering if there was a point where forgiveness became ridiculous, and whether some things could ever be put right. He was starting to feel swindled, as if some expert had told him that he'd just bought a fake. He wanted to go home.

25

Concentration

Even though his OT timetable said that today was the day for Woodland Workshop, the old girl of Weybridge College told her confused clients gathered in the dayroom that whatever they were down for yesterday, they would do today. Tomorrow they would do what they should have been doing today, despite the fact that there was not usually any therapy on a Friday. Several minutes of questioning and demands for further explanation of this irregular arrangement could have been an advert for the necessity of the session that they were having today, not yesterday or tomorrow called, 'Improve your Concentration'. As he was leaving the room, Jack, still banned from therapy, called out that the only thing that would improve anyone's concentration was to 'get 'em off that effing brain-scrambling medication.'

Dan was sitting on the windowsill, plucking the best of the petals from dying flowers and giving them to the goats, who accepted them with their soft lips as graciously as if they were the world's rarest delicacies. He was in need of a session to reduce his concentration, which was fixated on the Elf and her story. He wasn't in the mood for OT today, but it seemed that there was no escape. It was to be taken by the ex-Weybo girl right now in this very room.

She invited them all to pull up their chairs into a semi-circle around her. He found himself sandwiched between Alec and Malcolm. The woman introduced herself as Judith, and said that if anyone wanted to say anything about the terrible incident in Oak before they started they could. Everyone shifted uncomfortably and looked at the floor, even Malcolm, who could have been expected to take the opportunity to retell the tale about the only occasion when he had ever contemplated taking his own life, whilst enduring torture at length as a prisoner of war. He, needless to say, would rather have died than divulge the secrets of his beloved country.

Dan had overheard him telling Jack this tale before the memorial service. It had irritated him then, with its implication that Marianne was some sort of namby-pamby deserter, and he was glad he didn't start going on again. He'd been pleased to hear Jack saying, 'I don't know where we'd be without heroes like you, mate!' even though the sarcasm had been lost on the veteran.

Judith was handing out photocopies of a sheet of prose which, if it had been in French could have been a second year comprehension test, and was about as interesting. She told them to study the text for ten minutes. Ten minutes! Dan's eyes skimmed over it in about ten seconds, taking in the bare facts of Mrs Smith's visit to the supermarket, and what happened on the way there and back. He understood that he was supposed to be memorising the contents of her trolley and the names of the people she met along the way, but his brain laughingly rejected this as a completely worthless exercise, preferring to ponder further the boundaries of mercy. If the Elf's uncle were standing before him now, what would he do?

Whatever happened to him (with the exception of the time spent in the black hole), the memory of his childhood was one place into which he could retreat, where he was safe, a bolthole. As if he could, in his mind at least, go back to that point and start again, every day if necessary. The idea of that sacred place in his head being desecrated by a vandal from the alien adult world was ... was, he couldn't even find a word for it, heartbreaking was all he could come up with, and it didn't seem to be enough. He tried to think about something else.

He looked at the old soldier next to him and found it strange to think that Malcolm's memory of wartime London, if indeed he really had any, would be in colour, not in the black and white that ages everything so nicely, turning it into an old picture book. He could see the images of bombed streets, of dissected, burnt-out buildings. If his childhood was the house that remained standing, the Elf's would be the one that had got blown to bits. But if everything were dependent on what happened to you when you were a kid, then what was his excuse? It wasn't as if he could say that it was all to do with Uncle So-and-So. Maybe it was to do with what happened along the way, a virus, or a latent tendency, a biochemical short circuit or... whatever. You could say the same thing about just about any complaint from a cold to cancer. This was different though, he thought looking around him. This was no ordinary hospital for an ordinary illness.

He still couldn't get his head round the word illness when applied to himself, but he had to admit that the unpleasant aspects of life were attacking The Feeling, breaking out like spots, pock marking its smooth face. His eyes strayed to the open window as the sun shot a golden arrow through the cloud cover.

'...And Dan, can you tell us what the weather was like?' Judith was asking him a question.

'Sorry, when?'

'When Mrs Smith set out on her shopping trip?' All eyes were on him.

'Sorry... I can't remember,' he said, even though he hadn't forgotten, because he had never known. He scanned the sheet in front of him for words meteorological.

'Don't worry,' said Judith. 'It can be quite difficult when you're not used to it.'

He came up with a total body blush as the only way to deal with the many feelings that welled up including hatred and the desire to tell her that Mr Thomas, who she was sure to remember, had been astounded by his powers of recall. Not to mention that he could have concentrated her off the bloody planet.

'Alec, can you help us out?' Judith turned to him, smiling.

'It-was-start-ing-to-rain-so-she-took-her-umb-rell-a.' He was giving her the evil eye and for some reason imitating a Dalek.

'Very good. Now Tim, do you remember what the first thing on her list was ... without looking?'

'A vibrator,' said Tim. Alec kept the spotlight on Judith, it being her turn to blush while half the group laughed and half looked shocked. Elizabeth looked as if she would have expected better behaviour from Rupert, who was laughing like a Grade 2 listed drain, while Malcolm, shaking his head, muttered something about the youth of today. Dan was just waiting for him to say that he rued the day National Service had been abolished.

Mercifully soon it was time for a break. Dan drank his cup of warm sugar solution and had a fag. To say that this session was tedious was an understatement. He rejoined the semi-circle reluctantly. Judith was talking about memory and how often, things learnt off by heart when young stay with us for the rest of our lives, like the Lord's Prayer, for example. She was going to ask each of them in turn if they could recite anything, a poem or song maybe, it didn't have to be long.

Dan wracked his brains. Now was his chance to put

her in her place. Predictably his mind went blank. Tim said he knew a limerick about an old man from Madras, would that be any good? Judith said that no, it wouldn't. Elizabeth said she could just about remember the Lord's Prayer, but she really didn't want to say it out loud. Grace said she knew a song called, '*Say a prayer for the boys over there,*' because her mum, who she said she still missed very much, used to sing it all the time. Malcolm joined in as she gave her rendition. Rupert took everyone by surprise by reciting a large and obscure chunk of Shakespeare with considerable effect, which he then ruined by confessing that he didn't have the 'foggiest notion' what it was all about. Alec, who usually had a lyric for every occasion, refused to open his mouth and sat glaring at Judith, who quickly gave up on him. Joan started to reel off the names that Dan remembered from church, 'Nancy Newell, Nellie Poppell, Florence Grey, Bessie Conway, Annie Lavinia Wright...' Judith stopped her, saying that it wasn't something that she'd learnt when she was young, was it? Joan said that it 'bloomin' well felt like it.' Just as Dan was piecing together the school hymn ready to make Judith squirm, she said that that was all for today and she'd see everyone the following week. Not bloody likely, he thought as he headed for the dining room.

The HDM was sitting on his own, toying with his lunch and looking miserable. Dan took his plate of what Gerry had called Lancashire Hot Pot and joined him, desperately trying to think of his name. Julian, that was it, he remembered, pleased to find that his memory was still functioning after all. He asked him what was up. Julian told him that Joanne had gone. He didn't even have her address and that now he had no one to talk to. Dan said that he could talk to him if he wanted. Julian responded with a long sigh and a shake of the head.

They ate in silence. His curiosity about other ward members had scarpered, scared of more ghastly revelations. It was as if everyone had their own personal Pandora's Box. Even if Julian had been forthcoming about his grim reason for being there, he would have soon been silenced by Rupert, who joined them, making his way over like a bull in a china shop, with much loud apology. He slammed his plate and cup down and said that he thought that had been 'bloody good fun.' Dan and Julian exchanged glances.

'Feeling better now?' asked Dan. He wanted to ask what drugs the guy was on, because he seemed to be getting over his depression pretty damn quickly.

'Do you know what? I am! In fact, I'm thinking about going home soon.'

'Lucky you,' said Dan, suddenly feeling that the fact that this man was free to come and go at will whilst he wasn't, was an injustice. The reference to someone leaving was obviously too much for Julian, who got up to go. Dan went with him, leaving Rupert to plan his Mediterranean holiday.

They went to the bus stop, Julian once again the HDM, if at a more sedate tempo. Jack was sitting alone looking cold despite the warmth of the afternoon.

'It's lunchtime Jack,' said Dan.

'Not hungry,' he grizzled. He and Dan sat smoking whilst the HDM walked up and down and round and round to his self-generated rhythm track.

Dan watched as postprandial strollers appeared from out of distant doorways like insects, setting off in different directions with what could have been mistaken for a purpose. Under the circumstances, it would be foolish to expect good humour and laughter, but nevertheless he was disappointed with the day. He decided it felt a bit like 'one of those days'. Not bad enough to be serious, but bad enough to inspire self-pity, making you feel worse. The initial feeling justified, because now you know, if you didn't already, that you are weak, and a wretch, with no regard for the greater suffering of most of mankind. In this case, for Marianne. The sort of day that probably couldn't be saved. It would be like this till bedtime, even if you met a few mates and had a laugh for a while. Not then a seriously bad day, when the sight of any mates would send you scuttling behind a bush to avoid inflicting yourself upon them. Just a dull ache of a day. The sort of day he'd aspired to when he'd been in the state that Marianne must have been in the other day when she... Thank God, there was the Elf, heading over.

She ran forward to meet him saying that the whole of Lime was on a downer as well. She said she wouldn't mind a game of table football, so they said goodbye to their gloomy companions and set off for the Games Room. Dan wasn't sure how he'd feel when confronted by Bill, but he needn't have worried, on seeing him, Bill gave a confidential nod and said nothing.

If the Elf was wondering why he was here she certainly wasn't asking. It may have been the holiday romance syndrome, or politeness, but he had the feeling that her determination to dismiss the past was more likely to be the reason. That was fine by him, in fact it was helping him with the laying down of the last year. It seemed pointless to keep stirring it up, now that the sediment was settling on the bottom, beginning to rot. Prodding at it with a stick at the moment only brought a foul bubble to the surface. If left in peace perhaps one day something valuable might reside there, like oil formed from age-old bones, leaves and tree-trunks.

The Elf was good at table football. She spun the handles with casual confidence, beating Dan hands down as he was frustrated again and again by his plastic team, dictated to by their restrictive pole. Same as everyone here, he thought, bound by bad luck, which despite giving a sort of safety in numbers, prevented movement in any other direction. If only one of his little players would cut loose and make for the goal, dodging past the hapless enslaved, to triumph.

Bill emerged from his office and asked Dan if he knew the right hand to a duet that was a variation on the theme of Chopsticks. Of course he did. Didn't everyone who'd ever played the piano? It could have been the theme tune to a collective other life and he launched into the top half with something like bravado. The Elf clapped enthusiastically and demanded to be taught.

He relished the opportunity of passing on this knowledge, however inconsequential. With Fran, he'd been the ignoramus. She knew something about everything – wine, music, architecture, politics, love, sex, life, death. She seemed to know more about him than he knew about himself, must have in fact, since she was always telling him what he'd really meant, when he'd honestly thought he'd meant exactly what he'd said.

Sometimes he would listen, absorbing everything, grateful to his beloved polymath. Sometimes he'd snap sulkily that he did know, even when he didn't, and sometimes he'd feel himself shrivel with each new unknown thing. To be able to show this girl anything, even this silly tune, was pathetically gratifying.

Time vanished into thin air with the music and it wasn't long before the tea trolley had come and gone. They decided to walk up to the church and then out by acute to a part of the grounds that she wanted to show him. They stopped to peer through its glass doors. Inside, a woman was taking the cards off bouquets of flowers. The Elf said she wanted to help so they went inside. The whole place smelt like a florist's and Dan inhaled it as deeply as he could. The woman explained to them that the flowers were from Oak and from some other of Marianne's friends. The Elf asked why they were here and not wherever she was. The woman said that her family hadn't wanted any flowers so they'd sent them here. They all stood in sad silence for a while. Dan thought better of suggesting giving a bale or two to Ash. The goats could have had a field day.

Dan stood by the Elf's side while she arranged one of the bunches in a vase. She said she really enjoyed it, it was all about balance and symmetry. Not mirror image type of symmetry, which was too boring a thing for nature – but a really complex sort of symmetry that we couldn't understand, just respond to like a picture or something. He asked her how she knew that, feeling that he knew it too, without ever having formed the thought, to which she replied that she wasn't sure, it was just obvious.

He smiled as he watched her concentration, moving an iris to the right, then left a bit, standing back then returning to it and shifting its position until she was content, a surrogate mother nature. He had to admit that by the time she was finished it looked good. The woman thanked her for her help and they walked out into the grounds, an asymmetrical silhouette against the sky.

He followed her into what resembled an allotment with rows of tall, slightly wilted flowers of varying shades of blue, which she informed him were delphiniums, and prolific sweet peas making butterfly-coated wigwams of their bamboo canes. She said it was the Horticultural Therapy garden, and that she was really annoyed with Jack for throwing a stone at the gardener, because he was ever so nice really. He told her that Jack had said he'd had a 'run-in' with him, but he didn't realise that he'd done that. She said that at the last session they'd been digging up a bed near the bus stop so that some flowers could be planted out when Jack had started going on about 'whitewashing a bleedin' tomb,' and getting pretty annoyed. The therapist tried to calm him down by doing this stupid thing with stones, when you have to say which one you think is you compared to the others that might represent your mum and dad or someone important in your life.

Jack had picked up the biggest one and said, 'This one's me!' then chucked it at him – it hurt him quite badly, apparently. 'That's why Jack was in acute when you were admitted,' she said.

'Why is Alec here?' asked Dan, he couldn't help himself.

'I dunno,' she said. 'Apparently he's been in and out for years, since he left school.'

Suddenly they heard a rustling coming from the direction of a long greenhouse with most of its glass missing.

'Pssst! Lovebirds, over here!' They looked at each other, annoyed that their privacy had been disturbed. They went over to the dilapidated building and looked inside. Anna was sitting on the far end of a trestle table that stretched from one end to other, amidst trays of thirsty seedlings.

'Thought you had the place to yourselves? Sorry to disappoint you,' she said. She looked unsteady and her eyes were more glazed than usual.

'Come and join us.' They leant through the glassless door, to see Krish and Spide huddled in a corner beneath her, as white as sheets. Spide had his eyes closed and was lolling against the wall whilst Krish was running his hand up and down Anna's leg. There was a strong smell of solvents in the air and on the floor next to them was a plastic bag and a spray can.

Why did something always have to come along and spoil things in this place? Dan's longing for so-called normality welled up again. Of course there was all sorts of shit going on everywhere, but here, well, it was just so concentrated. It was an emotional assault course.

'You must be crazy!' said the Elf.

'We are, that's why we're here, just like you ... want some?'

Dan took her hand and led her away. She said that she couldn't understand how anyone was into that and at least winos were into a chemical that was made from fruit.

They went their respective ways, it being, they reckoned, almost time for supper. She said she was hoping that her mum would come tonight. It was Woodland Workshop tomorrow, so she'd see him there. Dan walked her to the main dining room on its incoming tide of people, then made his way back to Ash, trying to keep the good bits of the day afloat.

By now it was unbearably close and stuffy. It had rained again, but not enough to refresh the air, which was damp, heavy and so thick it was almost liquid. It was horrible, cloying, if only the wind would pick up and blow it all away. Every breath that he took seemed too short, shallow, as if there wasn't enough oxygen to go round. In the distance the trees were shrouded in rising mist like a tropical jungle. Suddenly he wanted it to be autumn, for it to be sharp and crisp and to need to wear a jumper.

This evening the hospital caterers presented the Woodlanders with their version of risotto, which amounted to lumps of rice dotted with big, pale green processed peas and lumps of Spam. IRA was giving it the sandwich treatment, dousing it with tomato ketchup which he assured Dan would help, seeing his expression of incredulous disgust as a solid mound of it was coaxed onto his plate by Colin. Dan took the watered-down ketchup, which flooded out of the bottle, ruining, if possible, his food. IRA was having his 'to go', reminding him as he headed off that it was Top of the Pops.

Dan abandoned the unsightly mess on his plate after a few mouthfuls and followed him, stopping at his room to grab a chunk of the giant Toblerone that he'd forgotten about, which, he remarked, was one good thing about the loss of his short-term recall facility. He'd been warned about people nicking other people's stuff, so he'd stashed his stockpile of goodies down his bed. He groped underneath the covers for the lovely big pyramidal box. It wasn't there... Maybe he'd eaten it all, no, he was sure he hadn't. He quickly checked on top of his locker, high enough to be out of sight, for his tapes and Walkman. Still there, thank God. So who the fuck had been down his bed? And how did they know to look there? Then he realised he was the biggest moron to ever walk the earth – hadn't it been Alec who'd told him that the best place to hide anything was down his bed?

He stormed into the dayroom on the warpath, to be told that Alec had gone out for the evening as it was his sister's birthday. There was an intergenerational row ensuing about which channel to watch. The oldies wanted to watch a programme about gardening on the other side. The youngsters were pleading for BBC1. Dan didn't care, still seething about his Toblerone. He knew it wasn't worth it, that he should just put it out of his mind. It wasn't so much the loss of the chocolate but rather the thought of Alec getting so intimate with his sheets that bothered him.

He decided to go into the office and ask Colin if he could look up his medication but the office was locked. Colin was still superintending the risotto eaters. He quickly lost the desire for academic research and went back to the dayroom, which was throbbing to the sound of Soul II Soul, Jazzy B addressing the room like a preacher.

Later that night, hot and restless, he tossed and turned, his one sheet as hot as fifteen blankets. At last, the storm broke. He sat up in bed to watch as the rain came. If he'd been sure that he could climb back in, he would have squeezed out of the window and stood in it. Instead he stuck his hands out as far as he could and let the rain fall onto his outstretched hands. Disappointingly few drops landed on his hot skin, even though from where he was sitting it looked like a downpour. Suddenly there was a flash of lightening. He counted one Mississippi, two Mississippi, three Mississippi, four Mississippi bars rest, before the celestial timpani came crashing in.

He wondered who else was awake, watching, waiting.

Was she awake, over there in Lime? Was she thinking of him? If only he could get inside her, or anyone's head – if only for a minute. Why did life have to be so lonely, no, not lonely, but so solitary, so solitudenous? If that was a word. Even if you sat next to the person that you felt closest to in the whole world and watched the most glorious sunset, you weren't really sharing it, were you?

As Woodland Park was lit up again as if the day had just nipped back for something, the darkness outside his window confessed that it hid nothing, no one. It was just plain old darkness, as predictable as solitude. Maybe all you had to do was just step into it, then, after groping around for a bit your eyes would become accustomed, and see that there was nothing to fear, perhaps even less than in the companionable daylight.

26

The kiss

The next morning there was a ward round and once again he found himself sitting in a small room opposite Sherlock and the aspirant Doctor Watson, who was sporting a huge spot that no normal person would have been able to leave untouched. He asked what mathematical feat they were going to ask him to perform today, fractions? No, silly him, that would be too useful, what about quadratic equations? The student wrote something down in his pad. He was asked for the third time if he thought he was ill. It was the tone of this questioning that bugged him. Why did they have to be so cold? If they'd been a bit more human, a bit more like the Art Therapist, perhaps they would have got more out of him. It was like being up before the headmaster. Even though your breath stank of smoke, when asked if you'd been smoking you'd say no. Of course you were going to say no. It was surely the most basic psychology in the world. Maybe they were taking that into account, it was impossible to tell.

He bit his lip. This was ridiculous. If it would help him get out of here then why not say, 'Yes, I think I am ill.' He couldn't, just couldn't give them the satisfaction, which, if he had been them, he would have understood. In fact, if they were him they would have been able to see the change that had taken place in his mind without him having to tell them. It was no longer a question of betrayal of The Feeling, it was pride, pure and simple. It must have been obvious. He had slowed down – there was no doubt about it. Regardless of whether he spat out his pills or not, the psychedelic delirium had waned. How on earth could he have sustained it in the face of all that had gone on since his admission? It was more of a downer than all the drugs in the pharmacy.

He muttered something about the fact that he may have been a bit happier than was realistic, but then again, in the face of it, at the time, it had felt completely appropriate. This seemed to satisfy them, more notes were made and they declined his offer of taking seven away from one hundred backwards. He even said he'd do it whilst drinking out of the wrong side of a cup, which made their mouths twitch into glimmers of smiles. He remembered to ask them about the medication and was told that he was on Largactil, which was chlorpromazine, Kemedrin, which was procyclidine, both of which would be gradually reduced and Priadel, which was lithium carbonate, a salt. They couldn't say how long he'd have to stay on that.

A salt! Back in the corridor he tried to remember chemistry lessons when they'd spent some time on salts. Carbonates, chlorides, chlorates, nitrites or nitrates, he couldn't remember the properties of these substances apart from the taste of the one you put on your chips. He envisioned the periodic table on the wall of the chemistry lab. He was pretty sure that lithium was up at the top with the really reactive metals like sodium and potassium. The dangerous ones that burnt very bright and whizzed about on water. Well, in that case, he wasn't too averse to the idea of it, it almost sounded cool. The others though, were highly suspect. Who the hell made up those names? Where did they come from and who on earth invented them? It was scary. Where were the laboratories full of stoned rabbits and monkeys with no memories? Who could do a job like that?

He went into the office and asked Gerry, who was emptying Colin's brimming ashtray with a disapproving expression on her face, if he could see the medication book which was on the shelf behind her, as thick as the Central London Yellow Pages. She said not now, he had to go and catch the minibus to Woodland Workshop. The minibus! Was this place in the outside world? He remembered the effort involved in looking normal when he'd gone out with Jack, and felt like giving it a miss. Then he remembered that the Elf was going to be there, so he hurried up the corridor and out into the fresher morning to join the others who were awaiting transportation, on the roadside between the main and the old building.

He went over to Tim and IRA who were sharing a cigarette. Benny was there as well, walking round in a circle listening to his radio, nodding his head and humming loudly. He was wearing the biggest pair of trainers that Dan had ever seen in his life, brand new and snow white.

'THIS TUNE'S BLINDING!' he hollered over the heads of the group. Other people were approaching. Dan recognised Tom and Mike. The Elf was coming over, with two girls that he didn't recognise, thankfully without Anna.

After a couple of minutes the minibus arrived, driven, to his dismay, by Judith.

'Does she take this group as well?' he asked the Elf as they got in and sat down together, clasping hands under cover of the basket case.

'No, she just drives us there. A man called Sal takes us. I think he works for the council rather than the hospital, I'm not sure.'

'What's Sal short for?'

'Dunno. I don't think its short for anything.'

'So where is this place?'

'It's in a youth club on an estate... What's with all the questions?' She looked at him sideways from behind what were, he noticed, rose-tinted spectacles.

'Just curious,' he said, hoping they weren't going to his estate. There was a youth club place behind his block.

They set off slowly and soon were on the other side of the checkpoint, Judith waving at the man at the barrier with a quick, jerky movement betraying the fact that she was not totally at ease behind the wheel of the nut mobile. They drove down the road, past the crystal shop, which Dan noticed was called 'Incensible', in the direction of the pub. He half expected to see Jack skulking towards it but instead saw Dave from acute with a woman who was crying. He nudged the Elf and pointed out the window.

'She doesn't look very happy does she?' she said. He agreed that she didn't, feeling strangely reassured that nurses' girlfriends shed tears.

Thankfully the minibus was heading in a direction that he didn't recognise. He looked out of the window at the shoppers reining in their kids as they darted about the shops selling miles and miles of sari material in all the colours of the rainbow. He would have preferred to be out in it, he noted with surprise. He suddenly wanted to go and do something normal with the Elf, like having coffee somewhere, or feeding the ducks in a park. An ambulance, siren wailing, was coming up behind them, forcing Judith to the side of the road. He closed his eyes as it passed and felt the Elf squeeze his hand. He squeezed back, hoping that she would stay in his life forever.

After another five minutes or so they were in the middle of a huge estate. Clapped out cars lined the streets and tired women overloaded with Kwik Save bags and babies were struggling homewards. Judith braked to avoid a football that was kicked into the street by a bunch of lads. The green expanse of the grounds of Woodland Park suddenly seemed luxurious in comparison. No wonder people went back in again and again. Maybe a lifetime of madness was better than a lifetime of nothing. Perhaps he could carve out a decent life for himself as a long-stay patient and become a fully paid-up member of the psychiatric social club. No, maybe not, he thought, looking at the girl next to him.

A man, dripping with golden chains like Mr T, was leaning out of a ground floor flat shouting at the boys to piss off before they broke his window, and they swaggered away, laughing, looking for somebody else to wind up. A bloke that reminded Dan of himself stepped onto the road to let them pass, carrying a portfolio and a plastic bag with a file sticking out of it. He wondered if the lads on his estate had looked at him with the same disdain, hating the college boy using their home as cheap digs, passing through with his white, middle-class, fresh-from-another-world-heading-for-another passport in his back pocket.

Judith brought the vehicle to a jolting stop by stalling it outside a squat grey building. Everyone piled out and went inside. At the end of the corridor someone had stuck a piece of paper with 'Woodland Workshop' scrawled on it, onto a door. It couldn't have looked more incongruous, nestling here in the concrete jungle. A handsome Asian man with thick white hair greeted them with a cheery hello and told them to sit down for a minute while he had a quick word with Judith.

Dan looked around at the room, which, he might have guessed, reminded him of the school woodwork room, full of tools, with the faint smell of pine shavings and PVA. It dawned on him that all the therapy (apart from drug and Electro-Convulsive) was arty, creative. He wasn't complaining. It seemed to confirm something that everyone knew deep down – that making things was so fundamental and good that you could all too easily forget about it, like exercise or apples. He wasn't sure where Concentration Group fitted into this theory. Thankfully, there wasn't any Business Studies Therapy, or Sport Therapy, which did surprise him – then again, it wouldn't have been easy to get a football team together. Half the team would be running around manically whilst the other half would be shuffling around, useless... But then, they could always link arms and make a solid defence like the table footballers.

The man called Sal closed the door behind Judith and turned to them. He told those that knew what they were doing to carry on, their stuff should be where they left it, and anyone new, or anyone who had finished something last week should gather round him. The Elf went to the wall of cupboards with IRA and the others. Dan found himself with the two girls he didn't know and Mike, who didn't recognise him. Even after he'd reminded him about Art Therapy Mike still looked blank, making him feel about as memorable as the invisible man.

The options were plentiful. You could carve, join, model, or make jewellery. There was even a small silkscreen press, but at least two people would have to do that, said Sal, otherwise it would be a waste of paint. Mike said he'd love to make a print, so Dan decided to do the decent thing and plump for that as well. The girls said they wanted to make jewellery, so Sal took Dan and Mike over to the contraption in the corner and explained its mysterious workings far too quickly. Mike told him not to worry because he knew all about printing presses.

To make something beautiful for the Elf was his intention. The first step was to make a stencil from a piece of cardboard. He stared at his piece of card in despair as Mike quickly drew a bold outline of a figure. He told Dan that he was a tutor at an art college, or had been until he'd cracked up. Thinking it might be expected, Dan asked what had happened to make him crack up and was relieved when Mike replied, 'Believe me, you don't want to know.'

A geometrical pattern, of course! Why hadn't he thought of that before? Relieved, he threw himself into his endeavour and in the blink of an eye it was break time. There was a machine outside offering hot drinks. The Elf chose hot chocolate and Dan had a cappuccino. They swapped cups and agreed that there was absolutely no difference between them.

When they'd finished she pulled him by the sleeve of his shirt over to where IRA was working, skipping break, such was his dedication. He seemed to be making something square and uninteresting. The Elf whispered to Dan, 'Remember I told you he was doing something amazing for his girlfriend?' He nodded. She asked IRA if Dan could see what he had made and he agreed, putting his pencil behind his ear in a most professional way and going back to the cupboard. He took out a shrouded object about a foot high and placed it on the bench in front of them. He said that he was making a plinth for it to stand on as he unveiled his masterpiece. Mike was watching and announced knowingly that it was Rodin's 'Kiss'. Dan recognised the piece. He was sure he'd stood before the real thing in some gallery with Fran.

'That's right,' said IRA with his pencil dangling from his lips. Mike was peering round it to see it from every angle, obviously seeing subtleties reserved for the cognoscenti. He said it was excellent. The master craftsman said nothing, making it quite clear that he didn't need anyone else to confirm it. The Elf turned to Dan with shining eyes.

'Isn't it the most beautiful thing!' she said. He looked at it, then at her, thinking that it wasn't perhaps the most beautiful, but beautiful it was for sure. But it wasn't its beauty that was the most impressive thing about it. It was its very being. The transformation of a lump of wood that could have so easily ended up as a footstool with enough left over for a pair of salad servers, into this encapsulated embrace – that was what bowled him over. IRA was showing Mike his sketchbook full of preparatory drawings of the sculpture, done on the last Art Therapy outing, while Dan and the Elf gazed at the wooden lovers.

Dan decided that he preferred it to the real thing. He liked the way you could see the marks of IRA's tools, as they moved round the thighs and backs in mechanical caresses. He wondered where this pose led. Did they fall onto a bed and take it further, or were they just getting up? They were stuck together somewhere in that desperate place, trying to defy their solitude.

Time was ticking by as he tried to blow his print dry. He realised he'd worked far too hard as Mike peeled away his simple design from the press.

'Christ, how have you managed to make such a mess?' he said, looking at Dan, who had paint on his clothes and his face, as well as on the bench, despite the newspaper. He took a cloth and wiped the smudges off the novice's face and told him that he really liked his print, which was kind, if an untruth. Dan could hear Bruce Forsyth's voice in his head saying, 'Didn't he do well?' as the audience shrieked with laughter at his disastrous attempt.

He was curious to know what the Elf had been up to. She said she'd show him on the way back. As they were all trooping out to the waiting minibus, the lads with the football were imitating the shufflers, laughing as they called out, 'Duh-uh … it's the loonies!' Sal told them to clear off, while Judith, looking flustered, hurried them on board and set off for the hospital, gears grinding.

Dan thrust his rolled up attempt into the Elf's hand, saying it was for her, even if it wasn't as good as IRA's carving. She said it was the thought that counted. She showed him a pair of earrings that she'd made, in the shape of eyes with green blobs of enamel in the middle. She said she couldn't wear them because the wire made her allergic, but she was going to attach them to some silver sleepers when she got out. She said that she had been making them for her mum's birthday but since she couldn't even be bothered to come and visit her, she was going to keep them for herself. Then she asked him to close his eyes, before placing something in his open hand.

'You can open them now,' she said. He looked down to see a shiny round metal pendant on a piece of beaded wire.

'Turn it over,' she said, smiling. Stuck to the metal circle, bejewelled with chips of coloured glass and surrounded by bands of enamel, was the orange Smartie lid with the D picked out in silver paint. He didn't know what to say, so taking advantage of being at the back of the bus he kissed her with as much passion as circumstances allowed, wishing they could be caught together forever, like IRA's statuette. Giggling and flushed, she held up her hair for him to tie it round her neck, which he did, envying it its closeness to her luscious skin.

Back in Ash, he toyed with his lunch like a lovesick teenager, whiling away an hour till they met up again in the walled garden. It started to rain again, so they sat cosily in the bus stop until Jack and the HDM appeared, still glum, not the sort of company that the lovestruck need. The Elf said that she'd promised to go and visit an old lady called Josie in geriatric, maybe he could come along too, she said it wasn't what you'd call cheerful, but she was really sweet and there were two really nice cats up there.

They went up the staircase, past Patients' Affairs, along another long corridor that he hadn't known existed, through a swing door and into the land that time forgot. Or if not time, then everyone else. The smell of neglected flesh hung in the torpid air as heavily as low cloud. Ancient ones were sitting dwarfed by huge wooden chairs, dozing after lunch with mouths open in their nodding heads. Four feline eyes surveyed the incomers with disdain from their laptop vantage points. The Elf went to the office and asked the nurse if she could see Josephine. The nurse pointed them in the direction of a tiny old woman who was reading a book.

'Hi, Josie, it's me, Kate!' she said, sitting down next to her, taking her crêpe-papery hand in hers. Dan decided to stay standing. He had a horrible feeling that if he sat down in that room he might never get up again. Josephine looked him up and down and asked if this was her young man. The Elf laughed and said nothing. She asked them if they'd like to see some photos and they said that they would. She reached down into a string bag and rummaged about till she found an old envelope. Dan caught a glimpse of the writing on the envelope. It was old-fashioned like his nan's, slanting forward and ornate, completely different from the bubble writing of his generation. Why was that?

She gave them a guided tour of her life. Could this really be the same person? Dan tried as hard as he could to bring it all to life in his mind – Josephine, her family, living and breathing, up to date in their own modern times. Did they seem older because they were monochrome, static? Would his past be kept alive by the millions of miles of home movies that his dad had produced? They stayed to have a cup of tea with her before stepping back into 1989. How horrible that life had to end like that, they agreed, how weird, that one day that number would be history, and Mrs Thatcher would be as distant as Disraeli. If the world didn't end, that was.

Later, the rain stopped and the sun came out, so they decided to follow IRA's example and make sandwiches of their fish suppers, rushing back to meet each other in their favourite place beneath the giant hollyhocks and the bindweed. By the time she got back from the main building with hers, Dan's was stone-cold.

'You didn't have to wait for me!' she said, sitting down

next to him, slightly out of breath and flushed from running. He looked at her face, trying to imprint its every detail on his memory. It must have been obvious that at that moment he couldn't have cared less about food. He asked what she'd be doing on a normal Friday night. She said she couldn't remember one, they were something that she looked forward to. He told her about the good times he'd had with Mat lately and all the big ideas they'd had. She said that there didn't have to be a size limit on ideas, that was the good thing about them – but yeah, she conceded, they could get a bit out of hand.

Benny and his wife came into the walled garden pushing their pram. The Elf went over and peered in at their little darling. His short wife, who was called Carol, said to her, 'I had the baby and he got the depression!' Benny gave a 'Ho! Ho! Ho!' from way up there, as if to say he was feeling better.

As they were saying their goodbyes for the night, they heard a noise behind them. They prised themselves apart and turned round to see Alec, glowering at them, his fists clenched by his sides.

'Leave us alone Alec, please!' said the Elf. Alec turned on his heel and stormed off.

'He's not in a very good mood,' said Dan trying not to be too bothered, but deciding against confronting him about the Toblerone. He walked the Elf back to Lime, just as Anna was going in. She took her arm possessively and led her away.

27

Home

Back in Ash, a few visitors were just leaving, and the goats were hovering expectantly, knowing that there were rich pickings in the newly stocked vases. Malcolm was taking the cellophane off a box of Newberry Fruits and was just about to offer one to Grace before Gerry rushed over to nudge him in the direction of Joan, who looked away with her nose in the air as he approached. Hurt, Malcolm offered Elizabeth one, which she accepted and nibbled at discreetly, as if it would be unseemly to exhibit any degree of pleasure in public. Rupert put a whole one in his mouth and made appreciative noises. Jack said he couldn't stand them. Dan took one, even though they were not high up on his list of favourites. Alec asked if he could take two. Dan could see that Malcolm was in a moral maze, there were hardly any left.

'If I were you, I'd go and hide them somewhere safe, Malcolm, like down your bed,' said Dan staring accusingly at Alec. Stoically, Malcolm said not to worry, rationing was over, if they got eaten, they got eaten. Alec was fuming, chewing frantically to get rid of the huge lump of jelly that was hindering a snide retort. Dan saw this and smirked, then got up and went over to the window to say goodnight to the goats. He felt like an early night, not that there was anything else on offer.

He heard a voice shout, 'Oi... Look out!' and a split second later he was brought to the ground, his legs kicked from under him. His chin caught the edge of the windowsill before he fell flat on his face. Everything went into slow motion as he felt his ribs being kicked, once, twice, three times. He wasn't aware of any pain at all – he could just feel the blows thudding through his body before he knew what was happening. Suddenly he felt a hand on the back of his head pulling it up, then smashing it back down onto the floor. He opened his mouth to shout out but nothing came out. Alec had both hands on his hair and Dan pulled away, feeling it being wrenched from his scalp. The next thing he knew he'd been flipped over and was on his back looking up at a fist before it came down on his jaw with a crack. He managed to grab one of Alec's arms but the other was still raining down blows. He tried to kick him off, as he was wrestled this way and that, as limp and helpless as a rag doll. Where the fuck was security when you needed them?

At this unfamiliar eye-level he caught glimpses of Joan's legs, and peoples' shoes – Elizabeth's sensible pumps, Rupert's brogues, a couple of pairs of trainers and a smart black pair that were so shiny that he could almost see his own reflection flash past. They had to be Malcolm's – so someone did buy the shoeshine in the shop after all.

Suddenly Alec was off him, pulled away by Jack. Dan looked up, putting his hand to his face as blood dripped onto his T-shirt. Jack had pinned Alec to the wall and was laying into him. He could see a crowd of uniformed men thundering down the corridor towards the dayroom. His back was throbbing. He lay back and closed his eyes, trying to get it together and on opening them again saw a pair of Doc Marten's by his head. Thinking he might be in for another kicking, he looked up to see Gerry leaning over him like a giantess.

'Are you OK?' she said, helping him to sit up.

'Yeah, no fucking thanks to you.' He shook her hand off his arm. Jack and Alec had been separated and were being held apart by the macho guys. The rest of the ward was sitting open-mouthed as they were marched up the corridor.

'Into the cooler for them, I'll be bound!' said Malcolm, coming over to Dan's side with his box of sweets. 'Here old chap, it's yours,' he said, offering him the last one.

'You keep it, honestly,' said Dan, getting to his feet unsteadily. To his surprise, the onlookers started to clap as if the whole thing had been laid on for their evening's entertainment. Gerry followed him into his room. He sat down on his bed and asked her to go away. She said she'd have to call the duty doctor to come and look him over, and did he want a cup of tea? He glared at her as she backed out of the room.

He began to shake violently all over. He ran his hands over his head and as he did handfuls of hair came away in his hands. He stared at it, almost feeling sorry for the redundant clumps. He pressed his nose tentatively and felt his blood still warm and wet dripping off it. One eye was throbbing. He closed it, then the other, holding his hands over them to make sure he could still see. His mouth tasted of blood but his teeth seemed to be OK, thank God. He hadn't undergone years of orthodontic work to have them kicked out in a fight in a mental hospital. He felt curious to see what he looked like now that he was sure he was OK, so he opened his door and headed for the bathroom.

Tim, just back from playing pool, was in the corridor, ready with a cigarette, which Dan took, his hands still shaking uncontrollably.

'What the fuck was all that about?'

'Dunno... I think he fancies Kate.' Tim followed him till

he was standing in front of the bathroom mirror. Every time he'd contemplated himself lately he'd seen a stranger and this time was no exception.

'Christ, you look like you've just done a couple of rounds with Frank Bruno mate.'

'Yeah, and I feel like it,' said Dan, moving his head this way and that to admire his injuries. One eye was swelling up and his top lip was thick, where it was dry and split already there were ruptures, and when he stuck out his tongue he saw that it was cut, he must have bitten it when he fell.

'I always thought that Alec was a bit of a psycho,' said Tim, as a man in a white coat appeared. He led Dan back into his room and checked him over perfunctorily, pulling up his T-shirt and prodding him, looking into his eyes with a little light whilst asking him if his head hurt and could he hear any buzzing noises.

'Like Pooh, you mean?' The man looked at him quizzically. 'You know,' said Dan,

"Pooh Hears A Buzzing Noise." It's a book.'

'Oh yes, of course,' said the doctor, making a few notes. He asked Dan if he wanted anything, a painkiller perhaps, or something to help him sleep.

'I've had my medication, thanks,' he snapped. Bloody typical. They wanted to knock him out so he'd forget all about it.

Later, he thought he was dreaming when he heard a voice underneath his window. He looked out to see the Elf's face shining out of the darkness like a moon.

'Tim told me what happened. Are you OK?' she whispered.

'Yeah, I'm fine, but I've had enough, I'm out of here...' He said this as if he had it all planned, but actually it had only just occurred to him there and then.

'I hope you weren't going to go without saying good-

236

bye to me,' she said, reaching her hand up to his.

'As if,' he said, reaching down to take it. 'Anyway, what are you doing over here at this time? What is the time anyway?'

'Not sure. I think it's almost ten. Most of Lime have gone to bed, what about your lot?'

'Dunno, I'll go and have a look.' Dan did a recce. It was quiet. Gerry had gone, and the sleeping beauty that he'd seen that night with Tim was settling down in her chair at the end of the corridor with Puzzler magazine. He went back into his room and leant out of the window.

'Elf, you still there?' Her hand reached up again. 'Your ward's going to be locked by now, aren't they going to miss you?'

'I put some things down my bed. I don't care. I'll stay here all night. It's not cold.' He suggested that he pull her up into his room. She couldn't stay out there, no way.

'Yeah, right,' she said, and they giggled, imagining themselves being caught together in his bed the next morning.

It was so easy, all he had to do was get out the window.

'Hang on a minute,' he said.

Without putting the light on, he pulled on his jeans and took his jacket out of his locker, trying not to have a noisy argument with the tangle of metal hangers. He reached up to where his Walkman was and took out the folded twenty quid that Uncle Paul had given him, from where he'd tucked it behind the tape, pleased with himself for thinking of this cunning hiding place. What else? he thought, as he forced his feet into his still done-up trainers. Fags, that was all.

He put his pillows down his bed, wishing he'd kept those bits of hair. He could have put them on the pillow to complete the picture. Now for the hard bit. The window was narrow, open as far as it would go, on an extendable metal arm. He clambered over the end of his bed and put one foot through, pulling his body out sideways. The window frames scraped against his bruises as he squeezed through, catching his jeans on the window lock and ripping them noisily.

'Fuck, Elf, I don't think I can get through,' he was wedged halfway in and halfway out. He hoped that the nurse was engrossed in her brainteasers.

'Yes you can! Breathe in!' She urged him on. He sucked in his chest and wrenched himself through, plopping out clumsily onto the grass like a newborn calf.

'You OK?'

He picked up his jacket and said, 'Yeah, let's get out of here.' He took her hand and they crept away, looking back to see if any lights had come on. They stayed close to the wall till they got to the bus stop.

'Where are we going to go?' she said. He thought about it. They couldn't go to the flat, he didn't have his keys, and there was no way Mat would be in on a Friday night. He couldn't face his brother, anyway he'd probably be out and about as well. Then he remembered that his parents were in the Lake District with Angela and Ron.

'Is there anywhere you can think of?' She shook her head.

'Ever been to Weybridge?' She shook it again. 'Come on then.'

He took her hand again as if he was picking up the reins of his runaway life, and they dodged from shadow to shadow until they came to the final hurdle of the barrier. The guard was watching telly. They bent down and sneaked out right under his nose. They resisted the urge to run until they were round the corner, then they galloped to the end of the road, jumping straight onto a bus that was heading for the West End. Panting, they went upstairs and swayed their way to the front seat. It was only then that the Elf saw the state of his face, and he winced as she hugged him.

'God, are you OK?' she said.

'I'm better than OK now,' he said, pulling her down onto the seat next to him and putting his arm around her.

They were excited, giggling with anticipation as if they were going to London for the very first time. The conductor came, annoyed that Dan didn't have anything smaller than a twenty, which he held up to the light to check. He looked at his face and said, 'You OK, son?' and handed them their tickets with a nod. They gazed out of the window at the familiar and unfamiliar world, huddled close together, heading for Waterloo, gateway to Weybridge.

She asked him if he'd managed to spit out his medication. He told her that he'd got rid of one pill but he wasn't sure which. She said the Bitch had practically got into her mouth to check that she'd swallowed hers. She'd had no choice and now she was really tired.

She put her head on his shoulder and soon she was asleep. He looked out at the shifting scene before him, the couples, the lights, the bustling city, all looking so purposeful. But was it? Was it worth all the effort, just to get up and do it all again week after week? He looked down at the Elf, feeling quite manly for once and thought that maybe it was. His eye was still throbbing. Talk about coming down to Earth with a bump. He'd heard of having the living daylights knocked out of you and wondered if that was what had happened to him. The bus stopped at the lights, he was up at their level and he stared into the redness, challenging it to come out and do weird stuff, but it didn't. To get the creature next to him to a safe haven for the night would mean negotiating with the world on its terms, and that was OK. It was as if he'd just got sick of the funfair with all its gaudiness and sweet things. He wanted savouries and documentaries. He wondered about Alec and Jack. He hadn't had a chance to thank Jack for rescuing him, now he thought he should probably thank Alec as well.

The bus made its way into the familiar streets of his part

of the world. He woke the Elf – they had to change. He looked around when he got off. It felt like only yesterday that he'd gone into that shop over there to get milk. He had to stop his legs from carrying him in the direction of the flat. They waited at the bus stop, looking around nervously. He was half-expecting a gang of security guards to appear and whisk them back to Woodland Park. Their bus came and soon they were at Waterloo. There was a Weybridge train waiting on the platform, so deciding to use the feeble excuse of not having enough time to get a ticket if a guard came along they jumped on, and sought out the demoted first class carriage. It was empty, cosy and old-fashioned. He opened the sliding window and they spread themselves about to put anyone else off.

Eventually they were moving, the train shuddering and screeching. The Elf went straight back to sleep in his arms. Dan watched the familiar stations go by, as unchanged and predictable as the road home should ever be. Christ, the last couple of months had been insane. He corrected himself – for the last couple of months he had been insane. Had he really just run away from a mental hospital? It's not the sort of thing you do every day. But what next? Maybe he would go back to college after all. It would only take someone to get pregnant and someone else to run off with a tutor to make what had happened to him old news, surely. Still, it was the bit before that that he couldn't face. Not yet anyway.

Weybridge station was quiet and there was no guard to be seen so they walked through and out into the open, congratulating themselves on the smoothness of the operation so far. The Elf said she needed the loo, so Dan stood alone, waiting for her. She came out smiling. She'd washed her face and said she was feeling wide-awake again.

'Not too awake?' he said, feeling sensible, but she said no, she actually felt quite normal. They walked through the warm night and soon they were in Dan's street. He was praying that Margaret and Ian, their next door neighbours and leaders of the Neighbourhood Snoop were away. Thank God, their caravan was gone, recently, by the look of the rectangle of pale grass where it usually stood. It looked like the new people on the other side were out as well.

'Have you got keys?' said the Elf, looking up at the dark house.

'No, but I know where there are some,' he said, relying on his dad not to have changed his ways. His dad's neurosis about keys was a family joke. He was constantly losing them or patting his pockets to make sure he had them. Then, as if they couldn't be relied upon to have done the job they were supposed to, he would go back to check locks ten times before he was satisfied. To ensure that there was always a way back in the event of having lost them, he kept a spare set in the shed.

They sneaked round to the back of the house. The key to the shed was where it was meant to be, in the fifth flowerpot down in the neat stack against the fence, Virginia creeper disguising it obligingly.

He opened the door, breathing in the dusty creosote-tinged dampness and found a torch. Caught in its beam was the evidence of his dad's loving concern for useful stuff, which was all neatly ordered. He wondered why the organisational gene had escaped him. He went to the little battered and paint-stained chest and opened the second drawer. His dad was no fool, he knew the best place to hide a stick was in a forest. He rummaged through the jumble of keys to long forgotten doorways, till he found the ones he was looking for, putting his thumb up to the Elf as he shut the door behind him.

Moments later they were in the kitchen. Dan locked the door behind them and breathed out, feeling safe, as if he'd just battened down the hatch on a typhoon. Not wanting to draw attention to their presence, he closed the curtains tight and went to the drawer where his mum kept candles. He found one, stuck it in a holder, put it on the table and lit it. The room was illuminated with a flickering light and he looked around at the stage-set of his past life as if he were a ghost. Nothing had changed – just an ordinary kitchen, clean and tidy.

He wondered how it was possible to ever arrive at this point in life, when drawers could be relied upon to hold candles and piles of ironed tea-towels and there would always be plasters in the same place, just in case. He smiled at the sight of the 'cock' jug from Spain, hearing his brother's voice saying 'cock-erel mum, please!' and the naff barometer in a horseshoe, which he was pleased to see was pointing to 'change', as usual. Come to think of it, the tops of the cupboards displayed a very strange mixture of things indeed, some nice, some decidedly nasty. It was as if the nice things put the nasty in question, and vice versa, so that in the end their accusation of each other rendered both ridiculous, till all that was left was either of practical or sentimental value. That really was his parents all over – and maybe it wasn't such a bad way to be. The Elf was looking at a plate with their photo on it, red-faced and merry, grinning from ear to ear in some taverna or other.

'Is that your mum and dad?' she asked.

'Yeah – a while ago now.'

'They look really happy,' she said, wistfully.

They sat down opposite each other at the kitchen table and smiled. The structure of the Elf's face was made plain by the candle's chiaroscuro. She looked so beautiful. Human, a woman, not like an Elf at all. She suggested putting the kettle on, which he did, and its rumbling crescendo echoed his desire, settling into a quiet hiss as the water boiled and he remembered her uncle. He made tea, resorting to his mum's emergency supply of powdered milk. She said what she would really like more than anything else was a bath, if that was OK.

They took their tea and the candle and went upstairs, Dan pointing out rooms as they did so. It was so quiet, so peaceful, the comforting smell of his dad's cigars lingering in the air. He wondered whether or not they'd been missed, but fuck it, there was nothing they could do about it now. It occurred to him that maybe he should ring, just to say that the Elf was OK, but she said, 'No, leave it.' So he put all thoughts of anything other than this stolen moment out of his mind, and turned the bath on, the boiler clicking into life.

As it was running he showed her his room, saying that she could have his bed and he'd sleep in his brother's old room, not meeting her eye.

'Yeah, whatever,' she said looking around at the memorabilia of a boy's life. He went back and turned off the taps, checking the water temperature for her. He told her it was ready and said he was going to go down and get another candle so she could take that one in with her. The bath looked wonderful. His aching bruises were crying out for a soak. He'd have one after her. He sought out his old towelling dressing gown and a towel and said he'd leave her to it.

Suddenly they were awkward, getting in each other's way as if it was their first ballroom dancing lesson. She dropped the towel and they both bent down for it, breaking the ice with the crack of their heads. They laughed, their faces drawn together magnetically. He tried to ignore the bruising on his split mouth while she tried to avoid it, melting into the door till they were weak. She lifted up his T-shirt and he pulled it over his head. She turned him round to see the boot marks on his back and made all sorts of sympathetic noises, saying that he was the one who should have the first bath, but then again they could always share it.

'Only if you're sure,' he said, trying not to sound too

keen.

Next thing they were looking at each other across the water, passing soap back and forth as he willed his eyes to behave respectfully. She seemed so at ease in her skin, and he said so, to which she replied, 'Don't you believe it!' She held his ankles and he cupped her feet in his hands as they both lay back, his head at a strange angle as he tried to avoid the taps. He told her about the first bath he'd had in the hospital with Gloria, and it turned out she'd had more or less the same treatment when she first went in, needle and all. The water was cooling. It was time to get out. They wrapped themselves in towels and went to his room with the candle.

Catching yawns from each other, they got into his single bed, and held each other, still damp, sticking together like limpets. To have done more than this would have been gilding the lily, he thought, but even if it had been on the cards, the medication still pumping through his veins had taken care of that possibility. He felt her breathing become regular as she fell asleep.

He looked round his room before snuffing the candle out with a dampened finger. God, if anyone had told him that one day he'd have been lying here, like this, with her, in this bed, he would have laughed in their face. Ever since the night that he'd lain there, waiting for the pills he'd taken to have their wicked way with him, he'd found it really hard to sleep in this bed, this room, this house. It had been like sleeping in a grave. To have two hearts beating under his sheets swung the scales way back in his favour, and as he held her, his bedroom seemed to reach out and put its arms around him, welcoming back its prodigal son.

28

Déjà vu

They woke up at dawn to the garden birds doing their thing. Dan went downstairs and made some tea, bringing it back up to bed. The Elf was sitting up rubbing her eyes.

'What time is it?' she asked.

'Just gone quarter to six, do you want to go back to sleep?' She shook her head, yawning.

'If they haven't missed us yet, they will soon,' he said, getting back in beside her.

'I never asked you what you were doing in hospital in the first place, God you must think I'm awful, it's just that you seem really together,' she said.

'Well, I think I am now, just about... You've helped,' he said, stroking her tousled head.

'Me? How?'

'You just have.'

She said he didn't have to tell her anything if he didn't feel like it. He gave her a rough sketch, saying that it seemed like nothing compared to what she'd been through and that he'd always felt a fraud – now he was even a fraudulent lunatic. She laughed, saying that hers wasn't that big a deal either, it was just like an upsetting film that she'd seen once. He told her that she could stop being brave, then he held her as she cried her eyes out, wishing that with every kiss he gave her he could cancel out a grope from that bastard. She said she'd never been in a bed with a man who hadn't tried to fuck her.

'Well now you have,' he said, hoping that he could be a touchstone, at the very least.

She got up and went to brush her teeth, coming back swamped in his old dressing gown. Sitting down in front of his stereo, she turned her head sideways to read the names of the LPs. She pulled out one by the Police, saying that she used to love it when she was at school. He put it on. The needle jumped over the scratchy record.

'I'll send an SOS to the world, I'll send an SOS to the world, I hope that someone gets my, I hope that someone gets my message in a bottle...'

He rummaged in a drawer and found an old pair of tracksuit bottoms that he'd forgotten all about. He pulled them on and they went downstairs in search of food. He found bread and butter in the deep-freeze. As he chiselled the rock hard butter onto some toast, she said, 'I won't be needing this anymore,' taking a few things out of her basket case, including the Smartie pendant, then tipping the rest of its contents into the kitchen bin.

They wandered from room to room. She said it was obvious how much his parents loved him – there were photos of him all over the place. Some of them made her laugh, like the one of him and his brother as kids, dressed in matching flares with tartan turn-ups.

'I can't imagine you being into the Bay City Rollers!'

'Nor can I,' he said, picking up the photo and staring at the boy he hardly recognised. They looked at more of him in varying stages of development, some slightly less cringeworthy than others. They seemed to be saying that there was more to his life than what had happened in the last year. And there weren't even any photos to bear witness to it, thank God.

They went out into the garden. Another pristine sky greeted them. She started to deadhead his mum's petunias.

'I never knew why people did that, does it just look better, or what?' he said.

'No, idiot! Didn't you do biology? It keeps them flowering. Stops them from making seeds, cos if they did, there wouldn't be any point in making more flowers, would there?'

'A bit cruel then, isn't it?' he said, thinking that there was definitely a poem in there somewhere. She laughed.

'Don't be silly. It's much nicer to have your flowering period strung out a bit longer, don't you think?'

He smiled, looking round the garden. He breathed in the air. It was cool and sweet, reminding him of camping holidays and the smell of damp canvas before the sun burnt off the dew. His eyes rested on the shrubs and flowers and the woods behind the back fence. He felt as if he'd just come out of the cinema in the afternoon, adjusting to a new, unexpected light. Nothing was glowing, nothing was dancing. Instead there were a thousand shades of green. Subtle, blending into the others, not trippy, still as lovely, but gentler. He resolved never to forget the way they'd looked a few weeks back, but the price had been too high. These were secondary colours, tertiary colours, demanding a different sort of attention, something steadier, more prolonged.

When the phone rang, they looked at each other without surprise. Dan went into the house. Bloody hell! It was seven thirty already. He took a deep breath and answered it.

'Dan is that you?' It was his brother's voice. 'What the hell did you do that for? I've just had the hospital on the

247

phone. Is that Kate with you?'

'Yes she is.'

'You bloody idiot!' He was hopping mad, 'This'll have really set you back, they were just about to let you out, you know.'

'I suppose they forgot to mention that I got beaten up?' He was getting angry now. Why hadn't he been told he was about to be freed?

'They said there had been some sort of fight but that you were OK.' Dan looked at himself in the hall mirror, smiling at his lovely big blossoming bruises, his alibis.

'I hope you haven't screwed that girl!' Dan told him to fuck off and put the phone down.

The Elf was waiting in the kitchen for the bad news.

'We may as well get dressed,' said Dan. They tidied up and went upstairs. He put on an assortment of his and his brother's cast-offs, and she pulled on her jeans and T-shirt. She asked him if he had an old coat, or something with pockets that she could put the rest of her stuff in. He dug out his old denim jacket and she tried it on, asking him if he minded her hanging on to it for a bit, turning up the sleeves.

Standing at the front room window, the Elf was the first to see the police pull up outside the house.

They hugged each other and went out through the kitchen. Dan put the keys back in the shed and the shed key back in the flowerpot. He looked up at the house and it smiled down at him like an old friend, tacit and complicit.

They were waiting by the front door when the two officers approached, cautiously. Dan was pleased to see that this time the car was a nice big Rover.

'You alright love?' said the first one as he came through the gate. The Elf nodded, then said, 'Aren't you going to ask him?' pointing to Dan. The second one said something into his walkie-talkie. They got into the back seat and soon they were off.

'Runaways are you?' said the driver.

'Not really,' she said, 'we would hardly have stopped there if we were, would we?'

'We just needed a break,' said Dan.

'We all need a break, mate,' said the other. The car fell silent, except for the crackles from the radio. Dan held the Elf's hand, stroking it with his thumb as he looked out watching his hometown peter out and become somewhere else.

'Have you got a pen please?' she asked, 'Don't worry, I'm not going to stab anyone.' The officers exchanged glances then the driver nodded to his partner, who handed over a biro.

She took out her cigarette box and undid the top, tearing off the flap of card. She wrote something on it in squashed-up writing, handed the pen back saying thank you, and then gave it to Dan. He looked at it. On it was a phone number and under that she had written,

'There is no greater disaster than not being happy. Since everything is perfect in being what it is, you've just got to laugh. I love you Dan. Kate xxx'

He bent his head down to kiss her hand without the policemen noticing, putting the card in his pocket. They both leant back and closed their eyes as the miles between Weybridge and Woodland Park disappeared.

29

Six months

The guard waved them through the barrier with his radio pressed to his face, talking into it urgently as if something really important was happening. The policeman swung the car into the car park in front of acute and got out.

'Looks like my mum's turned up at last,' said the Elf, as they noticed the beat-up mini. Security surrounded the car as they got out. One of them had to hold back her mum who looked as if she were about to attack Dan.

'You little shit!' she shrieked at him, 'What have you done to her? If you've so much as touched her I'm going to kill you, I swear!'

'Shut up Mum!' The Elf was in tears, 'He hasn't done anything wrong... Get off him!' she yelled at the security men who were leading him towards the open door, where Dave was waiting with a pained expression on his face. She ran after him, trying to say something, before her mum and another guard pulled her back. Dan heard her mum say that she was taking her home, right now, it was all agreed.

Without the benefit of hallucination, the place had changed. It still reminded him of a McDonald's but now it seemed repulsive. It was as hot as hell. He was marched in the direction of the TV room. In the corner he saw Jack, crashed out on a yellow chair. He put his hand up to wave, before it sank back down like a becalmed flag as he conked out again. Dan sat down and put his head in his hands, before hearing someone clearing their throat in front of him. It was Dave, leaflet in hand.

'Dan, we are holding you under Section 3 of the Mental Health Act 1983 ... blah, blah... You can only be kept in hospital for longer than 6 months if your doctor thinks you need to stay. If your doctor thinks you should stay longer he will talk to you about this at the end of the 6 months...'

Dan looked up at the flushed antipodean.

'Six months!' He took the leaflet, scrunched it up into a ball and threw it across the room. 'Do me a favour!'

Dave sat down next to him.

'It's only a formality, mate, I shouldn't be saying that, but you broke your section, that's what happens. I'm really sorry.' He looked at his black eye.

'That eye OK?'

'Yeah ... is Alec in here too?' Dave nodded in the direction of the locked room. Dan got up and went over to the hatch. Alec was sitting alone in the corner, rocking back and forth. On seeing Dan he sprang up and did an imitation of him on his first day begging for a fag. Dan lit one, sat down in full view of the captive and puffed on it like a Havana cigar.

He refused the offer of food and sat watching TV. Jack was coming back to life, just enough to flick two fingers up at the image of Mrs Thatcher on the screen.

'Hey, Jack thanks for helping me out,' said Dan. The hand waved again. Just then efficient footsteps announced the arrival of Dr Holmes and Pizza Face. The doctor was holding out a phial of the orange liquid.

'Dan, would you drink this for me please?'

'Don't suppose I've got much choice, have I?' He took the potion, turned to Watson and said, 'This'll make a nice little case study, won't it?'

Christ Almighty, I'd forgotten what this was like, he thought, as about two minutes later he felt himself being sucked down, spinning, falling like in a dream, as he clung on to the chair, breaking out in sweat. He tried to get up, but felt his legs buckle underneath him, so he flopped back down and sank into the blackness.

He woke up to the sound of the tea trolley approaching like a scrap metal merchant lumbering up a cobbled street. As he sat up a new packet of fags fell to the floor. There was something written on it. He struggled to focus then smiled. It said, 'Wha'appen? Easy. Laters. MAT.'

'Your mate came, but you weren't receiving visitors,' said Jack, handing him a cup of tea, his shaking hands making it rattle against the saucer. 'I put plenty of sugar in it, mate.'

'Cheers Jack.' He drank the tea-flavoured syrup. Any minute now all the side-effects were going to kick in. He made his unsteady way to the loo and then went into the office to enquire as to the whereabouts of the rest of his things.

'It's there,' said Sue, pointing to a plastic bag.

'Any chance of going out in the garden?' he asked, but she said no, he'd slept through outdoor time. He took his things into the TV room and sorted them out, before putting them back neatly, thinking about the garden shed, and the night before. He put on his Walkman, but the music dragged as once again the little light grew dim. He asked if he could go and lie down but he was told to wait until bedtime.

Supper was spaghetti hoops, which he moved around his plate, thinking about the Elf and hoping that her mum wasn't giving her a hard time. Jack sat down next to him with a slice of dry toast on a plate.

'Dens of despair in the house of bread mate, dens of despair,' he said mysteriously. And with a heavy sigh, took one bite of his toast, put it down, stood up and said, 'I'm off for a smoke.'

Dan went back to the TV room and pulled a chair over to the window to look out at the evening sky. Out of the corner of his eye he saw a bush move and suddenly three shadowy figures appeared. He put his hands up to the glass to look out. It was Tim, IRA and the HDM. They were waving, putting their thumbs up and gesturing to him to keep quiet. Contact having been made, they stood looking at each other not knowing what to do next, before giving more waves and raising their fists in solidarity as if he was a political prisoner, before they disappeared back into the shrubs. Dan was touched. He wondered if maybe he should try a hunger strike. Maybe not, he thought, craving sweeties.

Before long the ward was ordered into a line and herded upstairs to bed, Sue and Dave unlocking and locking doors behind them, waiting while they used the bathroom. Dan was put in the same room as before, as if it might have been reserved for him. He wanted to relive the night with the Elf, but crashed out instantly, the little blue light disappearing like the dot on a TV screen at closedown.

The next morning Dr Holmes was back to see him. Her tone had changed. He didn't apologise for doing what he did, saying that he would have been mad to hang around after his kicking. She was nodding, writing things down. He realised he was talking to her as if he, or was it she, was a normal person. He said that all he wanted to do now was go home to his flat. To his surprise she kept nodding, saying that another doctor would be along shortly to make an independent assessment. Before too long a young guy stinking of fags appeared. When Dan said he was dying to get out, he nodded and said, 'I bet,' as he signed his discharge papers.

When he came out of the consultation room his mum, dad and brother were there. They jumped up as he approached, looking appalled at the sight of his face. His mum rushed over.

'Darling, this is all my fault, I should never have agreed to go away.'

He told her he was fine, why had they come back? They could have finished their long weekend. His dad said they'd headed home as soon as they'd got the call, not knowing what to expect, but finding everything in order apart from the kitchen bin being full of plastic knives, sachets of sugar, inkless biros and empty lighters, with a little basket next to it. He came over and hugged him.

'Ready for the off, son?'

'What, you mean that's it?' said Dan. Obviously everything had been sorted out without him having anything to do with it, which, he decided, shouldn't really have surprised him. Still, he could hardly believe it, what about Section 3? Suddenly he felt ... what was it? Short-changed? No, that would be ridiculous... What about the Elf? They told him not to worry, she was OK. His brother said he'd managed to get hold of her mum and they'd had a chat. He said he was sorry he'd said what he did about, you know, he just didn't know what to think.

Dan gathered his things and went over to Jack who was sitting sadly, looking at the floor.

'I'm off now Jack. I just wanted to say goodbye, I...' Jack looked up at him and took his hand.

'Told you I had a good feeling about you mate. You mind how you go, now, and think of old Jack now and again won't you?'

God, this was awful. It looked like Jack was going to cry.

'You'll be out soon ... then we can go for a drink or something,' said Dan. Jack looked up at him again and said that that would be nice, then stood up and put his arms around him, squashing Dan's bruises against his shoulder.

'Now get your arse in gear and get out of here before they change their bleedin' minds!' he said, turning away.

He went over to the hatch and waved to Alec, who waved back, moving his hand from side to side like the Queen. His parents were waiting, looking more anxious to get away than he was. Dave patted him on the back as he stepped out into the world, free.

They got into the car and went over to the pharmacy. Dan said the place gave him the creeps so his mum went in with his prescription. He told his dad and brother that he'd be back in a minute, ran across the grass into the old building and down the corridor to Ash. Most of the olds were at church and the ward was quiet.

IRA said, 'Nice one!' and Tim said, 'Wicked, alright for some!' The HDM looked as if he'd lost his sticks. Dan went into the office. Colin was flicking through the Sundays. He looked up when he came in.

'Well who's a lucky boy then! Happy now?' Dan saw the fat medication book behind his head and realised that he never did get round to his bit of research, or repay the woman in the shop for that matter. The nurse came over and shook his hand vigorously, then stood back and said, 'Now look here young man, you've got to try and keep that head of yours together, d'you hear?' Dan nodded.

'Good.' He promised to say goodbye to the music man, and to the Art Therapist. And the rest of the ward.

'Especially Eustace,' said Dan.

'You can always come back and see us sometime,' said Colin, 'But don't make a habit of it!'

Dan made his way up the corridor, looking back into the dingy dayroom and seeing the goats munching in the distance. He remembered a poem – he couldn't remember who it was by, about a man in a dungeon and how he came to love his gaol and the spiders that kept him company... No, he wasn't going to get sentimental about a mental hospital for God's sake! What was he like? On the way out, Anna was sitting on the steps. She looked up at him.

'You off then?' she said.

'Yeah.' He didn't know what to say, as if he'd just passed his 'A' levels and she hadn't.

'Sorry if I've been a cow,' she said, fiddling with her hair.

'You haven't.'

If only he could think of something meaningful to say, something that would wrap everything up neatly, something really wise that she would forever quote as the turning point in her recovery...

His Dad tooted the horn.

'Bye Nice Boy,' she said.

'Bye, take care,' he said, but she was already walking away.

He got into the back seat of the car next to his brother. They were silent until they were on the other side of the barrier. He turned round to look back, feeling numb.

That night he buried his nose deep into his pillow desperate for the merest whiff of her. God, it had only been the night before last.

30

The end

They wanted him to stay longer, but after three days he insisted that it was time for him to go back to his flat. His mum gave him a hundred quid to keep him going until he went back to Uncle Paul's.

'Before you go back to college,' said his dad, as if there were no two ways about it.

Even though he said he could manage, they insisted on driving him back. He could feel their hackles rise as they drew up outside his block. They waited for the lift, laden with more fruit than he could ever eat. When it arrived, Mat stepped out.

'The wanderer returns! Good to see you mate, check ya laters!'

His mum said it was nice of him to offer to check him.

'Check doesn't mean check like that Mum, it means see you later.'

'Oh,' she said, sounding puzzled.

Reacquainted with his keys, Dan opened the door. The flat smelled of fresh paint and was as clean as a new pin.

'We decorated it for you,' said his dad cautiously, as if awaiting an explosion.

Dan looked around in amazement. He felt a mixture

of relief and disappointment. He'd wanted to see the evidence of his madness with a clear head, but then again, perhaps it would have been embarrassing. He went into the tiny kitchen. God! A full size fridge! Margaret and Ian's little one out of their old caravan had gone. In its place stood a microwave oven. He opened his cupboards. They were stocked up with tea, coffee, powdered milk and tins of his childhood favourites, like 'red soup'. He felt a lump rise in his throat. He turned to his parents, speechless. They asked him if he was sure he was OK, making him promise to take his pills. He knew they were frightened of leaving him with bottles full of medication, even though they'd talked about it and he'd done his best to reassure them. They embraced, and saying that they'd phone later, they left. He heard the lift's mechanism grind as it took them away.

He looked around at the flat. It was like a new page. He almost felt as if he should tiptoe around. He went to the wall of windows and pulled them open one by one and looked out at the same old scene. He saw a pigeon take off from the opposite block and fly over, swooping down, landing onto his window ledge and side-stepping along till he was standing in front of him. It didn't seem possible, but sure enough, it was Pidge, with his one missing toe. The bird looked up at him with his beady eye as if to say, 'Where the hell have you been?'

He went to the cupboard and opened a packet of biscuits, crumbled half of one and held out his hand hopefully before scattering it in front of him. He watched as the bird pecked at it, more falling to the earth than he got down his throat, seeing the greens and purples of his neck feathers and the dappled greyness of his wings. The sun played upon his back, but nothing happened. He wasn't the Holy Spirit – he was just Pidge, nothing more, nothing less. His phone rang – it was Mat.

'Wanna check out some sounds?'

'Yeah! But in a bit, I've got a call to make first.'

He put the phone down and took a folded bit of card out of his wallet. He wiped his hands on his jeans, picked it up again, and dialled.

www.amandanicol.co.uk

Badric's Island

Onetime soap star, Rachel lives in hope of decent work instead of being cast in TV ads. As she dreams of escape and a less complicated love life, other peoples' dramas play out in her front room. A bit of Direct Action eases her conscience, until things go wrong. But then there's no such thing as bad publicity...

'Where's the film, where's the TV series? The dialogue sparkles, Rachel says things that we all think but are too timid to express and the description is wonderful. It's like one big long glorious rant with a few in-breaths!'

'Funny, feisty, smart feminist fiction for women sick of being told that we're worth it.'

More at www.amandanicol.co.uk

Dead Pets Society

Mike's writing 'Offsetters' but when her dog Harry dies, she loses the plot. Her piece of the natural world has gone forever. Is it too late to save the rest of it, or are we all going down with our masters?

Powerdown or technofix? What's the world coming to? This is about eco-anxiety, climate change, how to be green, oil spills, the sea, walking, seagulls, the internet, conspiracy theories, writing books, a stupid love affair, grief, hope, allotments, human beings, their dead pets and the social imperative to reconnect with the laws of nature before it's too late. It's a call to conscious evolution!

'The ecological research is impressive, it's about real life and it's funny. Everyone should read it.'

'Essential reading for anyone who even suspects they care.'

More at www.amandanicol.co.uk

Lightning Source UK Ltd.
Milton Keynes UK
UKOW02f2153040416

271529UK00001B/6/P